DAUGHTER OF THE WINDS

A novel by Jo Bunt

The dead die once. The disappeared die every day

Ernesto Sabato – Argentinian writer

Prologue

Trapped. Enveloped in solid, unrelenting darkness, it was hard to know whether my eyes were open or closed. Deepest, undiluted black surrounded me as the fear gripped me. The chances of anyone finding me here, in the heart of the Ghost Town, were slim. Nobody knew where I was. I had made sure of that.

The air was clotted with brick dust and it was becoming more difficult for me to breathe now. Dry air clawed at my throat but I couldn't muster enough energy to cough the irritant away. Something dense and cold lay heavily across my left arm and the lower half of my body. It pained me to suck in the oxygen I needed to maintain consciousness. I knew that my grip on the physical world around me was becoming more tenuous by the second. My legs weren't moving but I could just about wriggle the fingers of my trapped hand. I ran my tongue over my swollen lips, metallic and tacky with blood. The taste made me swell with nausea but I breathed slowly through my nose until the sickness passed.

My right arm was unpinned and I lifted it up fearfully to see how much space I had to move in. Barely twelve inches off the ground, the back of my hand struck something cold and rough. Sliding my arm from side to side, I was able to discern that it had once been part of the building that I had been exploring when the accident had happened. My breath was coming fast and shallow now. Tears pricked at my eyes. I mustn't panic.

I tried to lift my head off the ground but pain shot through my back and legs. Turning my arm around, I bent my elbow and dragged my free hand up to my shoulder. So far so good. I reached upwards tentatively but found an impenetrable ceiling. Bracing myself against the cool confines of my tomb, I pushed with pitifully little strength in my one free arm but nothing gave way. I was cold, uncomfortable and in pain. My legs were wet. I hoped it was from the rain that had been pelting down earlier, but I feared it was my blood seeping away, taking with it what little life I had left. It looked like my stubbornness had finally led to my very literal downfall.

It was too late now to ask "What if?" But even so, I started thinking about what had led me here and how, just a week ago, I had pictured a far different ending. It was ironic that I would die here, in the exact spot where I was born. The exact spot where I should have died all those years ago. It goes to show that you can't cheat death. He will catch up with you eventually.

Chapter one

The frost-dotted window gave me my first glimpse of Aphrodite's Island. From this height it looked uninhabited, the beaches empty and smooth, the sea clear turquoise and unruffled. Everybody else on this airplane was looking forward to a week of two of warm weather and cold beer. I was looking forward to finding out my real name.

"Ladies and gentlemen, we will shortly be beginning our descent into Larnaca International Airport. The weather on the ground is warm for this time of the year at twenty-eight degrees Celsius. Please remember to take your hand luggage with you. The crew and I would like to thank you for travelling with us today and wish you an enjoyable stay in Cyprus."

I closed my eyes and concentrated on my breathing until I felt the jolt of the wheels touching *terra firma*. I unlocked my eyelids to squint through the small airplane window, not sure what to expect. The usual feeling of overwhelming disappointment settled over me. There is never that explosion of culture and vibrancy that my heart craves. An airport is a functional site, or so my logical brain tells me, but I am always eager to walk out of the airplane slap-bang into the bustling heart of a Moroccan market or to hear the caressing whisper of the Atlantic Ocean.

Waiting for the others to disembark, I looked at the Cypriot landscape hovering above the shimmering tarmac. Faded yellow fire engines crouched in the shade poised ready to pounce at the first sight of flames. Sun-baked men gutted the belly of the aircraft causing the contents to spew forth in an undignified cascade of luggage and pushchairs. Dry land, dotted with the dull green stubble of parched vegetation signalled the perimeter of the airport. Above us a solid blue impenetrable ceiling pressed down upon our craft.

I side stepped out from under the overhead lockers with my shoulders stooped and headed for the impossibly bright light streaming in through the door. The perfectly painted mannequin at the door bade me farewell like an old friend and wished me a good holiday. *'Unlikely,'* I think, but instead I say. "Thank you. I'm sure I will."

In the taxi I peered out of the window, hungrily devouring what I could see of Cypriot life but the narrow streets were empty. Between villages, the arid land stretched into valleys and across tapered outcrops. White goats clung to small pools of shade watching my progression with indifference. As we neared Protaros, shiny white hotels and resorts protruded like badly healed scars on the brown skin of the land. Long before I expected it, flashes of sun on sea dazzled my eyes and I felt my stomach tighten.

I instructed my driver to drop me off near the beach and I stood on the side of the street unsure what to do next. The beach beckoned me and I took a moment to imagine the warm sand pushing up between my toes. I glanced down at my jeans that now felt too tight and oppressive in the afternoon warmth and decided that the shoreline would have to wait.

I dragged my case and my aching legs into George's Taverna.

"*Yasou*," I offered in guidebook Greek as I approached the open door.

"*Yasou*! You are most welcome. Please sit." A small brown man gestured to the nearly empty room.

"*Efcharisto*. Thank you."

I chose a partially shaded table away from two couples basking in sun and lager on the terrace. I could still see the beach from here but I wouldn't feel the pressing heat as keenly. The sea bounced and swayed with turquoise undulations as speed boats skimmed by.

Ignoring the proffered menu I asked the friendly Greek man, "Could I just have a jug of water and a Greek salad, please?"

"Of course. Just one minute." He deftly swept the unwanted menu under his arm and scribbled on his notepad before nodding and walking away. Surprised by the lack of people in the primely located restaurant I looked at my watch. Taking into account the two hours' time difference it was a little past four o'clock. Neither lunchtime nor dinnertime here, but at least it gave me time to collect my thoughts in relative peace.

I took out a black Moleskine notebook from my bag and stroked its smooth warm cover tenderly. The favoured notebook used by such greats as Picasso, Van Gogh and Hemingway was incongruous in such humble surroundings. I placed it carefully and precisely by the side of my cutlery along with my Cross fountain pen with its eighteen carat gold nib; an extravagant first wedding anniversary present from Dom. He always knew how to make me feel special. Well, he used to.

What had happened to that carefree couple that had been so much in love, oblivious to the rest of the world, caring only for each other's company? I alternated between thinking I couldn't live without him and thinking that we'd be better off apart. The shine had come off our relationship lately and I didn't have the energy to make it gleam once more.

To assuage the discomfort that was often present when

dining on my own in a restaurant, I picked up my pen and, opening and smoothing the first page of the notebook, wrote 'George's Taverna: Traditional Greek Salad'. I may as well keep up the pretence that I was here for work purposes. I wasn't sure whether I was trying to convince the waiter or myself but it served a purpose of sorts.

The jug of water came first and as the Greek man poured the water, clinking ice into my glass, he glanced at the book.

"English?"

"Yes."

"Holiday," he stated.

"Not really." I hesitated, not sure how much to reveal. "I'm a writer. I write about food for a British magazine."

"Aha! Then you don't want salad." He placed the water jug on the table and threw his arms up in mock outrage "A salad is *simple*. Anyone can make a salad, I will bring you our mezze."

"That's very kind, but, as lovely as that sounds, I really would much prefer a salad. Perhaps another day," I said carefully to avoid committing myself to anything.

"But you will come back for our mezze tomorrow?"

"Well, let's see how you manage a 'simple' Greek salad first, shall we?" I joked weakly.

The small, stocky man roared with laughter and slapped me on my tense shoulders.

"You will be back tomorrow. My wife, she make the best Greek salad in the whole of Cyprus. You have come to the right place, Writer Lady. I am George."

"Oh, is this your Taverna?"

"Yes. My father had this bar first. He also had the name of George."

I held out my hand to this man whom I instinctively liked. "Pleased to meet you George, I'm Leni."

"It is my pleasure to meet you." He offered his small, lined hand and shook mine vigorously. I felt mildly embarrassed that my hand, though more slender, was a lot larger than his. His skin felt dry and rough under my palm and, as we pulled our hands apart, they made a rasping sound.

What George lacked in height he made up for in charisma. He couldn't have been much more than five feet tall and yet he filled the expansive café with his presence. His face was creased with age like a piece of paper that had been screwed up and then smoothed out again. There wasn't a single fleck of grey in his brown-black hair. Whether that was the product of good genes or 'Just for Men', I couldn't tell. I guessed that he was about fifty years old but I could have been wrong ten years either way. He half walked, half danced his way to the back of the restaurant as I looked around at my surroundings.

It was a two-storey taverna with stairs in the corner by the small unmanned bar. Brightly patterned ceramic tiles in blues and greens separated the simple watercolours that adorned the walls. The decor was rudimentary but pleasant. In the centre of each table were small white salt and pepper pots with tomato sauce bottles in the shape of tomatoes. While I was still appraising the room, George was back and displaying the Greek salad before me with pride. It was piled high with glistening green olives, and interspersed with chunks of cucumber, beef tomato and thin green semi-circles of pepper. In pride of place, at the summit, was a thick slab of salty feta cheese encrusted in a green herb.

"Can I get you anything else? Chips?"

"No thank you, George. This looks lovely."

Often, when people found out that I was a food writer they would go to that extra effort, put extra food on my plate, and while that is all very nice, it didn't always give the true picture of their meals. Quite often, they confused me with a food critic and tried to waive the bill in return for a good review. Sometimes it was better just to go and receive your meal like a regular punter. But even then, it could backfire on you when you start asking about the provenance of the food. If a waiter or kitchen-hand thought you were an awkward customer and you might find more than you bargained for in your Vichyssoise.

It comforted me to be on a work assignment in Cyprus whilst also undertaking personal research. I was on safe ground with writing. Everything else was a mystery of unchartered waters and I wasn't quite ready to find my sea legs. I'd been working as a freelance writer for two food magazines in the UK since I graduated from University. Even though I'd fallen into the job by accident I couldn't imagine doing anything else for a living. And, with any luck, I wouldn't have to.

This particular series I was working on involved getting

to know the 'true' food of a country and comparing it with the UK's version. It was fascinating to explore how we've adapted other countries' traditional dishes for our British taste buds. The curry that we get in England bears very little resemblance to the ones dished up to the family in India.

One of the great things about living in the UK, if you're into food, is that we have access to such a wide variety of foods and cultures without having to board an airplane. My editor, Clare, suggested mainland Greece might be better than Cyprus but I'd managed to convince her that Cyprus would be an interesting study. I would be able to sample both Greek and Turkish approaches to similar dishes as the northern half of the Island has been firmly under Turkish control for nearly forty years. She acquiesced and a week later I was on a plane to Cyprus. If she suspected that I had ulterior motives for this trip, she didn't say so.

Dom said he would come with me if I'd postpone the trip another couple of weeks, work being crazy at the moment, but I was itching to get going and to do something productive. And, come to think of it, he didn't put up as much resistance as I'd been expecting. He was probably as sick of me moping around the house as I was. Perhaps a bit of time apart would do us both some good and help put things in perspective. Or maybe we'd realise that we could live without each other after all. The thought was depressing. I blinked away the vision of Dom's face and returned to the dish in front of me.

Olives, cucumber, white onion, lettuce, tomatoes, feta and, disappointingly, a *dried* herb of some sort. I lifted up a forkful and sniffed; saliva flooded my mouth. Oregano. The first mouthful was almost painful as my taste buds reacted to the saltiness of the feta and the sweetness of the tomatoes. The richness of the extra virgin olive oil smoothed the passage to my eagerly awaiting stomach. I screwed my mouth up at the thought of tasting the white onion, anticipating an overpowering and unwelcome taste that would linger for the rest of the meal, and well into the afternoon. Trying it anyway I was surprised to find the sweetness cutting through the rich oil, and I nodded appreciatively.

I tried to pace myself, to savour the flavours, but it was deliciously fresh and I was so very hungry.

"Good?" enquired George, refilling my water glass as I paused to catch my breath and to appreciate the simple gustatory sensation.

"Oh, yes. Perfect. Thank you."

"You wait till you eat our mezze!"

"Looking forward to it," I said as I finished the rest of the salad by chasing the olive oil round the plate with a final tomato.

While the flavour of the salad was still popping on my taste buds George returned and picked up my plate, which had a few olive stones littering the rim.

"George? Do you know anyone who has a room that I could rent for a couple of weeks? I don't want to stay in one of the big hotels. I'd prefer to stay somewhere a bit more, er, I don't know, genuine? Do you know what I mean? Perhaps with a family?"

"Maria's sister has rooms."

"Maria?"

"My wife. She's the big boss here." He smiled before continuing. "There are some rooms in the house but there is also a room away from the main house which is not bad. It is not so far from here but it is away from the beach, towards the mountain."

"Sounds great. Can I take a look?" I asked, eagerly sitting forward in my chair.

"Sure. I can drive you up there in half an hour, if you like?"

"Oh gosh, no. No. There's really no need." I shook my head smiling at his hospitality. "You've already been far too kind. If you could write down the address for me I'll get a taxi up there."

"Of course. No problem."

"Thank you. And one more thing, George?"

"Yes?"

"The bill."

George waved his hand dismissively "Pfft!"

"No George, seriously, I must pay you."

"I will add it onto your bill when you come back tomorrow night. You look like an honest woman. This way I make sure that you come back for the mezze!" He walked away laughing to himself and I smiled at his disappearing back.

George was one of those *likeable* people. Even when you didn't want to talk, they would always make you smile whether you wanted to or not. I had come here expecting to be fully anti-social but I had suddenly found myself agreeing to come back for dinner the following night. I could never resist a good meal.

Chapter two

Cyprus, 1974

"But *why* do I have to go?" whined Pru, jutting her chin out and balling her fists up at her side.

"C'mon, Sweetheart, we've been through this. It isn't safe for you here. There could be fighting in the streets of Famagusta any day now. Think of the baby."

"Think of the baby? *Think of the baby!* I do nothing *but* think of the bloody baby! How about we think of *me* for a change, Eddie? I'm eight months pregnant in a foreign country with no family and no friends. I don't want to leave our home to go and stay God-knows-where with God-knows-who."

"Right." Eddie sighed, bowing his blond head. "And when

you've come to your senses, the buses will be picking people up from noon. Our pick up point is the corner of our road and *Jules Verne*. And remember, it's one *small* bag per family. I'll see you after work."

Eddie turned on his heels, avoiding Pru's glare. He hated arguing but sometimes there was just no getting through to her.

"Screw you, Eddie!" shrieked Pru.

"That's what got you into this mess in the first place," he muttered as he stalked out of the flat, car keys jingling in his hand.

"Bastard!" screamed Pru, looking around frantically for something to throw, but her husband of five months had already disappeared down the stairs and out into the street below. The sound of her voice lingered in the sparsely decorated room until it gave way to silence.

The young woman sighed and flung herself into the orange armchair by the open balcony doors. This wasn't what she'd imagined her life would be when she left Bedford on a grey February day to go to Cyprus with her handsome army husband. The sun had been a welcome change but she was having trouble adjusting to the food and the lifestyle. For weeks she had persisted with making the same food Mam used to make. Roast beef, Yorkshire pudding, egg and bacon flan, steak and kidney pudding, but nothing turned out like it should. Pru reached out to the side-board and grabbed her favourite 8-track. There was a moment of fumbling and then *Tubular Bells* filled the tiny room.

She let out a huge sigh as the melodic tune lifted her spirits. If it wasn't for the interminable heat she could almost imagine that she was back in her bedroom in England listening to music on her headphones. She liked her apartment. It was one of the only things she *did* like in Cyprus. There was a small balcony from which you could just spot the sea through the gap between the grand hotels. They were quite close to the famous Argo Hotel where, rumour had it, Raquel Welch was staying at this very moment. It pleased Pru to think of herself as a neighbour to the great and the good. Richard Burton and Elizabeth Taylor stayed there sometimes too. Yes, thought Pru, this was definitely the right neighbourhood for her.

Pru counted herself lucky to have been able to secure this apartment. They'd managed to negotiate the rent down because of that God-awful stench that hung heavy in the streets. According to the boy across the road, it was due to a pig's head that had fallen off a truck. When the local council had come to investigate they simply kicked the head further into the bamboo.

The smell had long gone now, even though the locals were still talking about it. The ants had probably stripped the meat to bone anyway. They were as big as bullets and, as far as Pru was concerned, twice as deadly. She often woke up to find they'd eaten the gusset off her knickers in the laundry. Eddie once woke up to find them covering his feet like a moving blanket of black sequins. She hated them passionately, but not as much as she hated the scuttling cockroaches. Disgusting armoured creatures, she squealed every time she saw one. Pru was meticulous in her cleaning of the flat and her extermination of the strange Cypriot insects.

Now that the pig head smell had gone, Pru could inhale the scent of the orange blossom and jasmine. Most Cypriots seemed to favour geraniums but Pru couldn't stand the overpowering smell. She missed English smells like freshly mown grass and Dad's greenhouse full of tomatoes, the smell of a Victoria sponge baking in the oven and of Pear's soap. She could buy some of these things from the NAAFI but the aroma wasn't quite the same after it had bounced off the tiled walls and floors.

Pru didn't believe for a single minute that they were in any danger here. How could they be? This was where Elizabeth Taylor holidayed. Pru had heard that there were problems between the Greeks and Turks on the island but she had never seen any outward hostility between the two. She and Eddie often headed into Famagusta's old town to eat where it was cheaper. The Turks ran most of the restaurants there but they were never anything but polite to the interlopers.

More than anything though, the main feeling Pru was experiencing was annoyance. She didn't see why she should be moving out of her apartment when the fight had nothing to do with her. And how about the rent? Would the army be reimbursing them for the time they would be paying for their apartment but not actually living there? She didn't think so.

"Why now?" she moaned. "Why wait until I'm eight months pregnant before you invade? Selfish bastards!"

She pushed herself out of the chair with a sigh and headed towards the bedroom to pack 'one small bag'.

Pru's idea of 'small' appeared to be larger than most people's and she could see several people looking unkindly at the case by her side. She sat on the wall in the shade and waited for the bus to come and evacuate them. In the midday heat, Pru's delicate skin could burn in ten minutes and her nose blister and peel. Hot weather didn't suit Pru. Sure, she liked the sunshine, the sea and the evenings warm enough to sit out in, but the summer sun was fierce and aggressive here. Even in the shade, the heat still made its mark on her and Pru's chest throbbed with the red rash of prickly heat. Pru was always relieved to watch the sun give up and slip soundlessly into the sea. Not that it gave as much respite as it should. Back home the arrival of summer would be greeted by the removal of one heavy blanket from the bed. No longer any need for warming pans wrapped in tea-towels under the sheets. Windows would occasionally be opened during the day but always closed by night time.

In Cyprus, however, the nocturnal heat danced around semi-naked bodies while the windows and doors hung open in the futile hope of catching a winsome breeze. There was no expectation of intimacy between Pru and her husband. The last thing she wanted was to feel another hot and clammy body against hers. It surprised her to find that the woman who lived downstairs was pregnant. How anyone managed to conceive in this heat was beyond Pru's comprehension. She was surprised the population hadn't died out years ago.

Discordant yapping alerted Pru to the fact that the local children were arriving home from school already. Pru wondered how on earth they were meant to get a decent education if they did such short days at school here. She was going to have to talk to Eddie about where they were going to educate their child. Eddie had never cared much for school but Pru had done well in her O-levels and had been studying for her A-levels when she had been forced to leave home, drop out of college and get a job. She'd dreamt of going to Art College to study Fine Art. But that was all behind her now. Pru ground her teeth in irritation at the thought. She wasn't sure who she blamed most; her Mum, Eddie or the baby. She did a quick calculation in her head and realised with horror she'd be well into her thirties by the time she got her life back. What fun could she possibly have then?

The smell of the fumes from the traffic turned her stomach and she was just about to head back to the apartment when a small white bus slowed down in front of her and wound down the window. The wheel arches were peppered with rust and the exhaust pipe was belching out thick black clouds. Disgusted by the thought that this was to be her lift, she reluctantly stood up to be first in the queue.

It was then that Pru noticed the face looking back at her from within the vehicle. A young boy, no more than fourteen, was pointing a rifle in her direction. Time froze as Pru noticed the minutiae of the scene unfolding before her. The boy had the smoothest of brown faces with the slight covering of soft dark down above his top lip. He could have been any one of a number of boys playing soldiers with their friends with a block of wood as a hand-gun. But this was no toy in the overlarge hands of the man-child before her. The rifle looked heavy in his lean arms. There was something in the way he cradled the weapon and the narrowing of his black eyes that left no room for doubt. The rifle was loaded and his finger was curled around the trigger.

This was a boy who should be kicking a ball in the park or climbing trees, but his lifeless eyes suggested that such childish pastimes had long since been forgotten. As they locked eyes, the rest of the world shrank around them. The open mouth of the gun expanded to fill up all of Pru's vision. The heat of the day was sucked away down the looming barrel. Pru tried to take her eyes off the gun and concentrate on her connection with the boy. She willed him to hear just one word.

No.

She thought she saw the muscles in his forearms tense and she braced herself for the explosion but she was unable to duck and too scared to even flinch.

No.

His eyes narrowed and his cheek pushed up against the armament almost tenderly.

No.

A shrill scream rose from somewhere behind Pru which made her jump and broke the connection between her and the would-be assassin. No one else made a sound or movement as the bus continued at its stately pace inches from their feet. The eye of the rifle slid from Pru to the man standing next to her, and then to the woman holding his arm. The boy was taking each person in his sights one by one. The strange thing, Pru reflected later, was that no one ran or took cover. Every man, woman and child stood motionless as a young boy decided their fate. It was the first time that Pru had even noticed the people who had been waiting by her side. And even though she knew that they were all in danger, she could only feel relief that the boy was no longer looking in her direction.

A sudden screech of tyres and a gritty dust cloud was thrown into the air. Satisfied that they had put the fear of God into the English people, the boys in the white bus sped off. Pru sat down suddenly onto the wall with her pulse booming in her ears. She felt the baby squirm within her and felt genuine fear for the first time. She let out the breath which she hadn't realised she'd been holding. She briefly considered locking herself in the apartment until it was all over but Eddie's words about there being fighting in the streets of Famagusta seemed all too realistic now. Perhaps Eddie was right after all. Not that she would tell *him* that, of course.

Layers of voices were asking each other, "Are you okay? Is anyone hurt?" Pru could hear them but didn't feel like answering. Every concerned step in her direction was met with a frosty glare. She didn't see why this should make them all friends when moments earlier they had been murmuring about the size of her bag. Nothing had changed, Pru reassured herself. Everything was still the same as before. Pru sat up straight, consciously lengthening her neck and pushing out her rounded breasts. A jumped up little boy playing 'soldiers' would not intimidate her. She pulled her long blonde hair over her shoulders and, knowing that she looked good, clasped her trembling hands in her lap and waited for the evacuation bus to appear.

Chapter three

Without even seeing the room, I knew that this was going to be the perfect base for me. The Pleiades was a low, uneven white block of a building. It was all on ground level but it spread out generously, oozing across the mountainside. The window boxes at the bright blue shuttered windows were exploding with fierce colour. They were brimming with geraniums of every shade of red, orange and pink bowing down before the white-washed walls, their heads heavy with masses of fiery blooms.

The late afternoon was still glowing with buttery sunlight and the warmth in the air was soft and comforting, even in the shade that was growing in front of the house. Sounds of people talking good-naturedly, dogs barking and the hum of a distant car reminded me that I wasn't alone in Paradise. Insects made their presence known by flitting in front of my face as I batted them aside.

The main road, if you could call it that, ran close to the front of the house. On what should have been the pavement sat an old lady, dressed head-to-toe in black, on a starkly plain wooden chair. I hadn't noticed her motionless form when I first stepped out of the taxi. She leant forward, stooping over her gnarled wooden walking stick. Her hands were a mass of liver spots and protruding knuckles.

"*Kalispera*. My name is Leni. George gave me this address. I am looking for Antheia. Are you Antheia?"

The wizened woman looked up at me and narrowed her hooded eyes. They were encircled with a milky white ring that confirmed her advancing years. Her hirsute top lip curled to reveal a gap where her front teeth should be. She muttered something unintelligible, but unmistakeably harsh, and spat on the pale dirt at her feet. With no more explanation she turned her skeletal face back to the empty road.

I stepped backwards, startled. After my initial shock, I fought back a laugh. After all, I wanted a more genuine 'Greek' experience away from the tourists and it appeared that I was getting exactly what I asked for. I made my way to the blue front door bumping my bag across the ground behind me. I could hear voices, both adult and child, from within. A roughly hewn wooden plaque announcing *The Pleiades* informed me that I was in the correct place but there was no doorbell or knocker. I tapped on the middle of the door, painfully aware as I did so that it wasn't nearly loud enough.

The voices continued inside the house but there was no sound of movement towards the door. I counted to ten and then tried again, louder this time. I didn't want to give up, and certainly didn't want to go back to the spitting woman at the side of the road, so I grabbed my courage with one hand and the door handle with the other.

"*Kalispera?*" I called shakily into the cool dark room beyond the door and my voice echoed back at me from the terracotta-tiled floors.

"Ahhhhhhh! Leni!" shouted a female voice, assaulting my ears with its force. "Come. Come."

A large doughy woman appeared in the arch towards the rear of the house and beckoned me. She disappeared back into the other room talking to someone in Greek. I closed the door behind me and followed timidly towards the hubbub.

As I stepped through into a large kitchen area an amusing scene greeted my eyes. Two young boys, with chocolate-smeared faces, were running around naked. One of them had a colander on his head and the other was brandishing a wooden spoon menacingly. There was a slightly older girl of about six standing on the table. The woman, who I assumed was Antheia, was pinning up the hem of the girl's yellow dress while holding pins in her mouth. One last twirl and the older woman nodded with satisfaction. She said something to the girl in Greek, slipped the dress off her slender shoulders and then lifted her off the table. The young girl, now in her underwear, ran out of the door following her two brothers while the hefty woman put her sewing kit away.

Another girl of about ten or more stood in the corner looking wistfully out of the half open window. She turned her head to me sadly and, when our eyes met, her face illuminated with a smile that brought light and warmth to the kitchen. I couldn't explain it but she looked so pleased to see me that I thought I must know her from somewhere. I shook off the unlikely thought and smiled back at her. There was a peculiar connection between us, and for a fleeting moment I thought she was going to embrace me. She took a step towards me but just raised her hand in my direction.

Antheia turned her attention to me as if she was appraising me with her enormous bovine eyes, which were topped by generous black eyebrows, and then she grinned so that her cheeks bulged and her nose wrinkled up. She was almost as tall as I was, which was a rare occurrence for me. To say she was plump would be an understatement, but I wouldn't really have called her fat either. Her face wasn't conventionally pretty but it held a strong beauty that comes with age and self-assurance. She had that allure that only women truly comfortable in their own skin have and I couldn't look away from her clear, deep brown, almost black, eyes.

"Leni!" she said as if greeting an old friend. "How are you?" Her Greek accent was strong but her English confident. "George telephoned and said I must look after his good friend, the writer."

I opened my mouth to respond but all of the air rushed out of my lungs as she squeezed me in an embrace. I didn't quite know whether to hug her back so instead a stood with arms limply and self-consciously by my side. By the time I decided that this was too awkward, and that I really should hug her back, she had let go of me.

"Come. You are tired. Let me show you your room and then I will make tea. I have PG Tips. That is what you drink in England, yes?"

She weaved her way out through the open double doors of the kitchen and through the shrieking whirlpool of children. She cuffed them playfully as we dodged past them and they squealed with delight. In front of me, an open terrace held uninterrupted views down the mountainside and towards the sea.

Despite the cries of the children at play, tranquillity washed over me. The house was set around three sides of a courtyard with the right-hand-side wing protruding further towards the sea than the left. The focal point of the courtyard was a stone trough and water pump and, judging by the pools of water on the ground, was still in use. A quick glance around me revealed that there were two sunshades canopying four assorted and mismatched chairs and a table each. I was almost overwhelmed by the smell of warming rosemary, and looking behind me, I found raised beds beneath the kitchen window holding aloft thick bushes of herbs with small purple flowers hanging between wide pungent needles. The older girl was watching me from the doorway, unwilling to play with the others but surely not too old for games. Much as I wanted to, I had no time to engage in conversation with her as Antheia had already crossed the courtyard and was descending some hidden steps. I hastened after her leaving the three youngest children encircling the water-pump.

A few yards down the hill, along a sloping track, was a grey stone cottage with its stooped back to the main house. As we rounded the corner I didn't know where to look first, the picturesque landscape or the quaint Cypriot cottage. There were only two windows in the entire building and they were hidden behind blistered wooden shutters on the front wall. Cracked irregular tiles paved our progress to the narrow door that stood lazily against the large grey stones. Dry, but fragrant, lavender bushes skirted the house, their elegant silver stems topped with violet butterflies. A small oblong table with a low, sun-bleached bench offered an invitation to come sit awhile. My legs started to ache at the thought of the possibility of taking the weight off them. A low level vibration in my thighs coupled with the throbbing of my tired muscles suddenly became very apparent. A sharp ache erupted between my eyebrows and I rubbed at it with the heel of my hand.

Antheia pushed open the door on surprisingly silent and well-oiled hinges and then took a step back. I brushed past her into the cool darkness. The room was sparse and dark but clean. The walls and floor were bare and all that was in the room was a double bed with a canary yellow bedspread, a hurricane lamp with a chunky, partly used candle, a box of matches and water jug. In the corner was a chair and, behind a crudely constructed low wall, a toilet and sink. There was the slightly bitter smell of toilet cleaner sharpening the air.

"I leave you now and get some tea and some biscuits. See? I know English people." She laughed, a round and hearty sound. "You tired?" Antheia questioned as she placed my suitcase by the foot of the bed.

"A little, yes. This is wonderful, Antheia. What does 'The Pleiades' mean?"

"Ahhhh! The Pleiades! They are stars that were the seven daughters of Atlas. Zeus made them… ah… *immortal*, yes? He put them in the sky. There are seven rooms here and each one is called after one of the sisters. This room is *Merope*, the youngest sister."

"Merope," I echoed. "I like it. It's lovely. *Efcharisto polo*," I mumbled, not at all confident of my accent and hoping my vocabulary didn't disgrace me.

The large woman beamed at me.

"*Parakalo*. You're welcome."

She bustled away with a wave that was more like a salute, leaving the door open. I listened to her footsteps crunch into the distance until there was silence. The cottage felt completely and suddenly remote now that I was on my own. The room had more or less everything that I needed. Briefly I wished that Dom was here to share it me with but I shook the feeling off. This was something I had to do on my own without a crutch.

I couldn't remember the last time I had done anything on my own but I had to stop relying on other people. They only let me down anyway. I was beginning to realise that the fewer people you let yourself get close, to the less you got hurt. If you give people the keys to your heart it's only a matter of time before they take advantage, let themselves in and trash the place.

I sighed. Even in the privacy of my own mind that sounded pathetic. The truth of the matter was I'd been hurt by someone I loved. They'd lied to me all of my life and now I felt like a fool. I never wanted to feel this way again. Crushed. Abandoned. Useless.

I opened up my case at the same time as kicking off my shoes and sloughed my jeans. The sticky heat had caused them cling to my thighs uncomfortably and it was a relief to be free of them. I pulled on my pale blue linen trousers and noted that they hung loosely off my hips. Part of me was pleased; who didn't want to lose a few pounds? However, they didn't look as good as they used to and it was more evidence, if any were needed, that I hadn't been eating much lately. Looking after myself wasn't my priority at the moment. Days passed when my only sustenance was wine and crisps. Not exactly an athlete's diet, and not what was expected of a self-declared 'foodie' either.

I hung my jeans over the wall that separated the bedroom from the toilet, poured myself a glass of water and lay down on the bed, planning to sit outside at any minute. Yes, any minute now. The bed was saggy in the middle and creaked as I melted into it. I could smell the soothing scent of lavender as it washed over me, even though there was no breeze to blow it through the open door. According to a story I heard when I was a child, the lavender was given its scent when Mary had hung Jesus' baby clothes upon the bush for them to dry. The scent of the baby's clothes imparted itself to the bush rather than the other way around. Some Christian houses in Greece still hung sprigs of lavender over the door for protection. Buoyed by the scent of the lavender I started to think that this was one superstition I could embrace as I let the aroma cradle me.

When I woke over an hour later, the sun was melting into the sea in a golden puddle. I eased myself off the bed and swam through the glow bare-footed to the open door. Before me on the little table, some food was laid out. It looked like I'd missed my cup of tea. I still hadn't spoken to Antheia about how much the room cost or how long I would be staying. The fact that I'd already fallen asleep on the bed was probably a clear enough indication to the Greek woman that I had made myself at home.

Even though I wasn't feeling hungry, I sat down and looked at the delights in front of me. There was a small carafe of white wine in the centre of the table by a larger jug of water. The water still had ice-cubes bobbing in it, suggesting that it had only recently been placed there. There was a bowl of green olives, a tomato salad, a basket of heavy-looking bread and a dish of sauce that was the same colour as hummus but thinner in consistency. I broke of a piece of the bread and dipped it in the sauce. The bitter, but moreish, taste woke up my mouth and I greedily reached for another chunk of bread. I searched my memory banks for the name of this sauce. Tahini, chickpeas and lemon juice. *Tashi* sauce! That was it.

I helped myself to a glass of dry white and felt the tension evaporating from my shoulders. I wouldn't say it was the best wine that I had ever had but I welcomed it more for what it represented than for its taste. It was a perfect accompaniment to the sweet tomato salad made with mint and hair-width strands of red onion. There was still considerable warmth in the sun and I basked in it, savouring those last moments until the sun would lose its fight with the dusk. I felt content in a way that I hadn't for weeks. Somewhere in the back of my mind the possibility grew that life would once more be manageable again and the task before me might not be an insurmountable hurdle.

I had been trying hard to keep my emotions on a short leash. I brought them to heel each time I felt pangs of guilt. Guilt for leaving Dom. Guilt for going against my mother's wishes. Guilt for misleading my editor. It wasn't like me to be so underhand but I was driven to do something proactive about this situation I found myself in. I told myself that, for once, I was going to be the one calling the shots.

I blinked and swallowed and tried to concentrate on the view of the sea in front of me but tears surged against the self-built damn and, with constant battering, broke down the edifice that had been protecting me. Tears bloomed at my eyes and flowed down my face.

The sheer beauty of my surroundings had rendered me vulnerable and I struggled to find a place for myself amongst all of this. I no longer knew where I belonged or exactly what my purpose was in life. The only thing that I was sure of right now was that I couldn't make any decisions about my future until I understood my past. I only hoped that I would find the answers here on this island. I'm not sure what good they'd do me though, but that was another problem. Answers first, consequences later.

Was Dom relieved to have the house to himself now, without having to walk on the eggshells that I scattered around myself? Was he pleased not to be my verbal punch bag every day? None of this was his fault and yet I seemed incapable of saying that to him and instead I lashed out at the one person I wanted to hold onto most of all.

I didn't know how I was meant to deal with the last few weeks. All I knew was that if I didn't do something constructive now I would crumble away as surely as my foothold on the life I thought I knew had eroded beneath me. Ricocheting between self-pity and uncontrollable anger, I had been unable to make simple decisions or carry out mundane tasks. On more than one occasion I had walked out of the supermarket empty handed because I found myself overwhelmed by the thought of what to have for dinner.

On some days I would sit down in the armchair and, when I looked up at the clock, would find that hours had passed without making the slightest impact on my day. I was still breathing, my heart was still beating, but in every other way I had ceased to live. Dom and the doctor colluded to prescribe me anti-depressants "to help me function a bit better". Naturally I thanked the doctor but really I wanted to scream in her face until my throat grew hoarse, "Of course I'm bloody depressed! Wouldn't you be if all this had happened to you?"

Of course, it wasn't just the bombshell that Mother had dropped on me about her not being my 'real' mother, it was the other thing as well. The other thing. The. Other. Thing. The baby.

I tightened my grip around the stem of the wineglass and with the back of my other hand I wiped my nose. I wanted to laugh out loud. What must they be thinking of me now? Dom, my mother, Dr Davidson. *Shall we increase the dose of anti-depressants Mrs Jeffries? You seem to be showing signs of independent thought and that will just never do…*

They would be tut-tutting about how I wasn't in my right mind but I'd never been so determined in my life. I would not be swayed or manipulated by any of them anymore. It was time to do what I wanted to do. Everyone else could go to hell.

Chapter four

Cyprus, 1974

"What's happening? Tell me what's going on! Do you know we were nearly gunned down as we waited for you? We're in the middle of a war zone here!" Pru shouted at the scrawny British soldier standing in front of her using his clip-board for protection. The young man looked at her warily but showed no sign of being about to answer the angry young lady in front of him.

"Tell me where you are taking us right now or I will refuse to take one more step. I demand to know what's happening!"

The other people who had been standing with her at the side of the road filed quietly onto the waiting bus.

"Sorry to have kept you, Miss. We're evacuating everybody before the Turkish invade the city." He motioned to the waiting bus with his clip-board and put his hand on her back to guide her towards the open doors. Pru slapped his hand away.

"For God's sake, I know *that* much. I want to know *exactly* where you're taking me. And how close are the Turkish really? And what makes you think they would want to hurt me anyway?"

"Ummmm…" began the soldier.

"Well, come on! I haven't got all day."

Under Pru's scrutiny, the young soldier began to stutter and sweat. He was immeasurably more comfortable facing an inscrutable enemy than dealing with beautiful, pampered women. At least he knew how an enemy soldier's mind worked. He hadn't a clue about women.

"The er… base, the army base. That's where you're going. And er… the Turkish are still north of here but getting closer and um… What was the other question?"

"Idiots. I'm dealing with idiots," Pru said, apparently to herself but obviously directed at the man in front of her. "I asked why the Turkish would possibly want to hurt *me*?" She walked past the soldier and onto the bus before the young man could mutter under his breath, "Oh, I dunno, I could think of a couple of reasons."

The bus rumbled into life and then jerked onto the main road. Someone behind her was smoking, and she inhaled deeply. She looked around her and recognised some of the people who had already been picked up. She nodded to Marjorie who was sitting with her three children cramped across two seats. Marjorie smiled but looked weary. Pru didn't have many friends amongst the army wives. She blamed Eddie for that.

Eddie was popular with the lads, particularly Marjorie's husband, but he hadn't really fitted in with the officers. Eddie was the type of character who was easy going to the point of infuriation and, while this was great at an army social event, these were not the qualities that an officer wanted to nurture in him and subsequently they tried to suppress that side of him. This all reflected badly on Pru, and she despaired at the thought that people felt she wasn't doing a good job of controlling her husband.

Because it had been made clear that Eddie would never make any progress in the army, Pru was never at the top of anybody's list of party invitees and was rarely entertained by the officers' wives. Marjorie went to these soirees and told her she wasn't missing much anyway. But Pru was jealous of the thought of Coronation chicken sandwiches with the crusts cut off and dainty mushroom vol-au-vents, light as a dandelion seed-heads. And oh, how sublime the sound of decadent puddings made with raspberries and cream and surrounded by sponge fingers.

She turned in her seat to look out of the dirty window and studied the landscape. The shops, the cafés, the houses – it all looked the same. If an invasion was imminent, it appeared no one had told the Greeks. Groups of men still sat under trees playing chess. Women were still sweeping their front door steps. She was sure she would be telling Eddie "I told you so" in a few days' time when they were back on their balcony, sipping Keo and slapping at mosquitoes on their sun-warmed skin.

It had been good between them at first. It had never been that kind of earth-shattering love that some people talked of. It would never be the kind of romance that would inspire doe-eyed men to write songs or poems but Pru hardly cared. Marriage was never a fairy-tale dream for Pru. It was a practical and logical step towards self-advancement and independence.

Eddie was handsome, witty and strong, and Pru was pretty, slender and smart. Visually they were a perfect couple. Pru had fine, delicate features and shimmering golden hair that hung in gleaming sheets to her waist. Eddie had a strong square jaw with a dimple in his chin, looking every inch the film star. Everyone said they were made for each other. No one questioned why they didn't wait for a summer wedding. The more naïve guests at the wedding assumed it was something to do with Eddie's deployment to Cyprus. Others, who were more worldly, noticed that Pru's waist wasn't as trim as it once was.

Of course the reason for the rushed wedding was also the very reason that Mam and Dad weren't there. Mam was disgusted at her only child's "carrying on" and washed her hands of her. Instinctively Pru rubbed at her left wrist, where her watch would have been if she still wore one, remembering the last time she saw her parents.

On her eighteenth birthday, Pru had walked back slowly from the bus stop as usual, thoughts alternating between her English homework and what she could wear to go to see *Cabaret* at the cinema with Eddie on Friday. She'd heard that Liza Minnelli was amazing as Sally Bowles.

As she walked up the path she caught a glimpse of movement behind the drab net curtains but thought nothing of it. She made her way round through the clanging metal gate to the back door. As she reached for the door it was wrenched suddenly and sharply open.

"Don't you step foot in this house, young lady!" Mam's eyes were burning with fury.

Pru stepped backwards in shock. Her eyes widened as her mother, angrier than she had ever seen her before, confronted her. She was wearing a severe bruise-coloured dress. Even though it was a cold day, Mam still wore a sleeveless dress as usual. The yellow skin on her arms sagged like a deflated balloon at her sides. A bulge by her collar-bone alerted Pru to the fact that she'd been crying. She always stuffed her handkerchief under her bra strap when she had a cold or was upset. Pru tried to read her mother's face to see what had upset her so much. Colour was high in her cheeks and her mouth was clenched to the point where her lips had all but disappeared.

"You heard me, young lady. I don't expect a daughter of mine to carry on like THIS." Mam held a white leather diary in her hand and Pru felt her stomach drop away.

"Mam... I…"

"No!" Mam held up her hand. "No more. I told you about that boy. There will be no carrying on in this house!"

"But Mam, you don't understand. You'd like Eddie. He loves me, Mam."

"You? Hah! Who'd love a selfish little madam like you?"

"Mam!"

They had never had a close relationship. Pru was horrified at Mam's lack of attention to her appearance and wondered what Dad had ever seen in her. Mam never cracked jokes, sang around the house or used makeup. Pru had heard other women say that on a sunny day all you noticed about Alice

Merton was her shadow. You could never smell the subtle scent of the rose garden over the aroma of fried fish that hung to her clothes, even when it wasn't a Friday. Pru used to think that birds didn't sing when Alice was around. But it was just that she couldn't hear them over her constant wheezing and the clacking of her false teeth that she'd been treated to as a twenty-first birthday present. Happiness seemed to know that it wasn't a welcome house guest in Alice's home.

Pru felt a sudden pang of sympathy for her mother. She wondered whether Mam was simply a desperately unhappy woman going through the motions in life. She reached out to her.

"Mam, I'm not doing anything wrong. I'm in love and I'm happy. You remember when you first met Dad? How exciting it all was? Well, that's how it is with Eddie and me. We want to get married."

For a moment Pru thought that Mam was going to spit on her. "What has love got to do with marriage?" She shook the diary in Pru's face. "If you don't stop seeing that boy you will leave my house today and *never* come back!" Mam shouted.

"It's not that easy, Mam. You'd like him if you gave him a chance," Pru whispered holding back the tears.

They both stood staring at each other in silence. Mam, standing on the doorstep, looked down on Pru with disgust written all over her face. But there was something else behind those eyes. What was that? Smugness? Satisfaction?

Pru blinked away the tears in her eyes and felt the fear and nausea start to be replaced with something stronger in the fire-pit of her belly.

"I will do exactly *what* I want to do *when* I want to do it."

"Then you can leave right now!" Mam screamed.

"Where's Dad?" Pru asked without any emotion in her voice that might betray her fear.

"He can't stand to look at you. You've let us down Prudence. I always knew you would, it was just a matter of time. Now get away from me before I do something I regret."

"No."

"I *beg* your pardon?" spat the older woman, unable to keep the surprise out of her voice.

"I said 'no'. Why don't you get out of my way before I do something *I* regret."

Pru pushed past her through the kitchen and went quickly upstairs two at a time to her room where she pulled open each of the three drawers and emptied their contents onto the bed. She stuffed as much as she could into her travelling bag and stuffed her Post Office account book into the side pocket.

"Dad? Dad?" she shouted as she emerged from the bedroom. Mam was blocking her path, her arms folded over her narrow rake of a chest, her sallow cheeks starting to flush with rage.

"Give me your arm."

"What?"

"Give. Me. Your. Arm!"

Tentatively, into the silence, Pru started to glide her left arm to her mother. With lightening quickness her talons gripped at Pru's arm and clamped down tightly.

"Hey!" shrieked Pru, trying to wriggle free from her grasp.

"And you are NOT leaving this house with that watch!" Her mother's scrawny fingers with their bulbous knuckles fought with the clasp.

"No! It's my birthday present. Dad got it for me. Where is he? Dad? Dad!"

"I've told you, he can't stand to look at you. He's gone out."

"Of course he's gone out!" shouted Pru, pushing at her mother who was now holding the delicate watch against her chest. "He can't stand to be around you any more than I can. You are a poisonous old cow who knows nothing about love. You take no joy from life and can't stand it if anyone else enjoys it. Well guess what, Mam? I *am* enjoying life and I'll enjoy it even more when I don't have to be sharing a roof with you!"

The slap, when it came, hurt more than Pru had expected and took her breath away. Even as she thought about it now her hand automatically rose to her cheek and she could still feel the ghost of the sting.

Eddie's dad, a fair and honest man, had gone round to try to reason with Mam before the wedding and to tell her about the baby, but nothing had changed. She said that they didn't want to be any part of it. Eddie's mum wouldn't go and see them though. "I wouldn't piss on her if she were on fire," she'd said and that always made Pru laugh.

Pru was brought back to the present as the bus shuddered, lurched and slowed down. The driver was looking closely at the houses to the right. Pru looked out of the window herself. She didn't recognise the area at all but it appeared to be residential. All the houses were built in the same style: square, white and squat with tiny windows and plain doors.

The door of the bus clattered open noisily and a uniformed man stepped aboard. Without looking up he started reeling off names from a sheet in front of him.

"Baker, Clements, Clarke…"

Surprised to hear her name, Pru called out, "But this isn't the base. Where are we?"

The smartly dressed soldier in the early years of his forties looked up.

"You're being placed in a safe house close to the base until we can assess the threat by the Turkish. I'm terribly sorry but there's not enough room at the married quarters on the base for all of you. Here." He walked up the bus offering his elbow awkwardly. "Take my arm. This is quite an upheaval for someone in your condition so let's see if we can get you a little more comfortable. Now if you'd like to come this way, you'll be staying with…" He checked the sheet of paper again. "Ah, yes, here it is, Mrs Fisher."

Pru followed him off the bus with unhappy resignation. She did not want to be sharing a house with another woman. Woman rarely liked Pru. She had experienced a fair amount of animosity from the plainer girls at school. Pru assumed it was because they felt inferior beside her undeniable beauty. More than one of her friends' boyfriends had made a pass at her over the years. She couldn't help how she looked. She never encouraged the admiring glances and compliments but the least she could do was be worthy of them. She felt that it was her duty to make the most of her God-given looks and enviable figure. Even by having a child so young, Pru felt she was giving her body the best chance of regaining its elasticity.

Pru licked her lips and pulled her shimmering hair over her shoulders ready to face the hostility of whichever unfulfilled housewife she had been placed with. The front door was open and Pru found herself face to face with the friendliest looking woman she had ever seen. The lines on her face were soft and gentle and her eyes were lakes of milky green.

"Howay in, Pet."

Pru looked at the woman in confusion.

"Come in, come in!"

"Oh. Okay."

"Sometimes I forget that I'm not in Newcastle anymore, you'll 'ave to forgive an old Geordie woman! He he!"

Without saying a word Pru followed the older woman through to the back of the house.

"Mek yerself at home while you're here. Toilet's just through there, and this is yer room, pet."

Pru was ushered into a spacious, homely bedroom on the ground floor of the house. There was a crocheted patchwork blanket on the bed and Pru let her fingers tease the holes.

Without asking, the woman started to unpack Pru's bag, refolding the few items of clothes she'd packed into the top drawer in the mahogany chest of drawers. Stunned and dazed to find herself in this situation, Pru studied the other woman impassively. She was wearing a pale blue housecoat over a brown polyester pleated skirt. Pru was amazed to see that she was wearing tights underneath and they crackled as the skirt and tights rubbed together. In this heat, thought Pru, that was just crazy. But the older generation were inclined to think that bare legs showed, shall we say, a certain lack of morals. Pru's own mother had accused her of being little more than a trollop for leaving the house showing bare legs protruding from her mini skirt.

It was difficult to place an age on Mrs Fisher. Fifties? Sixties? All that was certain was that Mrs Fisher was a good deal more mature than Pru in more ways than one. Pru couldn't see what they could possibly have in common and hoped that the war didn't last too long or she was likely to be the first casualty of this war to die of boredom. This wasn't at all what Pru had been expecting. She didn't like the idea of sharing a house with an old couple any more than she relished the idea of sharing it with a young couple. Tomorrow she would have to get on to the CO.

"I'll put the kettle on for a brew while ya freshen up," smiled Mrs Fisher. "Anything to eat, pet? Mebbe a buttie?"

"Actually, yes, a biscuit or something?"

"Coming reet up."

She closed the door quietly and padded away leaving Pru alone with thoughts of her balcony in Varosha. She'd give them forty-eight hours to sort themselves out and then be back in her apartment by tea-time. Determined, she stood up and went to find the Geordie woman. She flung open her door and nearly collided with a hot cup of tea. "Prudence, I'm so sorry hinny, but there's a man here who says he needs to talk to you reet away. There's been some bad news, pet."

Chapter five

I stretched out and was reminded that I wasn't in my own home as my toes hit the wooden footboard at the base of the bed. I lifted my groggy head off the feather pillow and squinted at my watch. There wasn't enough light to see by but I could hear birdsong close by and knew that a fresh day had begun without me.

Despite my puffy eyes from the previous night's breakdown I felt slightly better than usual. I was still tired but not exhausted. I was still emotional but not heart-broken. I was still seeking direction but not lost. I rolled onto my back and looked up at the cracked ceiling. I couldn't recall any dreams at all. Half thoughts formed in my mind as insubstantial as mist. I tried to follow the gossamer threads of translucent pictures but they wouldn't lead me to anything tangible.

Most mornings I woke trying to free myself from a nightmare, still coated with sweat and balancing on the knife-edge of a panic attack. Images, smells and feelings lingered from my dreams seemingly more real than the Egyptian cotton sheets that cocooned me. The dreams all followed the same format. First I would be running, then I would be trapped and it would be pitch black. Sometimes I'd be in a cave, sometimes underwater, sometimes in a coffin. But always, always, I could hear a baby crying and I couldn't get to it. Then just as I thought I was going to die, there would be a bright flash of light and I would wake up. But not last night. No dreams.

Today was the start of it all. I wanted to find people who had lived in Famagusta at the time of the Turkish invasion. Perhaps they would know who my parents were. Perhaps they would know what had happened to them. As I slipped out of my creaking bed I wondered if I would be able to get a trip into Famagusta's Ghost Town to track down the apartment where I'd been born.

I opened the door of my humble home-from-home and smiled at the view. It was quite simply perfect. I leant on the doorframe and folded my arms against the chill of the new morning. There was no one between me and the sea. Yes, there were trees and rocks and roads but I felt like I could have reached out and trailed my fingers in the blue water.

People talk about a tranquil sea being like a sheet of glass but to me it looked like the blue satin sheet of a freshly made bed, decadent, unrumpled and oh, so inviting. It was calling me to stretch in it, lie in it, roll around in it. I could smell the seawater from here, or was I just imagining that? I licked my lips and could taste the saltiness. If it were closer I would have dived into the water then and there, but for now I would have to content myself with paddling in the glossy water with whichever of my senses could get me the closest.

My view down the mountain towards the sea was unencumbered by any people or buildings. The usual English suburban morning punctuation of car doors slamming was gloriously absent here. The sky was cloudless but still muted and in reflection the sea was deep blue with a thread of gold running through it. There was freshness to the morning but it still gave the assurance of heat to come. The day held such promise and limitless possibilities.

It took me less than ten minutes to wash and dress for the day. It's amazing how different you can feel when you start to do something conducive rather than sit around and mope all day. I pulled on a cream sundress over freshly shaved legs, something I'd done for the first time in weeks, and pulled a thin silk cardigan around my shoulders.

It felt ridiculously self-obsessed to be spending time on self-grooming. I battled against the feeling that important, life-changing things had happened and vanity had no place in this new world. But then there was that other voice. The one that said, "Have you seen yourself?" and "What will people think?"

I slipped on my gold trimmed flip-flops, the best of a bad bunch at the airport, and admired my freshly painted deep red, almost black, toenails. I decided against washing my hair this morning and I let it fall past my shoulders in messy voluminous brown waves, having found its natural curl in the damp heat of the night.

I picked up my makeup bag and considered my naked face. At home I wouldn't even think about taking the milk in off the doorstep without applying mascara first. My mother-in-law mistook my insecurity for vanity and said, "Get over yerself! Who's gunna stop their horse 'n' cart to look at you?" There was no getting away from the fact that she thought I was shallow. I spent too long in the bathroom preening myself and not enough time checking on my elderly neighbours. It was clear to her that I had my priorities all wrong.

What she didn't understand was that I was crippled with self-doubt about my appearance. Getting out of the shower, I would catch sight of myself in the steamed-up mirror, and see the sagging outline of a body past its best. When Dom was out I would wax my top lip, pluck at stray hairs on my chin and shave my bikini line. I was disgusted by the way I looked: skin too pale; hair too dark; breasts too large; feet too big; mouth too wide. It was a battle every day to get myself in a fit state to leave the house. Lately I'd stopped trying. No amount of potions and lotions could change what I was on the inside: a failure.

Squinting into the powder-covered mirror of my compact, I moved my head from side to side looking at my face, oval section by oval section. Applying makeup now would be inharmonious with my naturally beautiful surroundings. With my middle finger I applied a generous coating of lip-balm on my full lips, the bottom one of which had a tendency to burn when exposed for too long to the blistering sun. The first time we were on holiday together in South Africa, Dom said it was because I pouted too much. And then, as I opened my mouth to protest, he had kissed me firmly, holding on to the back of my head as I struggled until I gave in to him and melted against his body. He was the only one who'd ever been able to poke fun at me and get away with it. I warned him that his charm and dimpled cheeks would only get him so far.

I frowned at my reflection in the small mirror at the light brown eyes glaring back at me with contempt. Thoughts of Dom in happier times were bittersweet. Would we ever get back to that place where we would laugh at each other's jokes and run our hands over each other's backs as we passed in the kitchen? There was a time when we couldn't keep our hands off each other but now I couldn't tolerate the thought of him touching me or seeing my useless, naked body. I ran my hand down over the front of my dress and a spongy, saggy tummy wobbled under my hand. It would take a lot of courage to get myself into a bikini again. Perhaps at my age those days were over.

My tummy had that desperate hollow feeling of hunger but I hesitated before going up to the main house. Would they even be awake yet? What was the protocol? Did I eat at the house? Was food even included in the price, whatever that may be?

The house still looked asleep as I approached it through the silent, shaded courtyard. I wondered about skirting around it and heading down the main road to go and find somewhere open for breakfast. As soon as that thought came to me, the kitchen doors were flung open and three children spilled out of them, jostling one another. They raced towards me, the young girl reaching me first amid cries from her younger brothers. She was the one who had been having her dress altered yesterday but I didn't know her name. Her chin length hair was unbrushed and tangled. Her mischievous smile and twinkling eyes gave her an elfish appearance.

"*Yassas*," she sang.

"*Yasou*," I replied.

"Breakfast," she said in heavily accented English as she took my hand.

It was a strange and slightly uncomfortable sensation to have a small warm hand in my palm but I allowed myself to be led while the other two children yapped around my ankles like small, over-excited terriers.

"*Kalimera*, Leni. You sleep good?"

"Yes thank you, Antheia." I looked around the kitchen expecting to see the other guests but there were just three of children and me. As if reading my mind Antheia said, "The holiday people eat in the breakfast room."

"Oh, I'm sorry. Could you show me where it is and I'll get out of your way?"

Antheia laughed at this and came and patted my cheek with her pudgy hand.

"You are not holiday people! Sit. Cypriot coffee or Nescafé?" While she made it a question, an answer did not seem to be required.

My new landlady poured me a thick cup of Cypriot coffee, complete with the coffee dregs from the *briki* and placed a glass of water by its side. What had George said about me? She must have got the wrong end of the stick and thought I was more of a friend than I was.

"You are writer, yes? I will teach you about Cyprus. It is beautiful country."

"Yes, but I write about food," I began apologetically. "I'm sorry, I think that I might have misled you. I have some writing to do and also a little… um… personal research while I am here. I only met George yesterday."

"I know," she nodded. "And this will be your home. You will have breakfast every day. If you want dinner you tell me in the morning and I will cook for you. On Sunday you help me cook dinner for my family and I will show you real Cypriot cooking. Yes?"

I couldn't help but smile as I didn't appear to have any choice. "Yes," I said, "that would be great. Thank you."

I tucked into the loveliest breakfast ever to have graced my unworthy stomach. Peaches with Greek yoghurt and honey drizzled over the top, alongside several slices of toasted bread and yet more honey.

"What you do today?" Antheia asked.

"I'm not sure, yet. Perhaps hire a car? I'd like to arrange a trip to see the Ghost Town."

"Varosha?"

"Erm... I think it's called Famagusta," I ventured.

"Varosha is part of Famagusta. The place that is now the forbidden zone is called Varosha. There is nothing to see. The buildings fall down. There is nothing there now."

"I know, but I would still like to have a look if I can. It fascinates me that no one has lived there since 1974. It's so mysterious, isn't it?"

Antheia shrugged and started wiping down the table in front of me even though I was still eating.

71

"It is no mystery. Turks come, Greeks leave. That's it. You want dinner today?" She scrubbed fiercely at an imaginary mark on the wood.

It was only subtle, like the shift in wind direction, but I sensed that the atmosphere had changed between us.

"No, thank you. I'll get something to eat when I'm out, if that's okay?"

"Sure." She shooed the children out of the kitchen and left me alone to finish my sticky breakfast. I drank as much coffee as I could and then picked up my bag and crept away through the back door. It wasn't easy to put my finger on why the sudden shroud of discomfort had settled over me. It seemed, at least, that Antheia didn't think much of my plan to get into Varosha. Perhaps I'd been naïve in thinking people would be supportive of my quest.

Replete and gastronomically ecstatic with splendid Cypriot fare, I put on my sunglasses and strolled round to the front of the house. I felt a little disappointed not to have seen the beautiful little girl from yesterday and wondered whether she was enjoying a lie in on this glorious Saturday morning. Another notable absence was the old woman from the day before. Her chair sat empty but just as unwelcoming.

She was the only person so far who had made me feel like the outsider I surely was. Perhaps if I explained to her that I was trying hard to reverse that situation? How I so desperately wanted to find somewhere to belong to. I didn't think it would make much difference to the old woman. She didn't care about me, and why should she? To her I was another tourist coming to spy on the Cypriots and to make light of their life and their troubles.

Not for the first time since my mother had explained the accident that led us to be in each other's lives, I wondered why it meant so much to me to 'belong'. I was neither British, nor Cypriot. I didn't know whether I had my biological mother's eyes or my father's temperament. I didn't know whether I had a rich family history of grandparents who fought heroically in the war or was related to farmers who had spent their lives working the stony ground. Was there a family history of madness? A predisposition to cancer? Did diabetes run in my family? Would I ever know and why did it matter so much?

I looked up from my dragging feet and was surprised to find myself in the town already. The main promenade was already busy with holidaymakers as I approached the gilded beach. I stood in the developing heat and watched as people dragged sun-loungers into position on the lemon sands and applied sun-lotion on each other's backs. Some were reading books whereas other brave souls were already taking a dip in a sea that had yet to warmed by the summer sun. Small children dug holes in the sand with severe concentration etched on their smooth, plump faces.

A thought struck me and I kicked off my shoes and walked toward a tall square structure at the back of the beach with a bright blue 'Boat Hire' sign. The sand was still cool under my hot feet and it shifted underneath me with every sliding step. Its golden ripples absorbed the energy I was putting into my progress so that I seemed to be making little headway.

"*Kalimera.*" I pushed my sunglasses to the top of my head, forcing my hair off my face. "Do you have any boat trips to Varosha today?" I asked rather too loudly and over-enunciated so that the shirtless, sculpted man-child in front of me could understand. I flashed my best smile and allowed my eyes to hover over his well-toned abs for just a moment too long. He looked back at me with a hint of amusement in his sable eyes. Oh Lord, he probably thought I was flirting with him. I guessed I was nearly twice his age, which made me feel desperately old. What age did a woman have to be before she was considered a cougar?

"Good morning. Yes I do. The next excursion is in approximately half an hour." He pointed at the handwritten sign to his right with the times of each boat trip clearly marked. Now I looked like an illiterate idiot as well as a cougar. My face started to prickle with the heat of my embarrassment. I thought about cutting my losses and beating a hasty retreat but the lure of Varosha was too strong.

"Right, yes, I can see that. Could I book a place on that trip please? The name's Leni Jeffries. Thank you. I'll be back in twenty minutes," I said, trying to maintain some air of control in the face of the Adonis whose grasp of English was as good, if not better, than mine.

I turned with as much dignity as I could muster and headed back up the beach towards the car-hire shop. Fearing he was watching me I forgot how to walk. I lifted my knees too high, wiggled my hindquarters too much and generally stumbled away from him in dismay.

Stopping to put my shoes back on I pushed open the stiff glass door of the hire shop. "*Kalimera*."

"*Kalimera*, how can we help you today?"

"I would like to hire a car please."

"Of course, take a seat."

"Thank you."

"This is a list of the classes of vehicles we stock. Are you wanting something in particular?"

"Yes." I looked at the list in front of me. I wanted a manual gear stick, small car but big enough to keep me safe if anyone crashed into me and, most importantly of all, air conditioning. I surveyed the list. Nissans seemed to be popular here. Nissan Note, Nissan Almera or perhaps I'd go a little wild and get a Suzuki soft-top jeep for thirty-three euros a day. So no one was more surprised than me when I said, "I'd like to hire a moped please."

A voice in my head was screaming at me, *What the hell are you doing? Do you know how dangerous these things are? You've never ridden one in your life!* The decision was such a bold one for me that adrenaline sped through my heart, causing it to thunder unnaturally loudly. Emboldened by the rashness of my actions I felt invigorated, as if something deep inside me had been woken up. Just as I tried to pinpoint the feeling it was lost to me and I was left staring down at a single key on an oblong key ring.

I was still shaking a little when I joined the boat trip with the keys to my shiny cream moped in my bag. The exhilaration of my newfound bravery battled with my 'head girl' disapproval at my rashness as I settled into the boat, stifling an inappropriate giggle. There were only four other people on the boat with me. I didn't pay much attention to the two couples but said the usual polite "Hello" and then took a seat towards the front of the small, brightly-painted wooden boat, next to the scuffed green cool-box. I sat alone, so very alone, and looked down at my wedding band. Just the mere presence of these two couples highlighted my solitude. I'd never been on holiday by myself before. I'd been on some solo work assignments but I usually managed to take Dom along with me. I'd never undertaken anything of such life-altering significance before without someone holding my hand.

Almost before I blinked, Famagusta's Ghost Town appeared apologetically ahead of us like it had been caught doing something it shouldn't have. At this distance it looked like a normal resort that had become a little rundown and dishevelled. Imposing hotels stood to attention facing the sea, ready for inspection. But the eyes of these buildings were blank. There was no one sunbathing on the beach and the waters were devoid of swimmers. An eerie silence hung around the bay and a tremor trickled down my spine and caused me to shiver involuntarily. I waited for it to hit me – the recognition, the clarity – but there was nothing. The boat skipped its way from crest to white crest with occasional sprays of water sprinkling my cheeks and eyelids.

I focused intently on the horizon, unblinking, and clasped the side of the vessel with two hands. Come on. This is where it all started. Shouldn't I feel something? I would have settled for any feeling at all. Elation. Despair. Anything to suggest some attachment to the town in front of me. My breathing continued evenly, my heartbeat quiet and steady. I was still just me and Varosha was still just a Ghost Town.

Our young captain started his well-rehearsed soliloquy about Varosha, which sounded straight out of a guidebook, and I half-listened to him as I scanned the horizon for clues that I feared wouldn't be there.

"This is Varosha, part of Famagusta known for its beauty. Famagusta was once a bustling and vibrant tourist destination for the rich and famous. In the early 1970s it was one of the most popular holiday destinations in the world. This hotel closest to us now is the Argo Hotel which was a favourite of all of the Hollywood stars in the 70s: Elizabeth Taylor, Richard Burton...." His voice trailed off as he could list more if he wanted to. "Elizabeth Taylor was often to be seen here on the terrace sipping cocktails wearing elaborate kaftans and headscarves. Unfortunately the lucrative and bustling world of Hollywood and tourism ended abruptly in the summer of 1974 when the Turkish people attacked the peaceful Greek citizens of Cyprus and forced them from their homes."

I looked then into the unmistakably biased eyes of our lecturer. His English was perfect but his understanding of the facts had a certain Greek slant.

"There is a fence around the town known as the 'Buffer Zone' or 'Green Line'. People are prohibited from crossing this line. Clothes were left on the washing lines," he continued, "cars are still parked in garages and electric light bulbs were left on until they finally burned out. The Turkish Army patrol the area but the Greek people are not allowed back into their homes."

"Why are they keeping the land?" asked the larger one of my male companions, seemingly genuinely interested.

"They use it as a bargaining tool. They will give it back if we meet their demands. But to meet their demands would be to acknowledge them as an independent country, which we cannot do. Nobody except themselves and Turkey recognise Northern Cyprus as an independent country. The international community classes Northern Cyprus as occupied territory and it is widely accepted that they are guilty of genocide in the war following the invasion of 1974."

Genocide is such a repulsive word. I looked to the sleeping town. People had died here. Thousands of people were still missing but I hadn't really considered them for longer than five minutes. I was ashamed at how self-obsessed I'd been.

"What a shame," cooed the big man's wife. "It looks so... What's the word Barry? Forlorn."

She was right: it was an apt word for the sight in front of us. It was strange to see that time had stood still and I itched to walk up the beach and have a good nose around. There's nothing more tantalising than the thought that you are the first person to set foot there in many years. It would be like unearthing a treasure of some sort. It might not be on a par with being the first person to explore the pyramids, but the treasure of a snapshot of history and of precious memories is more valuable than diamonds. What I wanted to discover was worth more than jewels: I was hoping to find myself.

"Nature is gradually taking over Varosha," our guide sighed. "Our once beautiful buildings are crumbling, the sea front is lapping at the bricks. Nature is the only one who is benefitting from this atrocity. Houses lie empty, gradually falling into a state of disrepair that they cannot return from. The curtains are falling from broken windows like yellow leaves in autumn. The only good thing about this town where nature reigns is that sea turtles now nest on the beaches in complete safety and the fishes thrive in these waters. In this at least, we can say that the Turks have not beaten us. Life will go on where Greek Cypriots can no longer live. We would rather the sea turtles made their homes on our beaches than have the Turkish pitch their beach umbrellas there."

"How do you get in there?" I asked, interrupting our guide's dramatic prose. All eyes turned to face me as if they'd forgotten my lurking presence. The question was greeted with silence so I tried another tactic.

"I would like to find out more about it. My parents lived there in 1974. I imagine their apartment is still as they left it and I'm, y'know, well, a little bit curious, to say the least." I attempted a weak smile and a careless shrug of my shoulders.

"There is no way in," our guide answered firmly. "There is a Turkish patrol to make sure than no one enters and they will shoot you if you are caught. Only Turkish Military and UN Patrols ever enter Varosha."

I'm not usually stubborn but I decided to try out my newfound rebellious streak.

"I've seen photographs and videos on the Internet that were taken from within Varosha." Pushing my point further, I continued, "And even from this distance I can see that the perimeter fence has been broken down over there." All heads turned to look where I was pointing and one of the women said, "Oooh, Barry, she's right."

My face remained turned to our guide who, tellingly, hadn't moved an inch or allowed his eyes to wander. He knew exactly which part of the fence I was talking about, that much I was sure of. I fought the urge to look away or to apologise. I'd had enough of people pulling the wool over my eyes. The only way I was going to stop people walking all over me was to stop acting like a doormat.

Expressive dark eyes held my gaze without blinking and I swallowed too loudly. I knew I wasn't his favourite passenger. I half expected him to raise his voice at me in rebuke but instead, when he spoke, his voice was quieter and measured.

"I'm sorry. Perhaps you do not understand. When I said there is no way in, I meant that it would be both illegal and unwise to attempt such a thing. That is not to say that there aren't any stupid people out there with a death wish. However, I for one, would not attempt to cross the Green Line, nor would I advise you to do so."

"Really?" I pushed

"Really."

He continued as if we had not spoken. "Even if a resolution was agreed tomorrow, these houses and hotels would have to be demolished and rebuilt before anyone could move into them again."

"Why is it a ghost town though?" asked Barry's wife. "I mean, if the Turkish control it, why don't they use it?"

"Some of the buildings are used by the Turkish army but Varosha is protected by a UN resolution which states that the town can only be resettled by its original inhabitants. The inhabitants of Varosha were almost entirely Greek Cypriot. Unfortunately the Turkish are allowed to live in Greek houses in the North of the island and treat them as their own. They are allowed to pull down Greek churches to make way for Turkish hotels. The resolution does not stop this. "

We sat in silence for several minutes and though I thought that I could feel the young man's eyes on me I refused to let him draw my gaze. I felt that I had angered him somehow but I didn't see why asking to get a closer look at the city could have had such an effect on him. Perhaps it suited him to portray the Ghost Town as an impenetrable fortress because it made his job as a tour guide all the more necessary.

"Ladies and gentlemen, we must now return to Fig Tree Bay."

It wasn't enough. I hadn't seen nearly enough. I hadn't really seen anything. I was feeling frustrated but I would have to find another way in. I hadn't come this far just to fall at the first hurdle. As the boat turned and started off in the direction that it had come from, I watched the hotels melting into a shimmering mirage behind us.

Back at the beach, I hung back a little on the boat for all the others to disembark, pretending to have trouble locating my keys in my apple green bag. Inherent politeness overcoming his annoyance with me, the young man held out his hand to help me off the boat. Apparently he was a better person than me. I refused his assistance and managed to stumble from the boat into the shallow water all by myself.

"I'm sorry if I angered you," I stated without an abundance of sincerity.

"I am not angry," said his perfect Cupid's bow lips, even though his eyes were saying something entirely different.

"Right. Look, I really would like to get into Varosha."

"There are parts of Famagusta you can visit which will get you closer but you will not be allowed into Varosha."

"Can I go over into Northern Cyprus on a day trip or something? Would that get me any closer?"

He sighed and looked at the sand. "Of course you *may* go into Northern Cyprus, I cannot stop you, but you will still not see

Varosha. It is off limits to everyone except UN Personnel and Turkish Military…"

"Yeah," I interrupted. "So you said."

I felt deflated and let down once more. It didn't look like anything was going to go according to plan. I bit the inside of my cheek; there was no way I was going to cry again. Not here, and certainly not in front of a complete stranger.

"I am sorry I cannot help you."

"Me too," I murmured.

I busied myself searching in my bag for an invisible item as I walked purposely away from him. If I looked up now there was every chance that the film of water across my stinging eyes would escape in the form of a teardrop and there was no way I was going to let that happen.

I bought crisps, a bottle of lemonade and some chocolate, which I placed carefully under the seat of my scooter and then I was ready to start her up. I'd gone for a vintage-inspired 125cc scooter and she (yes, it was a 'she') was beautiful. Top speed was 60 mph so perhaps it wasn't that wild after all. I had been assured that it was a simple 'twist and go' moped with an electric push button start that even I would master within five minutes. As I looked appraisingly at her, I started to smile. It was just about the craziest thing I had done in a long time but she was gorgeous. I decided to name her Rita, as in Hayworth, and sat astride her.

I am not known for my rash behaviour. I don't make snap decisions, throw caution to the wind or believe in chance. I like words like "planning" and "certainty". There's nothing like a fast-paced fiendish Sudoku with a cup of Assam to reaffirm my sense of order in the world. No alternative answers, maybes or best guesses, just solid, hard numbers with the *right* answer.

Even when I'm cooking I'm a 'numbers' person. I'm more Delia than Jamie. There's no "glug" of this or "handful" of that in my kitchen. If the recipe calls for a tomato to be peeled, I peel it. Tablespoons, millilitres and grams keep my kitchen shipshape. My soufflés rise to order; my steaks are pink to perfection. Chance is a dirty word and dirt isn't tolerated in my kitchen. Or my life for that matter. I think that is one of the reasons that I love food and cooking so much. While you can just throw things together for supper, if you get stuck there's always a cookery book to offer inspiration or to tell you exactly what to do. How many situations in life come with such a comprehensive manual? Just follow the recipe: weigh things out, use the right ingredients cook at the stated temperature for the correct time. What could be simpler? There is something so reassuring to following a recipe, knowing that by correctly following the steps you are led to a most sublime and delicious outcome.

Five minutes later I was back at The Pleiades unwinding the tension from my shoulders. Instead of going through the main house I slipped off my cream domed crash helmet and skirted the side of the building. I had a spring in my step as I slipped down to the little cottage and to the awaiting view.

I hurriedly kicked off my shoes, almost bouncing with the exhilaration of a fear overcome. Doing something daring and out of character was intoxicating. My head felt clearer, refreshed. I could no longer feel the sharp pains that had ridden my shoulders for the last few weeks. I poured myself a glass of lemonade and headed back outside to the bench with a bar of chocolate and a map under my arm. I spread the map out before me over the rough slats of the crudely fashioned wood that served as a table.

It was a simple map given to me by the scooter hire company but

it gave me enough of an impression of where I was in relation to

the rest of the island, and Varosha in particular. As I cast my

eyes over the plan in front of me I greedily stuffed the warmed,

softening chocolate into my mouth. Simple pleasures. It only

took a moment to identify my location and my proximity to the

Ghost Town.

I really wanted to give Mum a call and find out exactly

where Lakira Street was because it wasn't listed on the map. No

place names or landmarks were shown on the faded section of

the map that identified Varosha. Perhaps Mum could have given

me some pointers, such as a school or a church. Which hotel

were they close to? I hadn't expected it to be this difficult to find

their apartment. I had mistakenly thought that the difficulties

would come later. I chewed at the hard skin on the side of my

thumbnail, a habit I thought I'd grown out of years ago. I

continued to stare at the map hoping that something would jump

out at me. But neither was there an 'X marks the spot' over

Lakira Street, nor was there a sign indicating a gap in the fence allowing for a covert entrance into the Ghost Town.

I was reasonably sure that Mum and Eddie's old apartment had been by the sea. Mum had mentioned how she used to be able to see and hear the sea from her balcony. I searched the map again. "Urgghh!" I thumped my palm down on the table in frustration, which caused the table to wobble on its uneven legs. In a split second my glass was on its side and rolling towards the edge of the table.

Without hesitation my arm shot out with viper-like accuracy and snatched it before it exploded on the ground. Relief turned to dismay as I saw that the content of my glass pooled in decreasing puddles across the map.

"Shit! Bugger! Bollocks! Arseholes!"

I tried to shake off the sticky bubbles but they seeped into the paper and hung heavily upon the printed grids. With its foot in the door, self-pity entered stealthily into my mind where it took hold with a vice-like grip. My 'can-do' attitude of barely ten minutes ago had fled and left me wondering what the hell I was doing here. I flung the sodden map to the floor and retreated into the cool shell of my room. I threw myself on the bed and squeezed my eyes against the anguish of my uselessness.

A cool breeze carrying the strong smell of lavender caused me to open my eyes. At the doorway stood Antheia's eldest girl, chewing on the end of one of her plaits.

"Oh! *Yasou*," I said as I sat up. "I was just lying down for a minute."

She continued to stare at me and I sat and looked back at her. Her hair, the same brown as her eyes, was in unruly plaits by the side of her face. They were bracketed with red ribbons at the top and bottom. She was about twelve years old, judging by her size, but something in her eyes suggested that she was older than she looked. Her blue and white checked dress reached the top of her dirty and bony knees and she wore white ankle socks with her sandals. We looked at each other for a long time before she nervously slid into the room. I gave her what I hoped was an encouraging nod and smile and she abruptly hopped up onto the bed beside me taking me by surprise. She grinned and starting telling me the most elaborate story in Greek.

"I'm sorry, sweetheart, but I don't speak Greek."

She nodded at me. "*Endaxi*," and then continued with her story. It seemed that I didn't need to be able to understand her for her to have an audience. She was an exquisite creature and despite myself, I reached out and stroked her hair as she talked. The touch of her hair hit me like an electric shock and she opened her eyes wide as if she had felt it too. I blinked away any sense of sentimentality and continued to nod encouragement at what I hoped were appropriate moments.

Eventually she stopped and placed her hand on her chest. "An-na."

"Hello Anna. My name is Leni."

She nodded at this and then continued with her story. I was sure this small brown girl and I were going to be great friends.

Chapter six

Cyprus, 1974

When Pru opened her eyes the whole room was buttery with late morning sun. Was the older woman still asleep? She flicked through her recollection of the previous night but couldn't remember her name although Pru could picture her face perfectly and recall her scent of perfumed talcum powder that made her feel nauseous. Since she'd been pregnant her nose picked up every aroma with a veracity that a sniffer dog would be proud of.

There were other names from yesterday that she had no trouble recollecting. The man was called Reverend Joy. The name didn't suit him. Pru saw his granite face as soon as she stepped into the sitting room clutching her cup of tea like a shield.

"Mrs Clarke?" he asked unnecessarily. Pru's eyes were drawn to this man's cavernous nostrils under his hawkish beak. Wiry hair protruded from dark hollows above his thin top lip. He seemed nervous, she noted, as he swallowed noisily and his jutting Adam's apple bobbed in his scrawny neck. She recognised him from the Easter service on the base but she wasn't a regular church goer.

"Would you like to sit down?" He motioned with long bony fingers to the armchair. His fingernails were too long.

"No, thank you, I'll stand."

Pru and the vicar continued to stare at each other, neither of them much impressed by what they saw. The roaring silence became unbearable and the Reverend cleared his throat to speak.

"Ehem. Yes. We've received a message from your mother. I went to your apartment but your landlady said I'd just missed you. I had quite a job to track you down actually." He smiled then. It was an insipid smile that showed no teeth and no warmth. Pru felt no compulsion to return the bogus grin.

She waited for him to continue. Pru could tell she was making him feel uncomfortable and she enjoyed the feeling of power she had over this man of the cloth. Seconds, as marked by the carriage clock on the mantelpiece, ticked loudly by. Before today, she had never noticed how slow seconds were when you stopped to count them. Pru raised the hot cup to her dry lips so that she had an excuse to break eye contact with the clerical man. His watery eyes were blinking too often and made her own start to twitch.

"I'm afraid I have some distressing news for you," Reverend Joy continued with a well-practiced frown of concern etched between his overgrown brows. "Your father has passed away." The ticking of the clock faded away. "I am very sorry for your loss."

Pru felt the world tilt on its axis and the force of cold air rushing into her ears. Her cup of tea left her fingers as if they were no longer made of anything substantial. She watched as the rosebud patterned cup twisted towards the floor and bounced off the carpet in front of her. Pru felt oddly removed from the scene as she watched amber beads of tea arcing through the air in impossibly slow motion. As the scalding liquid splattered on her bare toes, Pru abruptly came back to her senses.

"Oh God! I'm so sorry. Let me clean that up. Where can I get a cloth? I don't know what happened then. One minute I was holding it and then..."

Sturdy arms stopped her mid-bend as she stooped for the cup with arm outstretched.

"Prudence. Leave it, pet. Are you okay?" Soft tones soothed in her ear and Pru turned with puzzlement to the woman she'd forgotten was there.

"It was the shock, that's all, it doesn't really burn at all now." Pru's voice faded out as the two women locked eyes and Pru saw the dumfounded look on the other woman's round face.

"It's nothing but a bit of spilt tea. Pay no mind. I'm talking about your dad, love. Why don't you sit down?"

"Of course." Pru knitted her brows together. She was still wondering how she should react to this news.

"I need to pack though. Again. I'll need to go home for the funeral and what have you." She looked quizzically at her trembling hands. When she looked up, Reverend Joy was pursing his lips into a thin, grim line.

"Your mother wishes me to inform you that the errr... The, erm, funeral was last week and that there is no need for you to make the trip, especially in your condition."

"Right," spat Pru, balling her hands into fists at her side and feeling her strength rush back through her veins. "*In my condition?* Did she really say that?"

"Well, it was implied in her missive, I think. I'm sure she was only thinking of your safety and that of your child."

"Then you don't know my mother, Reverend." She suddenly felt nothing but hate for the woman who had given birth to her, though the fire soon dissipated and Pru sank to the chair in defeat.

Silence expanded between them until Pru spoke, quieter this time. "Did the letter say how he died?"

"Yes," Joy said, pleased to be able to impart some important information. "She did. I'm afraid he finally lost his battle with cancer."

Pru began to laugh mirthlessly and it was only the shocked look on the Reverend's face that stopped her.

"That doesn't happen overnight, does it? Cancer? I mean, she knew didn't she? And she didn't tell me? Well, that just about says it all."

"Well..." the reverend began, flustered and blinking rapidly.

"Right. If that's all then, I think I'll lie down for an hour or two. It's been quite a day."

Pru didn't actually remember getting to bed. The two large brandies she had swallowed without tasting had helped round the edges of her grief. She sat up in the bed stiffly and looked about her through puffy, half-closed eyes. It reminded her a bit of Eddie's parents' house, but even friendlier somehow. There was a scallop-edged crocheted mat under the figurine on the drawers. The figurine itself was of a woman in a bonnet holding a basket over one arm and in her other hand she held the hem of her dress, revealing her underskirts. On the window ledge there was a pomander in the shape of a pink, heeled boot. There were no signs at all that she was in Cyprus. There had been no attempt to embrace the local style.

A cold cup of tea from the night before lay untouched on the bedside table and she took a sip to wet her lips. The familiar presence of a full bladder suddenly made its mark on Pru's consciousness and she eased herself from the bed to search for the bathroom. Her attempt to open the door quietly was floored as she opened it directly into her protruding belly and then swore loudly.

"There's a lav just through the kitchen there, pet. I'll get the kettle on."

Pru jumped and took a moment to spot the originator of the soft Geordie accent.

"Thank you Mrs....?"

"Betty." And then each one of those lines on her face creased in a warm smile as she walked ahead of Pru into the kitchen.

Pru followed as quickly as she could but it always took a while for her hips to wake up in the morning and the aches were something else today. Once, quite early on in her pregnancy, she had vowed never to walk like a pregnant woman. She was sure that the pregnancy duck-waddle wasn't a necessary part of the process. Now, nearing the end of her pregnancy, she realised that the choice wasn't hers to make.

When she emerged from the bathroom, Betty was at the cooker melting a huge lump of lard in the frying pan.

"Not for me, thank you. I don't eat breakfast," Pru said as she tried to slip away, embarrassed at the state of her un-combed hair.

"Ya do now. Sit down, I'll make you a brew." Betty laid three rashers of bacon side by side in the misshapen and grease-coated pan and reached for the white-shelled eggs. Uncharacteristically, Pru didn't even consider arguing with her and instead sat at the kitchen table to watch Betty at work. She was exhausted and spent.

"How ya feeling, pet?"

Pru thought carefully before answering the question.

"I'm fine, thank you. I think it's normal to be tired this late on in the pregnancy."

"I wasn't talking about that. I was meaning about your–"

"I know" interrupted Pru, effectively closing that line of conversation.

After a few moments of silence in which Betty studied Pru, the older woman shouted over the sizzle and hiss of the bacon, "Eddie looked in on you this morning. He didn't want to wake you but said he'll be back for dinner, mind. Poor bairn looks tired. Did you manage much sleep? Get all the rest you can now because as sure as eggs is eggs, that wee bairn will be keeping you on your toes when it's born. They don't care if you've had a bad day or a late night."

Relieved that the conversation had moved on to a topic she didn't mind talking about, Pru asked, "How old are your children?"

"Mine? Oh no hinny, I don't have any."

After a momentary pause while Betty poured an amber stream of hot liquid into another rosebud cup, she said, "Turns out that it wasn't in the plan for us, no matter how much we wanted it." She looked over her shoulder at Pru's uncomfortable expression and handed her the tea. "Now if I don't feel bad about it, pet, you certainly shouldn't! You'll never hear me complain about it. I've got the best life I could hope for, thank you very much. And it means I get to keep my hourglass figure too." And she laughed while turning her ample hips from side to side in an exaggerated figure of eight.

"Nah, I was a bit past my best when me and Bern married. He's a bit younger than me, see? Got meself a toy boy! By the looks of it you can only have a few weeks to go. Not the best time for war, eh? It'll be over before we hear any shots fired, though, you'll see."

"What happened though?" asked Pru. "I don't understand. The Greeks and Turks are friends, right? They work side by side, they live side by side..."

"Do they?" Betty raised her eyebrows as she flipped the hissing bacon over.

"Well... Yeah," said Pru, less certain this time.

Pru leant her elbows on the table and held her cup of tea against her lips as she thought about Betty's question. At the army stables where Pru was a regular visitor, even though her pregnancy stopped her from riding, both the Greeks and Turks worked together, but now she stopped to think about it, the Greeks had the slightly nicer jobs while the Turks shovelled the manure. But she had never seen any animosity between them. She realised now that she didn't know many Turks. The restaurants that they ate in were mainly Greek-owned; the woman they rented their flat off was Greek; the family she bought fruit off at the side of the road was Greek; all their local acquaintances were Greek rather than Turkish.

"I still don't get it. It's plainly stupid," she said finally, making up her mind that they must all be idiots.

"Well, the Turkish were unhappy, we all knew that, but I'm not sure them Greeks expected this. But then, if you poke a hornet's nest, you get stung." The older woman sighed as she placed cutlery and a bottle of HP sauce on the table. "There's been trouble fer years and it's finally boiled over. Eat up."

"But why aren't the British army doing anything?"

"Oh I dunno, pet, but what *can* they do?" Betty asked kindly. "If we side with the Greeks now and have war with the

Turks, we'll be in all kinds of hot watter. It isn't our country, pet. This is a politicians' war. Let them do the talking and in the meantime, we'll pray that not too many young'uns lose their lives because of some old men's hunger for power."

"That simple?" asked Pru through a mouthful of salty bacon.

"Let's hope so, pet. I've no desire to get back to Newcastle just yet. Now get that inside yer," she nodded at the plate in front of Pru. "And then get dressed. I want yer help oot in the garden."

Conversation over, Pru was left alone to finish her breakfast. She resented the fact that Betty expected her to do some gardening but she was softening towards the other woman. And, she had to admit, it was nice to be eating proper, lard-cooked bacon again. Betty had even cut off the rind and fried it separately so that it could coil into crispy spirals.

The news from last night was tapping at her subconscious and she knew she would have to let it in at some point. She was well aware that she should feel something over Dad's death and the fact that she didn't get to say goodbye to him. She pushed her bacon around her plate, smearing brown sauce across the circumference and strained to remember that last time she'd seen Dad. It would have been the morning of her eighteenth birthday. She remembered that it had been sunny, despite the chill in the air.

She opened her presents at the breakfast table over bitter marmalade-dressed toast. She clearly remembered the slender oblong box that Dad slid over to her from beneath the red knitted tea cosy. By the twinkling in his eyes she knew that he was pleased with the gift so she was expecting something special.

It was the most delicate and exquisite watch with a real leather strap. The face was white with roman numerals around the outside. She couldn't stop looking at it and bolted down her breakfast in order to get to college and show it to all of her friends her new timepiece. *"It's a timepiece, not a watch, Little Bean."* Did she even thank him for it? Did she tell him she loved him as she flounced out the door feeling like a woman? She could only hope so.

It was over half an hour later when she joined Betty in the garden in the same clothes that she had arrived in the night before. Whereas the interior of the house may have been like stepping into a semi-detached in middle England, the garden was all Cyprus. There were white and blue tiles on the garden wall and huge cracked terracotta pots around the patio filled full of bright, bowing stems of orange-red geraniums with lush tiered leaves. In the raised bed on one side of the garden there were numerous cacti, some with vicious spikes, while others looked soft enough to stroke. The other side was abundant with tomatoes, none of which were the smooth spheres that Pru was used to. The colours ranged from yellow to purple, and some were pear-shaped while others were more like ridged, small pumpkins.

"There's a bowl on the table. Could you fill it with toms? The boys'll be back soon."

The whitewashed walls dazzled like they had absorbed the very rays of the sun and were radiating the golden glory themselves. The whiteness was enhanced by the violet-blue of the midday sky and Pru had to shade her eyes to be able to focus on the task in hand. Somewhere at the bottom of the garden Pru could hear the sound of a lone cricket and as the baby squirmed inside her, an extension of her body, she felt something akin to contentment.

When the task was completed, Pru sat at the table in the shade with a glass of weak orange squash. She could still smell the pungent bitterness of the tomatoes on her fingers. She had been surprised to hear from Betty that there were rations and Pru had been delivered to Betty's house yesterday with a box of dried goods like rice, biscuits and some tins. Betty didn't seem to be worried about lack of food and was boiling some ham and potatoes for lunch while humming a tune that Pru had never heard before.

"Not too much for me, Hinny," boomed a man's jocular voice from the kitchen that made Pru jump. She looked towards the door and found herself hoping that Eddie was home too.

"You're late. And dirty!" came Betty's voice with a chuckle. "Get cleaned up! Eddie, pet, you look tired. Prudence is ootside, why don't you go sit down. I'll bring you a drink."

"Thanks, Bet." Pru was surprised to find that her heart soared at her husband's voice.

Eddie pushed aside the multi-coloured strips of plastic that served as a back door during the warm summer months and smiled boyishly at Pru. "All right?" His crooked smile and tilt of his head made Pru flush.

Pru smiled. "Tired. You?"

"Shattered."

Eddie kissed the top of her head and sat down next to her with a grunt, placing his tanned hand on her thigh.

"Where were you, Eddie? It's been terrible. No one would tell me where we were going. I thought I was going to have the baby then and there. And then I get here to be told that Dad has died. Where were you?"

"There is a war going on, you know?"

"Do I know? Are you seriously asking me that? Someone tried to shoot me, Eddie! Shoot me! Can you believe it?"

Eddie sighed wearily but didn't answer her straight away.

"I am sorry about your Dad. I didn't know until Bet told me. You know I wouldn't leave you if I didn't have to."

"Why should you put your work before me, Eddie? It's just not fair that I–"

Eddie leant over and kissed Pru firmly. She resisted at first, trying to keep her mouth closed against his insistent tongue. She was furious with him and would tell him so as soon as she could open her mouth to talk. Feeling his stubble against her smooth skin and his hot lips against hers, though, caused Pru to give in to his kisses. She would chastise him later.

"Pru! Lovely to meet you." Suddenly the man whose voice she had heard in the kitchen was upon her. Pru pulled away from Eddie in an instant and regained her composure. The colossal man held out his hand in what Pru assumed was a handshake but as soon as her hand was in his he hauled her to her feet and hugged her.

"I see you've met Bernie," laughed Betty as she came through to the garden with a tray of food. "Sit down, you old fool."

The men tucked into the food while Betty bombarded Bernie with questions about the fighting.

"Well y'nah how me and the kid here," Bernie nodded in Eddie's direction, "got Makarios out of the country last week?"

Pru didn't want to show her ignorance or her disinterest in what her husband was involved in. "Erm... Tell me again how it happened."

Pleased to be given an open invitation to talk some more, Bernie swallowed a large mouthful of ham and began.

"He's a good bloke, whatever they say. He made sure this group of school kids were oot of the presidential gaff and safe before he fled, y'nah? And he could've bin killed. We had no idea where he was until he turned up in Paphos. All we were told was the Greek military had overthrown the government. We were sent to get him to this RAF fighter jet and that was it. He was away. It's anyone's guess now what'll happen. I heard that some of 'em higher up wanted to intervene but have been told to stay put. They say it's been coming for years. There was all that trouble in the sixties. Each side blames the other. The Greeks should never have got rid of Makarios because now the Turks think that the Greek military are going to align Cyprus with mainland Greece. I can't see why they would want to anyway. Any more ham, hinny?

"The Turks tried to get wor support for their 'peace operation'. Ha! When we didn't give it they invaded anyway. Turkish troops landed on the Northern coast in the early hours and they are pushin' the Greeks oot a their homes with more force than I'd say is strictly necessary. But that's what happens when the fighting starts. 'Peace' isn't in the forefront of their minds and anyone who says it is, is a lying bastard. Pardon me French love.

"It's frustrating for us that we just have to sit by and watch it all. We're gathering intelligence and keeping tabs on where the Turks are but what else can we do, y'nah? Listen to me blitherin' on. Any mustard, hinny? Anyway you've got bigger things on yer mind. Sorry to hear about yer Dad, pet. Got any brothers an' sisters?"

"What?" asked Pru, surprised to find herself suddenly included in the conversation. "Er, no. Only child."

"Sorry to hear that."

"Don't be. I'm not."

"Even so," Bernie continued, "not nice that it falls on your shoulders to take care of your Ma."

112

"It doesn't. Fall on my shoulders, that is. No, she has made it clear that she can cope on her own." Eddie reached out and entwined his fingers with Pru. He didn't say anything, but that gesture was enough to let Pru know that he knew how much she was hurting. Sometimes she wondered what she would do without Eddie. No one else knew her quite like he did. And there was no one else left to care anymore.

The next few days were a welcome break for Pru. The four of them slid into an easy routine together and Pru helped Betty with the house, cooking and garden.

Pru was becoming impatient, even excited, to have this baby. She hadn't had a great relationship with her own mother but was certain that it would be different between her and her own baby. An only child to a couple who had had her too late in life to enjoy her energy, she craved the family life that she had never had. Her mam and dad weren't just a different generation to her but, it seemed to a young Pru, a different species. Mam's maternal instinct failed to be roused when a screaming baby had invaded her life when she was just embarking on her forty-fifth year. Dad wasn't a man of many words and if he wasn't on the allotment, he was reading the *Sun* newspaper or nodding off in his armchair. But there was still a bond in this silence that had the young Pru following her dad to the allotment and back every day.

"Pass me the dibber, Little Bean. Ha'penny for every slug you find and put in this jar, Little Bean." She missed Dad. What hurt her more than anything was that he hadn't stuck up for her when Mum had kicked her out of home.

Her thoughts were interrupted abruptly when Betty swung open her bedroom door with a flourish. She brought a morning cup of tea with a beaming smile on her face. "Morning! Ceasefire! Thank God for that, eh? You can get back home now and get on with bringing that bairn into the world. Let's get you packed up."

"Right. Yes. Well that's good, isn't it?" offered Pru half-heartedly.

Betty laughed. "You don't sound too happy aboot it!"

"No, I am. It's just... well, I've got used to being here now."

"Ha! And you were such a sourpuss when you arrived here, looking down yer nose at us."

Pru coloured with embarrassment and looked down at her cup of tea intently.

"Bless yeh. I'm only joking." Betty pinched her cheek "I'll never be far away! And just you try keeping me away from that bairn when it comes," she chuckled, and together they packed Pru's bag ready for home.

Neither of the women knew that this would be the last time that they would see each other without the weight of tragedy on their shoulders.

Chapter seven

The sun was fleeing west by the time I arrived at the taverna. In the restaurant heads bobbed and bowed over plates of green olives. With rising panic I wondered whether I should have booked, after all, it was a Saturday evening. George did say to come by tonight, but how firm an arrangement had that been?

"Writer Lady. You are welcome!"

A sigh of relief escaped my mouth too loudly. The swarthy man held my upper arms and kissed me on both cheeks.

"Good evening, George. Are you able to squeeze me in tonight?"

"Of course! Come. Your table is upstairs."

I followed George up the same stairs that I'd noticed on my first visit. Three sides of the room were open to the gentle breeze and most people were sitting at these outside tables with natural air conditioning and beautiful views.

I followed George past a couple holding hands across the table, gazing at each other with the fresh budding of love in their eyes. The next couple we passed were a more familiar sight to me. They sat in dense, foreboding silence. Both were looking in the vague direction of the sea and twisting the stems of their wine glasses. Their constricting wedding rings were choking the sensation out of fingers once used to cajole and caress.

I almost walked into the back of George as he stopped and motioned grandly to an oblong table set for four people.

"Oh. I will be dining on my own tonight, George," I said with a touch of embarrassment.

"I know. But you need much space for mezze. No?" He laughed that warm, throaty chuckle that made me smile with him. "And, anyway. There must be two people for mezze. For you, Writer Lady, I allow it to be one person. But don't tell the boss!"

"Thank you, George. That's very kind of you," I said as he pulled a chair out for me. "I am very much looking forward to it."

"Drink?"

"White wine. Whichever you recommend, and some water as well, thank you."

"Certainly. Would you like the fish mezze or the meat mezze or a mixture of both?"

"I'll have the fish mezze tonight, George."

"Of course, you can sample our meat mezze another evening, yes? My son, Stefanos, will serve you this evening."

George picked up the three unwanted wine glasses from the table as I laid the red paper napkin across my lap.

"And The Pleiades? It is nice, yes? Antheia is looking after you?"

"Yes, it's wonderful. Absolutely wonderful. Thank you so much for fixing that up for me George."

"You are welcome. I must see to my other customers. Enjoy your meal." He nodded at me.

"Thank you."

I exhaled and allowed my shoulders to drop away from my ears. The sea, still rich with the orange glow of the sun, was to my left and the hubbub of the restaurant was to my right. The sky was opulent with a pink haze the colour of Turkish delight, wisps of cloud powdering the confectionery.

From my elevated position I looked down upon the deserted beach. The day's detritus of a discarded shoe and a handleless yellow bucket lay unwanted on the sand. I took a deep breath in through my nose. There wasn't even the faintest scent of the sea tonight. Either that or I had already acclimatised and now took the scent for granted. The rich aromas of the kitchen pervaded the night air and mingled harmoniously. There was still so much residual heat in the day that I flung my shawl onto the neighbouring chair before getting out my notebook and pen.

Saliva flooded my mouth in anticipation of the delights that would be presented to me tonight. I watched with ill-disguised envy as dish after dish was brought out by the young waiter and placed before eager diners. Every time someone came up the stairs with his arms laden with succulent dishes my heart give a small skip with the hope that it would be my food. I was so busy studying the young man serving the next table that I didn't notice another, taller man sidle up to me with dishes lined up his tanned arms.

"Good evening. How are you tonight?"

"Fine, thank you." I smiled up at the waiter and found myself looking into the dark eyes of my tour guide from earlier in the day. The open smile on my face slithered away.

"Oh. It's you," I tried to say lightly while holding my chin aloft and keeping my gaze steady to cover the fact that I was inwardly cringing. The young man in his crisp, white shirt with one too many buttons undone at his chest placed the dishes carefully in front of me.

"I am Stefanos. My father has asked me to take special care of our *important* guest." I could almost hear the inverted commas he placed around the word 'important' as if he begged to differ on that point. "I am sorry that I had not been aware of who you were on the boat today," he smirked.

"Would you have treated me any differently?"

"No." A waitress appeared at Stefanos' side with a tray.

"White wine? And *nero*. Enjoy." She placed the drinks on the table and left but not before she fluttered her eyelashes in Stefanos' direction.

"So," he began, ignoring the dishes he had just placed down. "You are staying with my aunt at The Pleiades. How do you like it so far?" His words were polite but the lack of warmth in his eyes betrayed him. His short sleeves were folded up to his elbows, revealing strong arms with leather bands on his right wrist and a chunky gold watch on his left.

"It's very nice, thank you." I sat up straighter, sucking in my stomach involuntarily.

Pleasantries dispensed with, Stefanos swiftly moved on to business.

"This evening I will be bringing a selection of Cypriot dishes. To begin with we have olives, taramasalata, hummus, tsatsiki, tashi sauce and pitta breads. My father says you would also like further information about each dish. Everything is home made. Please ask me any questions you may have about the ingredients or method of cooking."

"Thank you, but I am familiar with these dishes."

"Very well." He nodded curtly and then left the way he came, his soft black shoes making no sound on the wooden floor.

I really hadn't been expecting to see the young man again and felt uncomfortable that not only had I run into him again, but that he was serving me my meal and was also nephew of the woman I was staying with. While he had been nothing but courteous, I still felt his chill of annoyance at with the way I had badgered him earlier about getting access to Varosha.

The smell of the dishes on the table brought me back to the sight before me. It was hard to be distressed when there was such delicious food to be savoured. I had always been a fan of this style of eating, be it mezze or tapas. There was something so indulgent about several dishes of sublime food in small earthenware dishes. It was rarely worth the effort of preparing so many dishes at home. This was certainly one of those occasions when I couldn't do better myself.

Ignoring the plate and cutlery in front of me, I reached for a chunky strip of pitta bread and dipped into each dish in turn. The tsatsiki was a world apart from the one I made for Dom and myself in England. The yoghurt was thick and creamy, the minutely diced cucumber was refreshing and the jade shards of mint lifted the dip onto its tip-toes. The hummus was richly nutty with a smooth rounded aftertaste. I left the taramasalata until last. Not because it was my least favourite; no, quite the opposite. I was such a fan that I dreaded that it wouldn't live up to my high standards. I was slightly put off by the colour. It was too pink to be natural so I gingerly dipped my little finger into to it and licked off the globule before it could plop back into the dish. It was tangy with the contradiction of fish and fresh lemon. I made a note in my book. I would have to get the recipe off George. I had never yet found a decent taramasalata recipe. It didn't seem fathomable to me but shop-bought always surpassed my own attempts.

Before I had finished all of the dips Stefanos was by my side again.

"And here we have Greek salad, artichoke salad, dolmades – vine leaves stuffed with rice, haloumi cheese and okra in a tomato sauce. Is everything okay?"

"Thank you, yes." I pointed to the carafe before me with a hunk of pitta. "Could you tell me the name of the wine?"

"Yes." He picked up the jug and began to pour it into my wine glass. "This is our house white. It is a chardonnay called Kotrotsos from mainland Greece."

"Kot-rot-sos," I repeated writing it down in my notebook. "Thanks. That's great."

He disappeared as silently as he had appeared and I was dining in solitude again.

I wrote down the names of the dishes as I ate but by now I had slowed down a little. There was still a lot to come and I wanted to be able to sample all of it. Mezze wasn't really the sort of meal you would normally eat on your own. It was a social meal for many people to share. There was no way I was going to be able to eat all of it but I would give it my best shot. I felt sure that good company was the only missing ingredient from this feast. Good conversation and laughter were an often underrated condiment for a perfect meal.

"And now we have the fish course," came the smooth deep voice behind me. I jumped a little but tried not to look surprised as I felt his warm voice draw a line down my spine.

"This is marida, a small fish to be eaten whole; calamari, deep fried squid, and grilled octopus in a red wine sauce. Can I get you anything else?"

"No, I don't think so Stefanos." He flinched at me using his name. It seemed altogether too intimate and I felt awkward at the sound of it being uttered by my own voice.

"Enjoy your meal."

I sat back and looked at the feast in front of me. There wasn't a spare inch of table to be seen straining under the weight of the ten or so dishes before me. I poured myself some more wine to cleanse my palate before starting to devour the calamari. I knew that I should take a measured approach to the meal but it was too delicious to stop at just one or two pieces. The only time I paused was to squeeze lemon juice over the crispy batter. Calamari was one of my favourite dishes. In fact, today, I would say there was nothing else I would rather be eating. The smell was enough to turn me into a ravenous beast but I reminded myself that with a mezze it is not obligatory to finish everything on the table.

I speared a slice of warm salty haloumi cheese with my fork and lazily bit off the end of it. The edges were slightly charred and caramelised. I knew from experience that it was better eaten while it was still piping hot. Cold haloumi had a tendency to squeak disconcertingly against your teeth.

Next, on to the dolmades which oozed a smooth green sweetness of olive oil down my chin that I dabbed away with the paper napkin. I picked up my pen and made a note that overall presentation could be improved upon but taste could not. "Delectable," I wrote.

My appetite hadn't been everything it could have been of late and so the dishes in front of me pushed at the sides of my shrunken stomach. Every time I thought I'd had enough and put my fork down, my taste buds convinced me to squeeze in just one more mouthful. I made notes on each dish as I sipped my chilled wine, and started to feel a bit more like my old self again. I was staring out to sea with my wineglass in my hand wondering what Dom was up to right now when the screech of chair legs brought me back to the present.

Stefanos sat across the table from me. His arms were folded and his gaze was steady. I looked back at him and raised an eyebrow. I was both curious and panicky at the sight of him sitting opposite me. I carefully placed my wineglass down and waited for him to speak.

"Is it true that you were born in the Ghost Town?" he shot at me.

"Yes, it is. Why would I lie?"

"Journalists are always trying to get across the Green Line into Varosha. They have a romantic notion of the city but they do not see it for what it is."

"And what is that?" I asked innocently.

"A symbol."

"Of...?" I prompted.

"Hatred."

We sat there in silence, our eyes locked. The silence between us was heavy but neither of us wanted to be the first to fill it. I felt tense. I had somehow wandered straight into a minefield and would have to navigate carefully if I was to escape unscathed.

I filled an empty water glass with wine from the carafe in the centre of the table and passed it to the suspicious young man across from me. He took it without a word of thanks.

"Stefanos, I am not a journalist. Really I'm not. I'm a food writer and I am in Cyprus to write about the food for a magazine in England. My interest in Varosha is entirely personal. I shan't be writing about anything I find there. That part of the trip is just for me."

"What do you hope to find if you do visit Varosha?"

"Answers."

"To what?" he sneered.

"Questions," I answered defensively.

It was Stefanos' turn to raise an eyebrow at me but I wasn't sure how much information I wanted to give away yet. I moved uncomfortably in my seat and rested my arms on the table so that I could make myself heard without having to raise my voice.

"My family's flat is there, untouched," I offered with a sigh. "It's still full of my mother's things, I guess. She had to leave in a hurry. She told me something about... about my birth.

Well, it's left me with a lot of questions and I'd like to see the place where I was born. I think it might give me some clues about where I belong."

"I doubt it," he scoffed.

"Why do you say that?" I asked alarmed.

"I doubt it remains untouched. The shops and the houses have all been looted. The Turks and the UN will have taken anything of any value by now. And the places that haven't been touched by man's hand have been crushed by nature. There are rats and wild dogs roaming the streets. Trees are growing through the roofs of houses. There are plants and weeds growing through the cracks in the pavement. Even if you could find the place where your family used to live, it would be unsafe for you to enter it."

"Maybe. But seeing as I can't get into Varosha, that all seems irrelevant now, doesn't it?" The bitterness in my voice surprised me.

Stefanos shrugged. "Maybe. Before the war, there were thirty-nine thousand people living in Famagusta – that's the name of the area that Varosha is in." He leant forward now, elbows on the table mirroring my posture. "Sixty percent of these people were Greek. In Varosha almost *all* of its population were Greek Cypriots. All of the island's best hotels were there and it was a very important source of income for my family. My grandfather owned a shop and a hotel there. The whole family, including his parents, lived in two rooms while they worked hard and saved hard to buy that hotel. They were a fine family in 1974. They had wealth, they were well regarded by the Greeks and the Turkish, and then they were forced out of their home. They lost everything and had to start all over again.

"By that time my grandfather was a lot older. He didn't have as much energy. The things he'd witnessed, the things he'd experienced... He couldn't do it all again. It destroyed him. He grew old overnight. He died not long after from a broken heart." Stefanos smiled sadly as he snorted through his nose and shook his head.

"I really am sorry, Stefanos." I almost reached out to touch his hand in comfort but stopped short and stroked the stem of my wineglass instead.

"The hotel he worked so hard for should have passed to my mother but instead she works her fingers to the bone in this shithole while tourists stuff their faces and forget to leave a tip. Not that she'd want that hotel, anyway. Not now. There is nothing for her to go back to now. What good would it be to us? The buildings are crumbling. It would take too much money to make it right again. We do not have that kind of money any more. There are people who lost a lot more than your family did – and a lot more than my mother's family did. If there was anything there for us do you not think we would all be fighting to get our homes back?"

"Well of course. I didn't mean to imply that you wouldn't. I'm just trying to understand more. Wasn't there a plan, a few years back, to give Varosha back to the Greek Cypriots who had lived there before 1974?"

"Yes. But most Greeks voted against it. They have rebuilt their lives, there are new hotels now. Also, who would be responsible for the upkeep of it? The Turkish government should have paid for the upkeep. The Greek government will not want to take on the spiralling costs of regenerating this area." Stefanos spoke with apparent animosity.

"But," I pushed, "didn't I read somewhere that in the analysis of the votes, previous Varosha inhabitants voted 'yes' to the UN plan?"

Stefanos paused before answering me, obviously weighing his answer carefully, and took a long slug of wine.

"You have done your research," he stated, looking down at his glass. "People are sentimental. They thought they would be going back to their old lives when the war was over. They left photographs, wedding dresses, things that they didn't need then and do not really need now. But as people get older, they want to be reminded of happier times."

We both looked into our golden wine, lost in our own thoughts. I eliminated the chatter from the other people in the restaurant and listened to the gentle "hush, hush" of the waves on the beach. Even though I hadn't lived by the sea since I was a baby, there was something so comforting about the inky blue.

"Stefanos?" I asked quietly. "At the risk of annoying you further, *is* there any way of me getting into Varosha?"

"I cannot help you. Please do not ask me this again." He responded with a hint of anger.

"Sorry. I just wondered whether you were giving me the standard answer you always give to tourists, or whether you genuinely can't get in. That's all. I didn't mean to offend you."

"It takes a lot more than that to offend me. I accept your apology."

"Hold on a minute," I raised my voice in surprise. "I don't believe I apologised. There's a vast difference between apologising and *explaining*."

Stefanos smirked and then drained the rest of his wine, before standing and walking away without another word.

"Infuriating man!" I thought. I didn't doubt for a minute that his family had suffered a great deal but his arrogance made it difficult for me to sympathise with him.

I sat for a long while then, alone with my thoughts. My appetite had disappeared and I no longer felt like eating what was left of the meal in front of me. I had to get into that town. Stefanos might be right; there might not be any of the answers that I hoped for, but until I tried I would never know. His family had been greatly affected by the war but at least he knew about it. I had no idea that my family had suffered at all until recently and now I was desperate to find out more, even if there was a chance that I might not like what I found.

It had been a month since my mother had dropped the bombshell on me that turned my life upside-down. I was in a vulnerable place already and had gone to her for help but what she told me ripped my world apart. I almost couldn't bear to think of her at the moment. On one hand I loved her as much as I loved anyone in the world. She had been there for me at every turn. And yet, on the other hand, she had deceived me. She wasn't who I thought she was. And if she wasn't who I thought she was, then who on earth was I?

I had never known my father and Mum had very few photos of him. Even their wedding photos had been left behind when we were evacuated from Cyprus. The only picture I had of them was a photo-booth picture taken when they were about seventeen and still in England. Mum was sitting on his knee and they were grinning at the camera, blissfully unaware of the heartache that the future had prepared for them.

It had been just mum and me for the longest time. Mum got plenty of attention from the opposite sex but never let anything get too serious until she met Jack. He asked her to marry him one Christmas, and although Mum looked annoyed at him for asking, eventually she said "yes". Mum and I looked at wedding magazines but even then I could tell that Mum's heart was never in it. She sought a divorce from my father, Eddie, in order to marry Jack, but said that if at any point I said "No" she would call the whole thing off.

In the end, it was Mum that called the wedding off. She said he'd ruined everything by asking her to marry him. She said she couldn't commit herself to anyone like that again. Before long, we were packing up and moving on.

Mum didn't talk about her past very often. From what I could gather, she had moved to Cyprus as a young bride with her doting husband Eddie, but, for reasons she had always been cagey about, things had gone quite quickly sour. She would never be drawn on facts, but would only say that he left her soon after she had given birth and she never saw him again. She didn't know where he was but the last she heard he had moved around a bit with the army and then retired to Cyprus to run a bar.

I had assumed that I looked a little like him. I certainly didn't look at all like my mother. She burned with a fierce blonde fire and clear fresh complexion that made her look years younger than she was, whereas I was tall and gangly with dark eyes and hair. I'd learned to love my long legs now but when I was a child I hated them. They seemed to grow before the rest of me, giving the impression of a new-born foal.

The snapshot I had in my drawer of Mum and Eddie in the seventies was in black and white but he certainly didn't look as dark as me. Of course I understood why now. He wasn't really my father. I suppose he never had been. After all, he had never held me, soothed me or cleaned my scraped knee. And now, as it turned out, he wasn't biologically my father anyway. The thing that broke my heart was the impact this news had on my relationship with my mother.

To find out that the only person in the world that I thought I could trust one hundred percent had been lying to me all of my life, well... it's difficult to put it into words. The pain is so sharp that mere words are not enough to describe the feeling. Any word that could come close would still have to be taken and planed until it formed a point that could slice into your heart and sever your dreams. Right now my foundations were unstable. It would only take one small push for me to crumble to the ground and lie there until the earth swallowed me up under the dirt and the moss and the fallen leaves.

Mum knew that I had returned to Cyprus but I'm not sure she fully understood what was driving me. We hadn't really talked much lately and I'd been dodging her calls. Dom had been talking to her in hushed sound-bites. I could hear him saying "she just needs space to grieve" and "she's got to take it one day at a time" and "I think she turned a corner today". But what did he know? He cooed and soothed but he couldn't truly understand everything I'd been through. It hadn't happened to him. It had happened to me. Of course, the news from my mother paled into insignificance against the backdrop of our other trauma. The other thing. The baby.

Without that, Mum probably would never have been forced to drop her own personal bombshell. Not only did her confession hurt me for its own sake but it was made imperceptibly worse by the timing, as if this news was overshadowing my own personal loss and pushing it out of the way, as if it didn't matter. I lost a baby.

Lost. Hah! That's a joke. "Lost" makes it sound inconsequential like a lost earing. Something misplaced, always with the potential to be found again. I did not lose that baby, it was taken from me. Following an interlude of elation and excitement, the ensuing heartbreak was of apocalyptic proportions to me. For Dom too, yes, and my mother, I suppose. We all suffered in our own way. I fell apart, Dom locked it all away, and Mum, well she managed to make it all about her as usual.

If I'm good at anything, it's compartmentalising. I can put anything into a metaphorical box, lock it up and push it right into a dusty alcove at the back of my mind. Every time I think of the baby I can feel the physical pain in my heart and my stomach so I shut down the thought, put it back in the box and decide to deal with it another time.

Dom and I had been trying for a baby for four years. Long years. As a woman who likes to be in control, for whom *que sera, sera* was a dirty phrase, I'd done everything expected of me. I lost weight, got fit, cut out caffeine and alcohol, started taking supplements and folic acid. I bought a fertility crystal, hung it in the bedroom window and started taking my temperature daily to monitor when I was ovulating. I made Dom cut out alcohol and take selenium tablets to boost his sperm count. A friend of ours joked that perhaps we should just think about having sex instead.

When nothing happened we sought the help of a fertility specialist who put me on drugs to help ovulation. Four months later and we got the result we'd been hoping for. I bought every book that Waterstone's had on healthy pregnancies and treated my body as an elite baby-making factory. My excitement was matched by Dom's as we started counting the days and stroked my blossoming stomach. For a few weeks I was content. A few weeks, that's all.

The twelve-week scan showed nothing in my womb at all. I quelled my panic and fixed the sonographer with a stern gaze.

"I'm sorry. It happens sometimes." She stroked my arm.

"What does?" I asked, forcing her to vocalise her doubts.

"Sometimes the body miscarries without us knowing it," she sang in a high-pitched, breathy voice you hear women using with pre-schoolers. "I'm afraid you aren't pregnant."

I flinched at the words. "I *am* pregnant. I *feel* pregnant. I know that I am."

"It is possible you still have some pregnancy hormones present but there is no foetus, I'm afraid." She looked resolutely away now as if she could sense that I was going to be one of those awkward patients. "If you could take a seat in the waiting room someone will be out to talk to you in a minute."

To be fair to her, she did look genuinely upset for me but I still felt she was just bad at her job. There had to be a baby there. There *had* to be. I could smell everything around me, I felt sick every morning without fail and my breasts were tender. There was no way I had lost this baby without knowing it.

The matronly lady who took us into a side room explained everything that the sonographer had said but with a harder tone, as if this was meant to convince me. I asserted my views that I had not had a miscarriage so she made me produce a urine sample for a pregnancy test. She returned within five minutes.

"You're still showing a strong pregnancy reading, which is concerning. There is a possibility that this pregnancy is ectopic."

"Ectopic?"

"Yes, it means the foetus is growing outside of the womb."

"I know what it means," I snapped. "What happens now?"

"I want you to come back in tomorrow so we can monitor hormone levels to see whether the foetus continues to grow or has indeed miscarried."

Dom and I gripped each other's hands with dread. The sickness I felt now had nothing to do with the pregnancy. It was pure, soul-crushing fear.

The following day's blood tests showed hormone levels still increasing but not at a level that would be consistent with a healthy pregnancy. Despite their urgings I refused to be admitted to hospital.

I knew then in my heart of hearts that the pregnancy was ectopic, although I didn't say it out loud. I'd had some pains in my side that I had assumed were normal pregnancy twinges. I just wanted to enjoy the last day of being pregnant even if nothing was going to come of it. The next day's scan showed bleeding in my fallopian tube and I was whisked down to surgery where they removed my fallopian tube, my baby and my future.

It was another one of those situations where words don't suffice. More than that, I don't even want to try and describe it. I don't want to even think about having to sign the consent form that said "sure, take my baby". I don't want to open those particular floodgates for fear of being washed away. Don't make me go there. I just can't.

When I awoke following the surgery I felt different. There's no way of explaining it to someone who hasn't been pregnant but there is a feeling you get when you are carrying a child. I had felt at ease in the world, like I had finally found my place within it. I felt altogether calmer, like my previous worries had all been put into perspective. Now I just felt empty. Physically and mentally empty.

Dom asked me to stop referring to it as a baby. He said it was never a viable pregnancy so there was no point attaching a personality to it. That's when I realised that he could never understand. A woman falls in love with her baby long before a man possibly can. From the moment of conception a woman's life is already changing but the man doesn't feel the impact until a long time later. Sometimes not until he feels the baby kick under his hand in his partner's stomach or, more often, not until he holds that child in his arms.

I turned to Mum but Dom turned to his work. Maybe that was the beginning of the end for us. Or maybe we would get through this trial and get stronger. Only time would tell. But first, before I could work on our relationship, I had to find out who I was and that quest had brought me to the island of my birth.

I looked around me then and felt suddenly exhausted. I motioned to one of the waiters and mouthed, "Bill please."

I knew what I had to do and I couldn't put it off any longer.

Chapter eight

Cyprus, 1974

Pru let out a yelp of surprise as she swung open her front door and came face to round flat face with her landlady who lived downstairs.

"*Kyria* Kostas! You made me jump!"

"This come for you." She held a narrow neatly wrapped brown parcel in her hands. She was unsmiling and looked weary standing before Pru. They had a perfectly amicable relationship but it rarely went past the polite acknowledgement stage. Pru didn't understand how this woman came to own the beautiful apartment block she lived in. Pru had never seen a husband around and Kyria Kostas' only income seemed to come from Pru and Eddie.

"Oh, right." Pru glanced down at it briefly and noted that it was covered with airmail stamps. "Probably something for the baby. Eddie's parents are going to spoil it and it's not even born yet." Pru was already annoyed with her unborn child for taking all of the attention. She had expected a little more reverence in her direction seeing as she was the person carrying and sustaining this baby.

The Greek lady nodded with her eyes half closed and turned to go.

"How's Helene?" Pru asked. She had never before enquired about the pregnant woman downstairs. Time spent with Betty and Bernie had made her crave company in a way she hadn't before. She was feeling in need of some sympathy for what she was going through. Perhaps it would help to talk to another woman.

"Okay. See?" Mrs Kostas pointed a crooked finger over at the row of trees to her right.

Pru tossed the package behind her into the hallway so it landed with a clunk and closed the door behind her, pulling it until she heard the 'click' of the lock catching.

Mrs Kostas was already halfway down the concrete steps by the time Pru turned back. Her landlady had never been very welcoming. Pru thought that, seeing as they were providing her with a decent income, she could act a little bit more grateful. Under the shade of the nearby Cypress trees Pru could see the blossoming figure of Mrs Kostas' daughter-in-law, Helene. Pru couldn't see her face but could see her legs that were set in the rather inelegant position that only a pregnant woman can appreciate. Helene was three weeks further on in her pregnancy than Pru was but the two women had shared little more than glances of the co-afflicted in this heat. From Pru's position on the steps she was still in the shade and lingered for a moment, bracing herself for entry into the heat-condensed air.

Gripping the warm, metal handrail Pru lowered herself down the last few steps and headed towards the trees. As she reached Helene, the darker woman raised her head and nodded. "*Yasou.*"

"*Yasou*. How are you?"

Helene shrugged and looked away.

Pru continued, "It's so hot, isn't it? I can't sleep at night. I don't know whether it's the baby or the heat keeping me awake."

"Is not so hot."

"No, well I suppose you're used to it, but it's a lot hotter than summer in England so I er...." Pru looked over in the direction that Helene was facing. There was a crowd gathered at the end of the road by the hotel.

"What's going on over there? More building work at the hotel? What is there to see? People here would cross the road to watch paint dry. They really need to get a hobby."

Pru squinted against the sharp glare of the egg yolk sun and shielded her eyes with her hand to focus on the scene that had so captured Helene's attention. There was a grand hotel a few hundred yards down the road towards the beach. Pru had been there once when they first arrived here. It had been someone's twenty-first birthday, she didn't remember whose now. She only remembered thinking that this was where she

148

wanted to live, not in married quarters like the other carbon copy army wives.

Pru could only make out shapes and shadows from this distance under the scowling sun. Workman were dancing on the watery haze of heat that was shimmering above the newly lain, sticky black road.

"They move the bodies," Helene stated bluntly.

"What bodies?" asked Pru squinting harder. "You don't mean dead people?"

"The bodies. They take them away now. The Turkish bomb come hit hotel. Many bodies."

"Don't be ridiculous! I hardly think... Are you sure? No one told me. They wouldn't have let me come back here if..." Thoughts whirred around Pru's head. Death and destruction so close to her beloved home didn't seem possible. She had only arrived back this morning but she would have thought Eddie would have said something. She would be giving him an earful when he came home tonight.

"Sit," commanded Helene, her hazel eyes never leaving the exhibition of devastation in front of her.

Pru, slightly stunned by the scene in front of her, and by being told what to do by the Greek woman, lowered herself onto the creaking wooden chair. Heat prickled her body and the ripples of realisation coursed through her body. Now she knew what she was looking at, the vista came into sharp focus in front of her unwilling eyes. The shadows she could see hanging from the windows weren't workmen. They were dead bodies. Her heart hammered in her chest. She'd never seen a dead body before.

Pru wrapped her arms tightly around her stomach. Half of the hotel was still standing but the other half had disappeared. There were no jagged lines of crumbling walls, no piles of bricks and mortar, it just looked as if half of the rooms had been scooped away. Pink-papered walls were now open to the elements. A bed sheet was draped in a nearby tree, snagged by dry branches as it attempted to flee from the horror. A man's body hung upside-down from one of the lower floors. His body was naked, either blown from his clothes by the impact or wrenched from his innocent slumber. He was European-looking.

Blond hair hung limply from his immobile head. A British flag still crowned the hotel but looked impotent rather than majestic.

"I didn't know the fighting had been so close. We've been staying up near the base. I only got back this morning," Pru whispered. "I mean, I hadn't heard. I thought it was miles away. No one said anything. When did it happen?"

"We see no soldiers. The planes they come from many miles. They bomb army shop too."

"The NAAFI?"

"Yes. Planes come round and round."

"But I was on my way there. I was going to cook a nice meal for Eddie. I... I know the people who work there."

The other woman exhaled slowly and rubbed the side of her curved stomach.

The only two places Pru ever shopped for food and household essentials were the NAAFI and the little shop by the side of the road run by a Greek woman and her daughter, Anemone, who sold the most delicious fruit. It was unfathomable to Pru that parts of her day-to-day life were being affected by the war. Luckily it had been all over so quickly and a ceasefire had been hastily agreed. She wondered briefly about her little fruit shop. The woman and her daughter were probably safe. They lived in one of the villages in the hills and brought their fruit down to Famagusta by cart every day. She didn't even know the woman's name but she was quite taken with the little girl.

Would they be back by the side of the road today in their makeshift hut that looked more like a bus-shelter than a shop? Pru had been planning on making a lemon meringue pie today. It didn't look likely now.

The two pregnant women sat in silence as the sun continued ascending the cloudless blue sky to its zenith. Mrs Kostas wordlessly appeared, bringing the pregnant women cool water and then disappeared again. Minutes later she was back with a salad and a bowl filled with thickly cut bread. None of the women spoke as the bodies were removed from the hotel and driven away. The food stood untouched. Mrs Kostas crossed herself and shuffled back inside.

Silence pressed down upon Pru until at last Helene broke the quietude, her voice croaky through either emotion or lack of use.

"The planes come. Early in morning. The childrens were on the roof when planes come from sea. They think this is very good, yes? But the planes, they go 'bang, bang, bang'. The childrens is okay, but they lucky. Next time maybe not so lucky. They go swim in the sea and come back with the... errr, the bang, bang, bang?" She held her fingers apart a little to show the size of the object she was referring to.

"Bullets," Pru answered. "Or shells, I suppose."

"Bullets," repeated Helene slowly, rolling the word over her tongue. "My husband, he is gone."

"Jesus! Dead?"

"I not know. He with father in Kantara mountains. He is not come for me. Big fighting in mountains. The Turkish planes big boom-boom bullets on mountains."

"Dropping bombs?" Pru suggested.

"Yes. The trees on fire. My husband he help the National Guards. I pray and I pray." Helene clasped her hands in front of her chest to emphasise the point.

"Well, it's all over now, isn't it? They'll work everything out, and we can get on with our lives. I'm sure he'll be back soon. It was quite irresponsible of him to swan off when you're about to have a baby. I wouldn't have let Eddie do it."

Helene snorted. "The fighting still not stop in mountains."

"Really? Can't anybody do what they're told in this country?"

"Men wait for this day. Five years, ten years. They hide guns in mountains. Greek people and Turkish they very different. You English think we are same. We no same. In North the Turks beat my grandfather with guns and shoot his dog. He lucky. In other place all men dead." Helene looked back towards the hotel.

Pru studied Helene's profile. There appeared to be a veil of tears over those amber brown eyes but she was not letting them go. There was strength in the way she held her head and the way her strong chin jutted forward that Pru admired.

"Well. Must be off. I'm sure you'll see that there'll be no more fighting now."

Helene gasped and grabbed Pru's arm.

"Look, I'm sorry that people are dying but it really has nothing to do with me!" Pru tried to pull away.

"Arrgghh! Baby." Helene bared her teeth and emitted a guttural sound.

"What? No. Just a false alarm. I had one myself, only the other day in fact. That really is hurting me you know. Could you just–"

Pru looked down to the floor as the amniotic fluid spread over the cement floor. No longer noticing the nails digging into her arm, Pru instinctively lifted her feet in disgust.

"Oh, shit!"

"The pains start in my bed last night but then stop. Aaaaaarrrrrrrhhhhhh!"

"Can you walk?"

Helene nodded with her eyes closed.

"Then let's get you inside."

Pru helped Helene to her feet but seconds later the Greek woman was crouched over and grunting.

"That's it. It's okay. It'll pass. Shallow breaths now," soothed Pru and then, louder, "Kyria Kostas? Kyria Kostas!"

The older woman appeared at the doorway wiping her hands on her apron. In a swiftness not usually associated with a large woman of such advancing years she was instantaneously at the other side of Helene gabbling in Greek.

"Okay then, I'll leave you to it. You know I'm just upstairs if you need me. Not that I can be of any help, I'm sure."

Helene linked her arm through Pru's and leant her considerable weight on her, baring her teeth in pain.

"Oh! Okay, um… I'll help you into the house and then I really should go."

They got Helene into the house and onto the sofa where Mrs Kostas crouched by her side and questioned her in Greek. Satisfied, she stood and beckoned to Pru.

"Here!" she barked.

Pru took up position on the floor and Helene took her hand while Mrs Kostas went into a back room. Another contraction shook Helene and her whole body went rigid, the veins on her neck bulging with the intensity of the pain that coursed through her. She gripped Pru's hand and Pru squeezed back.

Between them, Pru and Mrs Kostas placed sheets under and over Helene. In turn, each woman washed their hands in hot, soapy water and put on a clean apron fresh from the basket of washing lying on the kitchen table. Pru followed Mrs Kostas in a trance-like state and then stopped suddenly.

"Wait. What are you doing? Shouldn't we get her to a hospital? You are not suggesting she does this here, are you?"

"Eh?"

"The hospital? We-drive-Helene-to-the-hospital?" Pru asked annunciating each word slower, clearer and louder in order to get the point across.

"Phfft!" Mrs Kostas waved her hand in a show of dismissal and chuckled dryly.

Turning to the younger woman, Pru continued, "Helene, I really do think it would be better if you were in a hospital. Do you have a car? Helene? Mrs Kostas? Is anyone listening to me? Oh bloody hell!"

Pru glanced at the open door. It was so tempting just to leave. She briefly thought that no one here was in a fit state to stop her leaving if she chose to. She looked from the door to Mrs Kostas and Helene. Of course, she thought, it might make things unnecessarily difficult with her landlady if she were to leave now.

Resigning herself to staying, for a while at least, Pru decided that it couldn't be too difficult to deliver a baby. Women had been doing it for years. They would probably be so grateful for her intervention they would most likely end up naming the baby after her if it was a girl.

"Okay then, I'll stay. But don't expect me to be down 'that' end. Okay?"

Time passed and the shadows lengthened. Cicadas began their nightly serenade but the heat refused to abate. Pru was holding a cold cloth on the back of her neck to cool herself down. She was just wondering about a nice cool bath when Helene screamed. Her cries echoed around the tiled house but the baby resolutely refused to come. Mrs Kostas mimed pulling Helene onto her feet and Pru stood to walk her around the room. After a few minutes of hobbling and back rubbing the labouring woman's legs failed her. She fell to all fours on the knotted rug, howling like a trapped animal.

Pru still thought that Helene would be better off in a hospital but had given up trying to push her point. She was starting to worry about the wearying dark-skinned woman. She didn't look she was going to have any energy left to push with. Pru was beginning to wonder if something was wrong. Did labour usually take this long? She had nothing to compare it to, but Mrs Kostas didn't seem worried.

The smell of bitter sweat mingled with the aroma of the pungent warm bushes of oregano by the open door. Somewhere nearby someone was cooking lamb and Pru thought of her own empty stomach. Would it be rude to excuse herself for five minutes to get a drink and something to eat? She had no idea how long she had been there. She wondered whether she could leave now but she could not tear herself away from the combined horror and beauty of what was occurring in front of her. Pru hadn't really stopped to think about what was going to happen when it was time for her own baby to be born. This was partly due to fear and partly due to Pru's habit of living entirely in the moment.

The woman who had sat beside her only hours earlier with serenity and grace was now on her knees with her face tear- and sweat-stained. The usually smooth skeins of chestnut hair were plastered to her forehead and hanging lank over her cheeks. Part of Pru was fascinated to see a birth first hand, seeing as she would be experiencing it herself very soon. But there was the fearful voice inside her head telling her to run. She was scared of what she might see. The pain that Helene was in made her look inhuman at times and Pru had whispering doubts about whether the young woman would survive the ordeal.

Helene closed her eyes and started rocking back and forth. She began to hum tunelessly as if oblivious to Pru's presence. Mrs Kostas was back by her side urging her onto the cushions she had placed upon the floor. She propped her up against the sofa and covered her once more with the sheet. Turning to Pru with the measured confidence of a woman who has witnessed such things time and again, she beckoned to her.

"Is time. Towels. Come."

Pru grabbed for the towels and held them out towards Mrs Kostas but the older woman ignored her and examined

Helene. She said something in Greek to Helene but she shook her head.

Mrs Kostas took Helene's shoulders firmly and looked straight into her eyes "*Nay.*"

Helene shrugged and nodded with reluctance, "*Nay.*"

Helene reached for Pru's hand again while Mrs Kostas took her place between Helene's knees.

This time when the contraction seized her the atmosphere had changed. This time it was not something to be fought but to be harnessed. Helene dropped her chin to her chest and strained.

"That's it Helene. That's it. Not long now. Nearly there. You're doing so well. Good girl. Great job." Pru was aware of the fact that she was gabbling and that Helene probably wasn't hearing a word she was saying but she had to talk to steady her own nerves. Moments later Mrs Kostas was beckoning her with a slight smile. "See?"

Pru, in spite of all her senses telling her not to, looked where she was pointing and could see the top of the baby's head protruding from the young Greek woman.

"Oh my God! I can see it, Helene. I really can. I can see the baby's head!" Pru shrieked.

The wonder at seeing a new life overcame her revulsion at the blood and mucus. "Not long now, Helene. Really."

But twenty minutes later and Helene's pushing was beginning to lose its power and she was visibly flagging. Mrs Kostas' Greek had now taken on a more urgent tone but Helene was weakly shaking her head. The experienced Greek woman took out a pair of scissors from the pocket in the front of her apron and nodded at Pru. Pru instinctively knew what she had to do and eased her arm around Helene's shoulders and gripped firmly. She looked away but squeezed tighter as Helene brayed and Mrs Kostas cut the skin that was impeding the child's birth.

Helene sagged into Pru's shoulder with a groan. "Why does it not come?"

"It will now. It will now. Come on, I know you can do this." Pru poured the soothing words into her ear.

There was a focused intent etched on Mrs Kostas' face as she worked between Helene's legs and then, with an almighty scream, Helene sat upright and squeezed with every last drop of strength in her body.

Leaning forward with her Pru was able to see as the baby emerged from its sheath and into its grandmother's capable hands. The baby was mottled grey with a dark plastering of hair on its head and although its mouth was open no sound emitted from it. Pru faltered. Was it alive? Had it been starved of oxygen for too long?

Helene held out her arms as the baby was deposited onto her stomach and, as she did so, the baby started to bleat, shakily at first but then with more vigour. Pru laughed with relief and sank back onto her heels holding her own baby-bump.

Still tired but now radiant and glowing, Helene peered down at the wriggling bundle in her arms and soothed it in soft Greek words. Tears of relief and joy trickled down her cheeks. That she loved this child was already evident in the way her eyes glittered and shone with maternal love.

Pru watched in amazement as the little hands opened and closed around Helene's finger. It kicked its slender legs trying out its new-found space. It was almost impossible to perceive that moments ago this child hadn't been in this world. Mrs Kostas took the baby from the mother and wiped it down before wrapping it loosely in a pale lemon sheet.

"Oh wait! I didn't ask. What is it? Boy or a girl?"

"Girl. Here," replied Mrs Kostas and handed her the baby as she went back to checking on Helene. Pru couldn't believe that she was holding a tiny person in her arms. She was so delicate and light.

"A girl! Oh, wonderful! She is gorgeous, Helene. I've never seen anything so beautiful in all my life. What will you call her?"

Helene looked up, her colour having settled now and her serenity having returned. "I wait for my husband. He give name."

"Here," said Pru reluctantly. "Hold your daughter."

Pru didn't doubt for a minute that Helene's husband would return safely. After what she had observed tonight she was sure that anything was possible. She stroked Helene's head and laid her hand on the baby's head before standing up. It took a moment for the blood to come back into her legs, and as she stood there looking down on the maternal scene before her and the three generations of females bonded by blood, she felt a sudden, uncharacteristic pang of sadness at her estrangement from her own mother.

"*Efcharisto*. Thank you," breathed Helene with a hoarse voice from the screaming and exertion.

"No. Not at all. I should be thanking you. It's amazing. To have seen this... well, it is just breath-taking. She's really beautiful. I'll leave you now, but if there's anything you need, you know where I am, okay?"

Helene was nodding but she was not taking her eyes off her baby. Mrs Kostas was already cleaning the floor and tidying up as Pru stepped outside into the warm night air. Reluctantly she started towards her own apartment wondering what time it was and whether Eddie would be home yet. She had been part of something amazing and soon she was going to be welcoming her own baby into the world. She couldn't wait to tell Eddie what had happened tonight. She could scarcely believe it herself that she had helped deliver a baby.

The sound of her key in the lock clattered around the tiled apartment. Pru strode into the living room in the half-light, kicking something solid that had been left on the floor. She had completely forgotten about the parcel Mrs Kostas had delivered earlier. She stooped to pick it up, intrigued to find out what it was, but found herself to be woozy with hunger.

"Food first, then presents," she told herself.

Completely in the shadows now, the little kitchen was almost dark. Without switching the kitchen light on she opened the fridge door and illuminated the small room. As she had never made it to the shop there was more space than food on the shelves. There were eggs, but she didn't feel like cooking them. Apart from that, there was some cheese and a few of Betty's tomatoes. That would have to do. She would cook Eddie an omelette when he got back from work. It wasn't quite the romantic meal that she had planned but Eddie would understand when she told him about her afternoon.

Placing the cheese on the kitchen side, Pru turned the cold water tap on and took a glass from the draining board. She put her other hand underneath the flowing water to test the temperature while her mind meandered around what had happened earlier. She was still marvelling at the memory of the sight of Helene's baby making her way into the world when her heart lurched at the sound of the clean break of glass followed instantaneously by the thud of the plaster behind her as it fell from the wall in a neat circle. It wasn't till she heard the gunshots, though, that she reacted.

She flung herself down to the floor as quickly as she could and held her breath waiting for any further sounds. In the intensity of the afternoon and evening it had been easy for Pru to forget that the Greeks and the Turks had been at war with each other. It looked like the ceasefire hadn't lasted long.

"Oh God! Helene and the baby!" she thought and started to move towards the kitchen door on all fours. She felt something warm on her hand and looked down. Puzzled by the amount of thick liquid on her palm, she turned her hand one way and then the other and saw something dark and sticky on it. Bringing it up to her face in the dimness she realised, with a jolt, that it looked like blood. She held it in front of her face in the weak light wondering if she had she cut her hand on the glass without noticing. She didn't know whether it was because of the sight of blood but she was starting to feel weak. She started on her way towards the door again but this time her legs didn't want to move. Sitting back on her heels Pru looked down at inky crimson mark on her dress. The stain throbbed and seeped over her stomach as she tried to brush it away with her hand. It was growing with every beat of her heart.

The panic rose up on Pru like a tidal wave and she screamed out, "Noooo! Help me! Someone help me. My baby! Oh God, please. No!"

Chapter nine

The sun was in full dominance by the time I woke up.
The crickets, already drunk on sunshine, were singing lazily as I
emerged from my cocoon. It was beautifully warm as I let myself
be drenched by the full light of the day. I felt the release of the
previous night's tension as if I had just sunk into a hot, deep
bath. I pulled on yesterday's clothes and headed up towards the
main house. Antheia was waving to me as I crossed the
courtyard.

"*Kalimera*, Leni. You sleep well?"

"Yes, thank you, like a log."

"A log? A tree? You English are so funny," she laughed.
"Come, there is coffee."

I tucked into the breakfast eagerly thinking about where I needed to go today while Antheia bustled around the kitchen.

"Today is Sunday," announced Antheia. She said it like this was important and I looked up at her expecting more, "And you help me in the kitchen today."

"Of course," I said, smiling, hoping that my face didn't betray the fact that I had completely forgotten. "What can I do to help?"

"We will be making kleftico for the whole family today. You start by peeling the potatoes there."

"Okay." I stood up decisively. My island explorations would have to wait until tomorrow. "So, talk me through the kleftico."

"You have cooked it before?"

"No, but I have eaten it in restaurants."

"Pah!" she scoffed "If you have not eaten it with a Cypriot family then you have not eaten kleftico." She chuckled to herself. "Lamb. Here, this place." She pointed to her shoulder. "Very important. You cook slowly for very long time. It go on the top of tomatoes, onions, many rosemary and salt. Turn every

170

hour of the clock. Cook all day long if you can. When I was little girl, we cook in big pots in the ground on hot, hot coals. Potatoes around the meat and they cook in the lamb taste. It is favourite food for my children."

"Sounds lovely."

"There is one other dish that we shall be cooking: afelia. You know this one?"

"I've heard of it, but never eaten it." I puzzled over the word. My mind conjured up pork, but apart from that I fell short of a recipe.

"Very special. It is made with coriander seeds. I will show you when the kleftico is in the oven."

We peeled the potatoes in silence, Antheia listening out for the sounds of her children.

"You will meet my husband at dinner."

"Looking forward to it. You have a lovely family."

"Thank you. My boys born at same time. One, two. I do not know your word for this."

"Twins," I say.

"Yes, twins. They make me work hard but I am happy to be blessed twice. You children?"

"No. I don't."

"But you want," she stated. I turned to face her, my surprise at her bluntness written across my bewildered face. "You are sad that you not have baby. It is not difficult to know this." She answered the question in my eyes.

I looked at her silently, not quite knowing what to say. She smiled gently at me and placed her hand on my arm. "You not look at the children. You not ask names."

"Oh, sorry. It's just–" I began in embarrassment.

"No. Not be sorry. English people, they talk about weather and children. You do not. You have bad things in your head. I can see through your eyes. You have mother's eyes so you will have child. Now – potatoes," she said, dropping my arm and returning to work.

Antheia didn't seem to need me to either confirm or deny her assertions. I admired her quiet confidence and got on with peeling the potatoes as instructed, leaving them in a bowl looking like newly shorn sheep.

The remainder of the morning passed companionably as she taught me how to make afelia and other Greek Cypriot delicacies. I wrote everything down as she told me. I had struck gold. Clare, my editor, was going to love all of this. I took some photos of Antheia preparing the food for authenticity to accompany my article before she headed off to church. I, however, went back to my little cottage armed with home-made lemonade and a plate of sliced tomatoes scattered with small, pungent, purple-green leaves of Greek basil and the frosting of angular sea salt bergs.

I fell asleep for perhaps a couple of hours and was woken by the little girl, Anna, smiling at my door.

"Hello, Anna. Is it dinner time?"

I mimed eating and she nodded.

"Thank you. I'll be up in a minute."

Anna stood there and carried on smiling.

"I need to get changed," I said, pointing at my clothes.

Anna nodded and then came into the room and sat on the end of my bed. It didn't look like she was going anywhere without me.

Feeling self-conscious and somewhat hurried, I pulled on my favourite linen trousers and a plain white vest top. I liberally sprayed on the Jo Malone perfume that Dom had bought me for Christmas and applied mascara and tinted lip-gloss. A long way from perfect but it would have to do.

The little girl took my hand and led me back up to the main house where an unexpected sight greeted me. The courtyard was filled with tables laid end-to-end and covered with white and red checked tablecloths. There were about thirty mismatched seats around the tables. At one end of the long table, a group of six people sat in the shade talking loudly in English. I assumed, correctly as it turned out, that they were the holiday guests. With their backs to me sat five dark men of similar build with grey streaks in their hair, who could only be Greek. There were six children running around the table chasing a Tabby cat and there were voices raised in laughter coming from the kitchen. Anna slipped from my hand and ran to the other children leaving me standing in the middle of the courtyard wondering what I should do. Did I join the other English people or sit with the Greek men? Neither option seemed quite right so instead I headed to the kitchen to see if I could help Antheia with anything.

As I stepped into the relatively dark kitchen, a figure collided with me.

"I am so sorry," I spluttered before looking up into the dark brown eyes of Stefanos. He looked amused.

"No problem," he said and he breezed past me into the glaring sun.

It hadn't occurred to me for one minute that he might be here today. I really didn't want to have to talk to him again. I rubbed at my arm where we had touched skin on skin, trying to brush the intimate sensation away. Antheia appeared before me filling my empty hands with two bowls of salad.

"I fell asleep. Sorry. I... er... wasn't expecting so many people."

She laughed good-naturedly. "To the table."

"Okay."

I turned back to the table and looked at the sight before me. If I had my entire family around for dinner I still would only have to borrow one chair. And that's not because I have lots of chairs. Including Dom's parents, brother and sister-in-law we would still only number seven. But I wouldn't be nipping round to the neighbours any time soon to borrow chairs as the only time my mum and Dom's parents had been in the same room was at our wedding and it wasn't likely to happen again any time soon.

I managed to put the bowls of salad far away from where Stefanos sat so that I didn't have to make small talk with him and then went back into the kitchen as lines of women came out with arms laden with food.

Antheia gave me a pile of plates to distribute. "Come" she said.

I followed her out to the tables where the noise levels were almost deafening and placed the plates in front of each person in turn. Antheia took my hand and led me to a strong-looking man at the head of the table.

"This is my husband, Andreas," she said.

The man stood and kissed me warmly. It felt mildly inappropriate as I felt his warm wet lips on the corner of my mouth

"We are pleased to have you," he boomed. He turned to the assembled table and said something in fluid Greek. The family looked up, some waved and others smiled their greetings to me.

I murmured "Yassas," feeling redness tip-toe up my neck on course for my cheeks.

Andreas said something to the assembled family, which must have meant something like "Tuck in" because a small cheer went up and everyone grabbed for the nearest food on overladen platters. I went for the empty chair closest to me and had already sat down before I realised that I was sitting next to Stefanos. He didn't look at me, even though he must have felt my presence, and began talking animatedly to the elderly man on his left. On the other side of me was a smiling woman who kept putting food on my plate and nodding but obviously had as much knowledge of English as I did of Greek.

I was glad to able to concentrate on the food in front of me. I had forgotten to bring my notebook but knew I wouldn't forget any part of this banquet. The kleftico was melt-in-the-mouth tender and could have been carved with a spoon. The potatoes were a mouthful of gloriously smooth nuttiness that needed next to no chewing before they dissolved creamily in my mouth. The feta cheese in the salad added the salty sharpness to counteract the richness of the lamb but then the pork afelia sent taste buds into spasm at the sourness of the sauce. I savoured each mouthful to make sure I could memorise each dish when it came to writing it up later.

The fact that one of my table neighbours was ignoring me and the other was simply unable to hold a conversation with me afforded me the luxury of being able to look around at my companions. I spotted George easily with his overblown hand gestures and hearty laugh. He waved when he saw me looking at him and I smiled back at him with genuine fondness. Antheia was sitting opposite him with one of the twins on her knee. The woman next to her had to be her sister. Though the other woman looked older, the profile was identical. How strange it must be to be able to look into someone else's eyes and see how you will look in ten years' time.

The old woman who usually sat out front was now bent over the table with lamb grease on her bristled chin. There was still no hint of a smile on her face or a ghost of any warmth in her eyes, even though she was surrounded by her children, grandchildren and perhaps even great-grandchildren.

"That's Yaiyai."

I turned a startled look at Stefanos.

"Sorry? Did you say something?"

"Yaiyai. She is my mother's grandmother. We all call her Yaiyai. It is Greek for grandmother."

"I see. Why doesn't she look very happy?"

"You like looking into other people's business don't you?"

I mentally kicked myself. I'd only said a dozen words to him but I'd already managed to offend him.

"Sorry. I didn't mean to... I just wondered, that's all. I thought it was me. She spits at the ground when she sees me coming."

His upper body shook with the effort it took not to laugh out loud. "It isn't you," he smiled and shook his head. "It is all English people."

"Really? Why? What have the English done to offend her?"

"Not just her, many people of her generation feel the same. They hate the English." Then, smugness clinging to his face like an overpowering aftershave, he added, "You don't know as much about the history of Cyprus as you think you do, do you?"

"Apparently not. It appears that there is a lot I don't know as I'm sure you'll be quick to point out."

"Obviously, I am happy to help."

We both went back to the meals in front of us. This time it was Stefanos' turn to pour us the wine.

"If you would like to know more about the history of Cyprus I would be glad to tell you about it."

"Thank you. How do you know so much about it? Is this something that is taught at the schools here?"

Stefanos shrugged. "Some of what I know is taught in the schools, some of it I have learned from my family, but I also study history at a college in England. For now it is useful when I am a tour guide but I hope one day to be a teacher and teach others about their heritage before it is lost forever. But now let us eat. We will talk later."

This was the closest I'd come to a civilised conversation with Stefanos and I found myself looking at him appraisingly. Perhaps he wasn't as objectionable as I'd first thought. The sleeves of his pale blue shirt were rolled up above his elbows, which made me wonder why he didn't wear a short-sleeved shirt if he never intended to wear the sleeves down to his wrists. He had remarkably fair hairs on his strong brown forearms as he ripped apart a loaf of bread and offered it to me with a lazy smile.

The afternoon stretched dreamily into the evening, and as the sun made way for the moon and the stars, the music started up from within the house. Amidst all these welcoming people I felt Dom's absence keenly. He would have loved all of this. A cry of "Writer lady!" made me jump.

"George! How are you?" I stood to place a kiss on his cheek.

"Me? I am blessed with a beautiful family, fine clothes and a handsome face, so of course I am well! Waa-ha-ha! You?"

"Good, thanks."

"And the mezze? You leave without saying 'Goodnight'." He wagged his finger comically in my direction.

"You looked busy. It was wonderful, George, thank you."

"No, no, no. Tell me something in writer words." He sat down in the empty chair recently vacated by his son.

"Well, where to start?" I sat down importantly. "The hummus was quite literally the best I have ever tasted; smooth yet embroidered with nutty highlights and culminating with a lingering aftertaste that had my taste buds begging for more. It would be tantamount to abuse to deny my mouth the chance to taste that hummus again. The fish dishes were sublime in their simplicity. The freshness of the fish shone through the other flavours that were only there to highlight the essence of the main ingredient. The genius was letting the flavours speak for themselves."

"Waa-ha! So it was perfect, yes?"

"No. I wouldn't say perfect. Presentation could have been improved upon and your pitta breads were overcooked on the griddle. They were charred in places which overpowered the delicate presence of the tsatsiki."

George roared his laughter to the skies which caused the others to glance in our direction.

"Writer lady, I like you. You come and work in my restaurant. I will sack my wife!"

"Where is she?" I asked, looking around. "I'd like to thank her for that meal."

"Oh no! She does not have anything to say to beautiful women who criticise her cooking and then turn the heads of her husband and her only son! Waa-ha-ha-ha!"

I raised my eyebrow in response but not being sure which point to challenge first I let it drop and simply smiled along with the joke. I firmly refused George's requests to dance and excused myself from the table with my head feeling heavy from the Greek wine I had imbibed. I headed down towards my little home carefully in case I missed my footing in my inebriated state. I thought about calling Dom, just to hear his voice, but then remembered I had accidentally-on-purpose left my mobile 'phone back in England.

I was so lost in my thoughts that I didn't realise I had company until I came around to the front of the cottage. At the table, on which stood a lit candle in a hurricane lamp, was the strong, handsome profile of Stefanos.

He made no attempt to explain his presence, just merely nodded as I came into view. I walked past him and into the cottage to get myself a shawl. The clear night was still warm but it was losing some of its intensity. The lack of streetlights on this part of the island meant that the stars were fiercely shining down on us. There were more stars in the sky than I had ever seen in my life. It was a shame that the only person I had to share it with was a man who could barely stand the sight of me.

When I finally sat down next to him on the bench Stefanos sat forward and asked, "So, where did your parents live?"

"Lakira Street. Do you know it?"

He shook his head. "I have never been into Varosha. The city came under attack many years before I was born."

"Of course."

"Drink?" he asked picking up a bottle of red.

"Please," I said, even though I had no intention of drinking anything else except water for the rest of the night.

"Why were they here?"

"Mum's husband, Eddie, was in the army – the 9th Signal Regiment. He was posted here. Mum moved out here with him when they got married. She returned to England shortly after I was born. I think Eddie is back in Cyprus but I'm not sure where."

"Is that why you are here? To track down your father?"

"Noooo," I said slowly. "He's not my father. My father was a Greek Cypriot. I don't even know his name. I hope that I might be able to find out who my real family is, or was, but I don't know if I can."

"And your mother? She cannot help answer your questions?"

"No, it's a bit complicated."

"She is ashamed, yes? Of her affair?"

"Oh God, no! No, it's not that! She didn't have an affair. She doesn't know much more about my father than I do, and you'll just have to take my word for it that she has her reasons for not wanting to talk about it. So, your turn. Why does Yaiyai hate the British?"

Stefanos laughed at this. It transformed his studious face instantaneously and he looked like the handsome young man that he was.

"Her memories from sixty years ago are clearer than those from yesterday. She still holds the British responsible for the death of her eldest son and she will never forgive them for that. He was an EOKA fighter. You know of EOKA?"

"A little," I ventured. "But I'm not sure I really understand the difference between EOKA and EOKA-B."

Stefanos sighed and his eyes hardened as if he was trying to condense all the information in his brain into a palatable amount for me to grasp. "Okay... so EOKA wanted the British out of the island and in 1955 there was an uprising. It lasted for four years. Firstly I should say that neither side was blameless but EOKA used some pretty dirty tactics and killed innocent people, the wives and children of servicemen. You have to understand that they were furious that they didn't have control of their own country. The British didn't really have any right to be here."

"And Yaiyai's son died in the fighting?"

"No. The British rounded up the troublemakers and interrogated them. They claim they did not torture them but fourteen Cypriots died during these 'interrogations'. One man was Yaiyai's son."

"No! Seriously? I hadn't heard that."

"What had you heard about EOKA?"

I cringed, unsure whether to be honest or not and risk offending Stefanos again but the wine had expanded my parameters and my confidence levels.

"Well, I thought… I thought that EOKA was little more than a terrorist group that targeted innocent people. My understanding is they were rewarded for their terrorism with the British ceding control to the Cypriots and just holding on to the two army bases."

"Hmmmm. You shouldn't tell Yaiyai you think of them as terrorists," he smiled. "Of course, this wasn't only a fight between EOKA and the British Army. EOKA murdered Turkish Cypriots who had worked with the British. They killed a Turkish Policeman in 1955 so the Turks targeted the Greeks living in Istanbul. Thousands had to flee from the city. When EOKA tried again to get the British out, TNT – that's the Turkish National Party – killed eight Greek Cypriot men from Kondemenos. They bombed their own press office in Nicosia and blamed it on the Greeks. Even after independence from Britain had been declared, the Turkish Navy was caught sending a ship to Cyprus full of arms for the TNT. Yaiyai hates the Turks just as much as she hates the British. Maybe more."

"So why are the rest of your family so welcoming to the British? Is it because of the money that they bring with them in terms of tourism?"

"Do you know that you keep answering your own questions before I have time to open my mouth?" he asked with a frown.

"Sorry! Bad habit."

"The rest of us have reasons to forgive the British and be thankful for their presence here."

"Go on," I urged.

"When the Turks invaded in 1974, my family did not want to leave their home and their businesses. One of my mother's sisters, Tula, had three children. Her two sons had gone to join with the fighting. Tula refused to leave until they were both home safely, she thought that they would not find her again if she left. So she stayed along with her daughter, Anemone. My grandparents had to leave them behind. They picked up all they could carry and they ran.

My grandparents had nowhere to go so the British Army opened up their bases and gave them shelter and safety. The Turkish stopped when they reached these bases. They didn't want to start a war with the British too, and so we are thankful that these bases existed."

"I see. What happened to Tula and..."

"Anemone?"

"Yes, Tula and Anemone?" I asked dreading the answer.

Stefanos bowed his head and sighed. "We never saw my aunt again, nor her daughter. We can only assume the worst. They are among the 1,619 Greek Cypriots who went missing. It broke my mother's heart. She was not close to her sister, there was a large gap in age, but she loved Anemone. They were more like sisters themselves. My mother looked out for her and played with her. She will never forgive herself for leaving her. She still haunts her dreams. She has nightmares about what happened to that little girl, but we will never know. She just wants to find her body and lay her to rest."

"I'm sorry. I had no idea that so many people are still unaccounted for. What about Tula's sons?"

"One of them died in the fighting but the younger one, Jani, was rescued by an off-duty British soldier. He had been shot and left to die in a pit in the mountains but this soldier, he found him and carried him to safety. He literally owes his life to the British.

"It is difficult for my family to talk about. Only eighty-seven bodies have been identified and returned to their families so far. The UN-sponsored missing persons committee are still searching and testing DNA but it is a long and difficult process." Stefanos paused and sipped his wine.

In the absence of anything to say, I did the same.

"My father remembers it all clearly. He was a young man in his teens when the invasion happened. He and my mother were not yet married but they were engaged. They want to move on with their lives and hope to see a day when North and South Cyprus are unified again. Hatred is a disease that eats you up from the inside. When the border controls were relaxed and we were allowed to cross over to Northern Cyprus, do you know what my mother did? She went to visit her father's old shop and spoke to the Turkish family who run it now. She wanted to see who lived there now and wanted to wish them luck."

"Wow. That's amazing. And what about the Turkish family? How did they feel about seeing your mother after all of these years?"

"They were happy. They gave her a box of photographs that her parents had left behind when they fled. They had kept it in case they ever saw my grandparents again. My parents will not hold a grudge against these people but not everyone is so... so...

understanding."

I mulled that over for a moment. I was amazed at how

forgiving people could be. It must have been difficult for Antheia

to see the place where she once had lived but she had still wished

the new occupants luck.

"So," I asked, "tell me, how does EOKA-B differ from

EOKA?"

"Right," Stefanos took a deep breath. "After the Treaty of

Guarantee in 1960 there was no more EOKA, but there were still

many on the island who wanted to take things a step further.

When Archbishop Makarios showed no signs of pursing *Enosis*,

EOKA-B began."

"Remind me again what *Enosis* is?" I asked, somewhat

sheepishly.

"*Enosis*. Closer links with the motherland. You know?

Becoming part of Greece."

"Surely it doesn't take a genius to work out that the

Turkish population of Cyprus would oppose this?"

"Leni, you are being a little arrogant. You think that you are cleverer than everybody else? Do you think that the Greek Cypriots are idiots? Sometimes people are so blinded by their own desires that they do not think of the consequences. When the EOKA-B and the Military Junta launched a coup against Makarios, nobody could have known how the Turks would have responded. They were just waiting for an excuse to invade and, yes, EOKA-B handed it to them.

"Many people feel that we were betrayed by our own motherland. People who should have been protecting us led us into a war where too many people paid with their lives. Everybody had an opinion. There is a saying in politics – 'Five Greeks, six parties'.

"The Cypriot people have paid a heavy price for this. They are still paying a price, both Greek Cypriots and Turkish Cypriots. They were all forced out of their homes and both sides suffered. Yes, it is true that you could blame the Greek Cypriots for overthrowing Makarios. But the issue here is the strength of the invasion by the Turks. We could not match their firepower. They had forty thousand troops when we only had twelve thousand. They had tanks, howitzers, destroyers, submarines, helicopters and combat aircraft. We had guns and tanks. That is all. Do you think that is a fair fight?"

Stefanos stopped abruptly and stared straight ahead. I could see the muscles in his jaw pulsing as he tried to control his anger. Even in the deepening darkness of the night I could see the hardness in his eyes. I had read some of the facts about the Turkish invasion of 1974 as I tried to research the country of my birth but to hear it like this from someone emotionally involved in the struggle made it hard to digest.

"I'm sorry, Stefanos. I didn't mean to sound..." My voice trailed off. "I don't know anything about the personal cost of war. I am only just beginning to find out about what it cost my family."

"Your family?" Stefanos turned on me with nostrils flaring and thinly disguised contempt in his eyes. "*Your* family? What do *your* family know of loss? You were safe within the boundaries of the British army bases, your family didn't see any fighting, your family aren't wondering what happened to their loved ones and whether they'll ever be able to find their bodies and lay them to rest."

"Don't you dare lecture me!" I snapped at him placing my hands with unnecessary force on the table in front of me so that the wine glasses rattled. Stefanos' eyes widened and he physically moved away from me with what looked like fear on his face. "You don't know anything about my family or about me." I stood up, hands shaking and voice quivering. "The woman that I call my mother was *shot* by the Turks. My biological mother was *killed* by the Turks. I don't even *know* what happened to my birth father. My whole world has been turned upside-down and I might not understand everything that happened, but I am *trying* to understand. I am *trying* to learn more. Why do you think I am asking all these questions? Eh? Why do you think I am desperate to get into Varosha? I don't know *anything* about where I came from or who my biological parents were. I am trying to get some answers. And what about you? You weren't even born then. How dare you carry around all this anger and resentment when you have lived a happy and harmonious life in the arms of your family this whole time? You have no understanding of real pain. You are like every bloody student I've ever met, thinks they know every-bloody-thing but actually have experienced NOTHING!"

He caught my arm and stood to face me. I could feel his breath on my cheek and smell his musky scent. I looked at his perfect lips that parted with a sigh and he took a step closer to me so that our bodies were touching. He let his hand slide down my arm and I shivered, suddenly breaking free of the trance I was in.

"Don't touch me, Stefanos!"

I shook my arm free and stormed into the cottage. I paused at the door and faced him. He looked confused and hurt standing in the shadows. An apology began to form on my tongue and I started to reach out towards him, wanting to run my hand over his firm chest. I knew the alcohol was impairing my decision-making skills but desire was taking over my cognitive reasoning. I watched as look of triumph crept into his eyes and he started to smile lazily, taking a step in my direction. I gripped hold of the door tightly in one hand. The smugness on his face ignited a rage in my heart as I realised then that I had fallen into his trap.

With a smile that didn't reach my eyes I slammed the door firmly in his face.

Chapter ten

Cyprus, 1974

When Pru awoke to the polite applause of the early morning rain, she had the feeling she had been battling with bad dreams all night. Rain, which had long been absent on this island, was an unfamiliar sound to Pru, yet she found herself comforted by its staccato beat. An unsettled feeling of foreboding was tapping at her consciousness and her throat was sore and scratchy. She tried a small cough, her voice sounding far away and not at all like her own, and pain coursed through her body with torrential force. Her stomach erupted with a fire that she was unable to name. With her eyes squeezed shut she tried a deep breath through her nose but her expanding chest met aching ribs and caused an arrow of pain to shoot through her left shoulder. But still Pru didn't open her eyes. She knew there was something she needed to remember but, with equal certainty, she knew there was something that she did not want to recollect.

While the shutters on her eyes were able to block out the sights in front of her face, the smells assaulting her nose were not so easily kept at bay. There was something different about her room today. The pillow under her head smelled starched and the air surrounding her was thinner, cooler and percolated by the scent of crisp efficiency.

A murmured statement. A man's voice.

"She's waking up. I'll get Eddie." There was the anguished scrape of a chair leg on a hard floor.

"Eddie's home," she thought to herself. "That's good."

"Hinny?" A woman's voice this time. "Can you hear me?"

Pru knew the voice but couldn't associate it with a face for the time being. "It'll come back to me," she thought and she burrowed her head deeper into the pillow and drifted away to sleep.

"She's lost a lot of blood and she's been given a heavy sedative. I'm afraid she might be coming in and out of consciousness for some time yet. But all the signs are as good as they can be at this time. Now, if you'll excuse me..."

"Yes of course, Doctor. Thanks."

Eddie looked at his fragile wife, lying prone before him. She was the most beautiful creature he had ever seen. Her milky skin was alabaster smooth. A rose-pink flush tinted her high cheekbones. Her eyelids pulsed with visions that only Pru could see. Her dry pale lips parted in a gasp then went slack.

Eddie had known as soon as he laid eyes on her that he had to have her. She had evidently felt the same and they couldn't keep their hands off each other. When her folks had kicked her out of home Eddie never once felt trapped by the situation. He had felt like it was always meant to be and it had strengthened their relationship. It was the two of them against the world now and they were unstoppable.

But as infatuation had been replaced by pregnancy, everything had changed between them. Where there had once been love was now mutual resentment. He realised now that they had never talked about the future and, as a result, they hadn't realised that they both wanted wildly different things. They didn't have much of a social life in Cyprus but on Eddie's days off they would head out to Fig Tree Bay on the back of the Suzuki and swim the few hundred meters out to the small rocky island where they would snorkel for hours, pointing out the rainbow of fishes darting through the turquoise waters, returning back to the shore with reddened shoulders and wrinkled skin on their fingers. They would then sit at George's Taverna as the gossamer of salt hardened on their skin while they drank beer and awaited the catch of the day. Some days they would be served the freshest calamari dragged up the beach from the little fishing boats, hung on lines to be dried by the sun. Once they were given sea-slug to eat. They laughed about it, wondering what the people back home would make of it and marvelled at how different their lives were to those of their parents. They would talk as the sun started to slip down the sky of how lucky they were and how life couldn't get any better.

But then, as the pregnancy progressed and Pru found she couldn't do the things she used to do, she seemed to get angry with Eddie. Everything he did would infuriate her. She looked at him with contempt. Her once smiling lips now curled towards her button nose in contempt.

Eddie would never have considered himself a needy man but it was apparent now that he wanted to be needed by someone. Pru withdrew into herself and Eddie searched out alternative forms of validation. He threw himself into his work, volunteering for all the overtime, the more dangerous the better. He was hand-picked to escort President Makarios off the island amid fears for his safety. The feeling of importance he got from this seemingly simple task glowed deep inside him and he stoked the embers of this fire as a man desperate for warmth on a freezing cold night.

Eddie squeezed the wooden arm of the chair until his nails ached and his knuckles stiffened. If he'd been home he could have stemmed the bleeding at the very least. She needed him and he had let her down. All this bravado, guns and fighting didn't make him a man. He had fallen short where it was most important. He had failed as a husband.

Eddie hated this feeling of helplessness. He was trying his hardest to contain the molten anger threatening to erupt from deep inside. He was scared that if he let go, he would never stop. Nonetheless he was sorely tempted to start kicking and punching inanimate objects. Perhaps even the animate ones too. He wanted to hear things break and feel them crumple in his fists. His thoughts whirled around his head with dizzying ferocity. They had shot her. The bastards shot her. Did they look through their sights at her and squeeze the trigger? Did they know what they'd done?

Eddie couldn't help but feel the army had failed the both him and Pru. While the British army were just watching and listening, a very real fight was going on. And that very real fight had come over his doorstep tonight. What would it take for them to get involved, and how many people would have to die? Somebody somewhere needed to take very real and immediate action against the Turks instead of viewing the whole scenario as part of a testosterone-fuelled chess match.

"I love you, Pru. Can you hear me?" he whispered. "If you can hear me, I want you know this one thing. I am *so* sorry." He stood, leant over the bed, kissed her forehead, stroked her hair and then left without looking back.

Pru tried to swallow but her throat hurt. She tried to lick her lips and found them rough and dry under her tongue. She was so thirsty but she couldn't move to get the glass by the side of the bed. She needed a drink of water so badly. Water. A fragment of a memory caught in her mind, enticing her, beckoning her, a snake in the Garden of Eden.

She could see herself in the kitchen with a glass. The tap was running cool water over her hand. No. Stop. The shutters came down abruptly on the thought. There was nothing there. She'd get a drink later. Right now, she was so tired. Somewhere across the room she thought she heard Eddie say he was sorry. So he should be, it must be really late by now. What time does he call this? Doesn't he know she needs her sleep? He should have been home hours ago. Pru sighed and drifted back into the hospitable arms of sleep.

Chapter eleven

I snapped awake from my dream and sat bolt upright like a sprung trap. Wheezing, I dragged the air down into my lungs in large gulps. I placed one hand over my heaving chest and panted. I dreamt that I was trapped under a collapsed building and couldn't get out. It had all felt so real. I could still recall the roughness of the rubble, the bricks on my body and the weight of them pressing down on me. I had been cold, so cold, and it was wet where I lay amongst the debris. In my dream it had been raven black and I couldn't see anything. My legs were trapped and somewhere I could hear a baby crying – my baby – but I couldn't get to it. Then there was a blinding flash of white light and I was catapulted into consciousness. Always the flash of light.

I blinked and my eyes adjusted to the reality of the honey-gilt room before me. I felt comforted that it had been nothing more than a dream, even though it still felt like a reality. Goosebumps rippled over my arms as the cooling air sighed on my sweating body. I sat slumped over for a minute, still waiting for the hammering of my heart to subside. It was one of those dreams that stayed with you. I knew them all too well. It had been a while since I'd had a nightmare like that one. It would hang around me like a shroud for the rest of this evening, making me feel uneasy and unsettled no matter how many times I told myself it was just a dream.

I squeezed my shoulders upwards and rolled my head from side to side. I seemed to have strained something while thrashing about in my dream and my neck had stiffened in response. I was mildly surprised to find that I was still fully dressed. I remembered now that I had only intended to doze a short while away from the harsh glare of the sun. I wasn't feeling as refreshed as I'd hoped I would. In fact, if anything I was feeling more exhausted now than before I laid down. I pushed myself out of bed and slipped out to the patio area with a blanket around my shoulders. It was beautifully and resplendently warm outside and the blanket was entirely unnecessary as anything other than a comforter. I sat on the bench with my knees up to my chin and thought about what had happened today.

An appalling night's sleep last night meant that I had been awake before the morning was out of the starting blocks. In Protaros I had headed straight to an Internet café where I sat for twenty minutes with a drink looking for information on Facebook and then on Friends Reunited until I found what I had been looking for. A quick Google search and I was a step closer to my prize. I had been surprised at how easy it had been really. All that information on thousands of people you hadn't met laid bare for you to pry into. I felt like a voyeur sneaking a peek at these people from the hidden safety of my Cypriot café and eavesdropping on conversations not intended for me. Knowledge is a heady drug that I craved as much as a flower seeks daylight. Without it, I was suffocating and withering day by day.

I hastily tapped out an email to Dom explaining what I'd learned so far and where I would be staying for the next couple of weeks. After a brief hesitation I hammered out a few kisses and pressed 'send'. Armed with an address and a flicker of excitement, I wandered the streets of Protaros until I found the place that I was looking for. I positioned myself in a café over the road where I could keep an eye on the building I sought. I snacked on the chips and souvlaki they brought me but barely tasted it as I watched for some movement or sign of life opposite me. It looked like I was going to have to return later.

Now standing outside the building, which was now teeming with a certain kind of fun seeker, and still groggy from my nightmare riddled sleep, I was nervous in anticipation of what the evening might hold.

"Forgive me, Mum," I said to the air as I stepped into the neon-bathed bar. This certainly wasn't somewhere designed to appeal to the locals of the island. The music was too loud and was blaring out 'classic' Brit pop. Oasis was all but drowned out by a group of men with their arms over each other's shoulders singing along with 'Wonderwall' in flat Northern tones. I hovered at the door and fingered the shoulder strap of my bag nervously.

This was usually the kind of place that I avoided when holidaying or working abroad. I never went into bars like this at home so I certainly didn't seek them out when I was away. But I was here with a purpose; nothing else would have convinced me to set foot over the threshold.

My eyes scanned the bobbing heads in the darkened bar but no one stood out. Now that I was here I realised that there was more than a slight possibility that he wouldn't be here at all and, even if he was, the chance of me recognising him was slim. The air was thick with the scent of spilt beer and cloying aftershave. I manoeuvred my way towards the bar through the throngs of people, my trainers adhering to the lager-lacquered wooden floor. As I tried to squeeze past a man in a Ben Sherman shirt too small for his greed-induced girth, he turned and said "Aye, aye! She's touching me up!" to much hilarity from the assembled crowd. I managed a weak smile and tried again to get past him. This time he purposely blocked my way.

"Hey honey! I might not be Fred Flintstone, but I could certainly make your bed rock!" he said with a raised eyebrow and eyes full of mirth and suggestion.

His mates laughed and cheered and while he basked in their admiration I slipped away.

"Tosser!" I muttered under my breath and squeezed through enough people to shield me from the oaf and to get me closer to the heart of the din where people were shouting orders to the bar staff.

I got to the bar as two over-made-up young women moved away from it clutching their alco-pops. One glanced disapprovingly down at my attire and then away quickly as if she thought that I was the kind of woman who would start a fight. She leaned in closer to her friend who glanced at me sideways from under her false eyelashes. I met her surreptitious glance with a brazen stare of my own as they scuttled away. I wasn't in the best of moods tonight, possibly because I was way out of my depth and getting tired of treading water. I glanced along at the bar staff. They didn't look old enough to drink alcohol, never mind serve it.

There were only three of them and they seemed to be overworked. As soon as they handed the change to one person they were already asking the next one what they wanted. Pint after pint was pulled as I watched. It was surprisingly busy in here for the off season, but it was about as close as you could get to the high season before the schools broke up, so it stood to reason that nearly everyone here was childless or single. A quick glance behind the bar confirmed that this establishment would not be featured in my culinary tour of the island unless Walkers crisps and pickled eggs counted as a Greek delicacy.

Several times I opened my mouth to order a drink and the barman looked past me to either a young man leaning over me or a young girl who out-cleavaged me. Time to take assertive steps. I put both of my elbows on the bar top and felt something sticky on my arms. I pulled myself up to my full height and fixed my eyes on the nearest barman.

"Yep?" asked the barman.

"Keo please."

"Bottle or glass."

"Bottle."

"Sure."

"Is Eddie in tonight?" I asked as nonchalantly as possible.

The tanned boy in front of me cocked his ear at me and I leaned in closer to shout.

"I said, is Eddie here tonight?"

The boy just looked puzzled and shrugged as we exchanged money for beverage.

"Damn!" Maybe I wasn't in the right place after all. Deflated, I turned around and walked straight into the chest of a tall, well-built man.

"Who wants to know?" came a clear strong voice that cut through the music easily without shouting.

I looked into his face. It wasn't quite what I'd been expecting. In the photos I'd seen of him, he'd been fresh faced with a pointy chin. This man was altogether rounder and softer looking but there was no doubting that, when I was born, this man had been my mum's husband. I had found Eddie.

Chapter twelve

Cyprus, 1974

Eddie watched as the sky began to concede its raven hue. On the horizon the first rays of light were seeping like watercolours into the velvet morning. He sat astride his motorbike with his helmet under his arm. It was time to go. He threw his helmet into the wadi and heard it skid on the parched earth. He felt the need for the wind on his face today. Eddie was restless and in no mood to play it safe.

The birds were stirring and singing loudly enough to be heard over the thrum of the bike's engine. A lizard scurried into the bushes as the wheels disturbed the dust. Twice he narrowly missed the fast black snakes who made the arid wadi their home. The faster he rode the bike, the more he could detach himself from the sight of his wife lying in the hospital bed, tentatively hanging on to her depleted life.

He knew where the pockets of Greeks were hiding out in the hills and set off to join them in their fight. Knowing the thirsty land better than the roads, Eddie was able to move up the country without coming across any checkpoints until he got to the hills. He knew it was only a matter of time before he would come across fighters of one nationality or another. As he kicked the bike on up the crumbling walls of the dry ditch and onto the road, he wasn't surprised to see armed men up ahead. He felt unusually numb. He didn't fear for his own life, possibly because he didn't much care for it.

Directly in front of him were four soldiers leaning on a tank. Eddie slowed as they motioned to him with their guns. From here, he couldn't tell if they were Greek or Turkish. He had to be patient. Eddie slowed down enough to take stock of the situation. As he got closer he recognised the tank was an American M48 Patton favoured by the Turkish army and the final piece of his plan fell into place. He clenched his fists around the handlebars of his motorbike and hoped his recklessness would pay off. He didn't want to show his hand yet.

Even before he spoke, they knew that he was British.

"Stop. What is your business?" came the stilted but technically perfect English.

"I'm a journalist. I'm here to report on the..." Eddie paused, thinking carefully about what he would call it.

"The peace operation?"

"Yes, the *peace* operation," Eddie said pointedly.

"Where is your camera? Your papers?"

Eddie nodded behind him to the pack on the back of his bike.

"Please stand here." The Turkish soldier pointed with his gun at the side of the road.

Eddie got off the bike, carefully stretching his legs as he did so, and stood before the man addressing him. He might have looked relaxed but every muscle in Eddie's body was thrumming with adrenaline and preparing for attack.

"You have weapon?"

"No."

The Turkish man beckoned one of the others over who flicked his cigarette butt away before patting up and down Eddie's legs and body. He nodded as he confirmed there were no weapons concealed on the Englishman's body.

Eddie took this opportunity to look at the men closely. The Commander appeared a few years older than the rest of the crew but that might only have been because of the authority with which he conducted himself. They were shorter than Eddie but all were wider and strong looking. There was a slightly bored expression on the faces of the younger men. Eddie knew that look. He had seen it on the faces of colleagues who were eager to join in the fight but were instead put on basic duties. Something that struck Eddie as he looked at them was the assured manner they all had. Not one of them showed any signs of being in the wrong. Not one of the men here felt like they were intruding on Greek land. He wondered if one of these men had fired the shot that had hit his wife and felt his gut clench.

"Where are you going to?" the first man asked again. He looked curious rather that suspicious.

"To the North, in order to see the Turkish troops in action."

With a nonchalant wave of his hand, he dismissed Eddie and went back to his station by the tank. As he turned his back on Eddie his gun swung loosely by his side. Eddie saw at once how he could grab the weapon and crunch the butt of the gun into the Commander's face before shooting the others as they stood uncomprehending in front of him. His hands twitched but the moment had passed and he let the men live. For now.

Eddie kept his eyes on his mirrors as he edged the bike away from the group, careful to proceed slowly up the road while he was still in their sight. As soon as he was behind the ridge of trees he kicked the bike up a notch and turned off onto a dirt track that he had travelled many times before. Even if the tank had decided to follow him, it couldn't go above thirty miles an hour and there was no way it could follow him up this narrow track. Within fifteen minutes the track became too rough and steep to ride on so Eddie pulled the bike off between the trees by what looked like an abandoned shepherd's hut. Shouldering his pack he set off again up the hill. He wanted to retrieve the box

217

and then push on to reach his destination before the heat of the day could disrupt his plans.

It took him some time to find the right place, and in his panic he thought that someone had beaten him to it, but there it was, in the cool and silent darkness of the hollow in the rock. The crate stood firm and square with the word EOKA stamped on it in four-inch-high inky black letters. Eddie had come across the box on a camping trip two months ago but had left it well alone then. Partly because he knew it was something that he shouldn't have seen, but mainly because of the arrow sharp scorpions who made these rocks their home.

Eddie seized the rope handles on either side of the wooden cube and dragged it from its concealed position. He almost dropped it when something dense and sharp landed on his foot but it was a stone, not a clawed, sting-wielding arachnid.

With a pounding heart, Eddie carried his prize to the shade of the nearby Cypress tree and dropped to his knees. His mind sifted through what he knew of EOKA. They were the National Organisation of Cypriot Fighters formed, and disbanded, in the 1950s set up with the aim of the "liberation of

Cyprus from the British yoke" They not only wanted rid of the British from the Island but their main aim was one of *Enosis*: the unification of Cyprus with mainland Greece. They were known for, literally, shooting people in the back: a sergeant walking his two-year-old son down the street; an army officer's wife gunned down in the street shopping with her daughter for her wedding dress; a young soldier who turned his back on a Greek-Cypriot workman to get him a glass of water.

The stories sickened Eddie when he was first posted to Cyprus but he had been unable to equate those isolated incidents with the men and women he had worked side by side with in this beautiful country every day. He had memorised the facts. They had been led by George Grivas and in 1955 they recruited the *spirited youth* of Cyprus and launched a number of attacks on the British areas of Cyprus including the broadcasting station in Nicosia, the Wolseley barracks and significant targets in Famagusta. This continued until the late fifties when a ceasefire was declared and EOKA was disbanded in order to pave way for the Zurich agreement. In August 1960 Cyprus achieved independence from the United Kingdom with the exception of the two Sovereign Army Bases, one at Akrotiri and the other, where Eddie and his regiment were based, at Dhekalia.

But, it appeared, they never quite forgot their hopes for Enosis. President Archbishop Makarios wasn't the leader that George Grivas had hoped for. He was disappointed with the lack of drive for unification with the motherland and in 1971 EOKA-B was born. By this time Grivas was so hungry for *Enosis* that he would kill both Turks *and* Greeks who were opposed to their ideology. If the British had hoped that Grivas' death in January would take some of the impetus away from EOKA-B's fight, they had been proven wrong. Six months later the Military Junta took direct control and launched the military coup that led to the installation of Nikos Sampson as dictator of Cyprus. The Turkish inhabitants feared for their safety under this new regime and retaliated by launching an attack on the Island. It was anybody's guess how that was going to pan out now.

The Army had given Eddie his orders, but he was never one to be told what to do. The army were not going to intervene in this war unless the fighting came anywhere near sovereign territory, but that was before the war became personal for Eddie.

He hadn't been there to protect Pru last night, but now he was going to make things right and make the Turks pay for what they had done. He opened up his backpack and took a swig of water while he decided on his next move. Judging by the sun, it was midmorning. He could still cover a substantial amount of ground before the heat became too heavy to walk through. Taking out his knife from inside his solid black boot, Eddie began to loosen the lid of the crate.

The sudden sound of gravel being disturbed had Eddie crouching low in the dust. His knife still poised in his hand, he retreated until his back felt the warm roughness of the tree trunk. His breathing and his heart sounded too loud to him and he forced himself to breathe slowly through his nose, making minimal sound. More sounds, this time from behind the bushes directly in front of him. There was more than one set of feet, but the noise level suggested two at most. The bush swayed and juddered in front of him as the branches were pulled and snapped. He turned the handle of his knife over in his hand and held the shaft firmly, ready to spring into action if his hiding place was discovered. More shuffling and the sound of heavy breathing, close to the ground. The intruder was stooped behind the thick bush but Eddie still couldn't get a visual on him.

Eddie moved slightly and soundlessly to his left in order to catch a glimpse of the man or men. He had no time to think what he would do if confronted; he would just have to react quickly to whichever situation he found himself in. And if that meant silencing a Turk permanently then that was fine by him. To be able to see what was behind that bush would mean exposing his hiding place. Eddie hesitated for a split second too long and the decision was taken from him. His heart shot into his throat as his assailant leapt from the bushes towards him.

He instinctively raised his arms above his head to ward off attack and prepared to spring up against the aggressor. The blurred form above him was momentarily silhouetted black against the white sunlight. The shock knocked Eddie backwards and he lost his footing, crashing against the tree. Recovering his grip on his knife he coiled as if to pounce before he realised his would-be attacker was on all fours, had horns and was grazing before him. The animal raised his head and looked directly at Eddie with eerie eyes which had oblong slits of black at the centre. Eddie exhaled and shook his head. Shitting himself over a goat? He had to pull himself together.

He allowed himself a small smile as he straightened his back against the tree and looked up into the branches above him. Jesus, he was losing the plot. He threw his knife into the ground so the blade landed with an honest thud in the dry earth four feet in front of him and reverberated contentedly with the impact. The goat gazed at him with cold, impassive eyes and ambled off. Eddie was going to have to come up with a better plan if he was going to survive out here.

With no warning, the back of Eddie's head smacked into the tree trunk as strong arms snaked round the tree from behind him and a hand clamped firmly over his mouth. Even if a shout could have been heard, it wouldn't have been possible as the other arm closed so quickly over his chest that he was momentarily winded and he felt his ribs pop.

Chapter thirteen

"Oh, er... hello. I'm Helen Jefferies."

He looked at me, his face showing no flicker of recognition. Silence stretched in front of me, begging to be filled.

"I'm Leni?" I made it a question. "Erm... of course, you don't know me but you know my mum, Prudence Clarke."

His shoulders tensed and the light went out of his eyes like a candle that had been snuffed out. Hardness crept into his clamped jawline and his eyes narrowed. I certainly hadn't been expecting this reaction from the man who, until recently, I'd thought was my father. He rubbed his stubbled chin.

"What d'ya want?" came his cold monosyllabic demand.

"I wanted to talk to you, ask you a few questions. Is that okay?"

"No. You shouldn't have come here."

"What?" I asked, shocked at the unexpected turn of events.

He turned and walked away into the crowd, and before I could follow him he was sucked up into the writhing bodies.

"Wait!" I shouted after him. "I just wanted to…"

"Shit!" I said to myself and took a swig from my Keo.

I hadn't expected that he would flatly refuse to talk to me or emanate such hostility. It hadn't occurred to me that Eddie might have any kind of grievance against Pru and me. I'd thought of Mum as the wounded, abandoned party for so long that it was something of a surprise to me that Eddie was anything other than contrite. If Eddie wasn't going to talk to me I was at a dead end. I'd come too far now to give up without a fight and decided to hang around in case he changed his mind or at least until I'd come up with a better plan.

I went outside in the direction that Eddie had stalked off in and, in doing so, passed my admirer and his friends. "Eh, Kev, she's back for more! Whey-hey!"

I didn't stop for them this time and instead barged past them to the sound of their mocking laughter. Eddie was nowhere to be seen. I decided to bide my time until the bar closed when it would be quieter. Perhaps when he saw my persistence he would waver and consent to talk with me. It was worth a shot and I had no pressing plans tonight, or tomorrow for that matter. He was going to have to talk to me if he wanted me to leave.

I found a seat being vacated just as I reached it outside. I slumped over the table toying with the idea of crying. It would be so easy to run away with my tail between my legs and flee back to my old life. I sat passing, or possibly wasting, time and nursed my beer until it had grown warm and flat, picking at the label on the bottle.

"Sign of sexual frustration, that."

"Pardon?" I asked wearily as I looked up into the alcohol-flushed face of Fred Flintstone again.

"Peeling labels off bottles. It's a sign of sexual frustration. I reckon I could do something about that," he sneered and grabbed his crotch.

I managed a half-hearted smile and turned away, focussing on the moths flittering around the orbs of light. Even out in the evening air I could still smell his beer breath and his sweaty, out-of-condition body.

His friends cheered and, bolstered by their amusement, he took this as some sort of encouragement.

"Are you a dyke, luv?" he laughed.

"Or a man-she," one of his friends offered.

"A chick with a dick! Is that it? Are you a lesbian? You're on the wrong island love, you should be in Lesbos." He found himself very funny but my patience had worn thin enough to snap.

"Listen arse-hole," I spun round in my seat but remained sitting. "Do not think for a minute that I am in your league. Even if I wasn't married, *which I am,* I still have certain standards. Maybe I'm choosy, but I don't think it's unreasonable to want someone whose IQ exceeds his waist measurement."

His friends, still standing nearby, issued a low whistle and a few uncomfortable laughs.

My challenger looked confused for a minute as if trying to work out the insult and then as I turned back to my beer he grabbed my breast. I shot up out of my seat and, without thinking, hit him round the side of the face. With dismay I realised that I was still holding my beer bottle in my hand and it had smashed into his cheekbone causing his face to split open like a ripe tomato.

The anger in his eyes thundered darkly and too late I realised that he had clenched his fist.

"Bitch!" he spat at me and punched me in the face. His fist met with my jaw and snapped my head backwards. My teeth ground together with the force of the blow and I fell to the floor watching the arcing sky in slow motion. The wooden chair I'd been sitting on a moment ago fell at my side with a clatter. I don't know what shocked me more: the fact that he'd hit me or the fact that I'd smashed him in the face with a bottle. Neither event made any sense to me. I would have apologised profusely if he hadn't retaliated so readily.

I tried to get up but the ground was shifting under my feet, I was aware of commotion all around me but I couldn't focus my eyes so I just put one arm over my head hoping to fend off any more blows that might come my way and rolled onto my side in a ball. I could hear swearing and slaps of fist on face but every time I opened my eyes to look in the direction of the sounds, they refused to give me anything to work with. The two lights outside the bar that had previously seemed so tame now shone like floodlights into my retinas and I blinked away the bright green imprints behind my eyelids. There was a hurricane materialising around me and I was blissfully tranquil at its core.

Suddenly there was stillness. My eyes gave up trying to focus on anything and I slipped into that tantalising space between reality and sleep, not sure which way to travel. I could hear an unfamiliar voice coming to me through the miasma.

"Can you hear me? Can you hear me?"

"Of course I can hear you," I thought, but I couldn't make the words come out of my mouth no matter how hard I tried.

"Take her through to the back."

I tried to say "No thank you, I can walk," but my brain hadn't found the way to make my mouth work yet. I closed my eyes and let myself be half carried, half dragged back into the busy bar. I was taken through a door that I hadn't noticed before. It was painted the same mushroom colour as the walls and had a combination lock on it. I attempted, half-heartedly, to resist but relented and let myself be ushered inside.

By the time I found myself slumped on an oversoft sofa my vision was a little blurry but at least I could keep my eyes open. I could now feel the growing pain in my face and my head. For some inexplicable reason, my behind and left hip were aching and almost certainly developing a bruise. I manoeuvred myself so that most of my weight went down my right side but I still wasn't comfortable so I pushed myself backwards, trying to even the pressure out.

"What did you say your name was?" Eddie was sitting in a chair opposite me, leaning forward with concern over his face.

"Leni," I said, although it didn't quite come out like that.

"Ellie?" asked Eddie

"No," I said, clearer this time. My jaw wasn't working the way it should be and I reached my hand up gingerly to the throbbing area. "Leni."

"You didn't *have* to pick a fight with the biggest guy in here to get my attention," he smiled.

I tried to return suit but instead I ended up grimacing and wincing simultaneously.

"Jeez. You didn't get that street fighting style from your mum. Not the Pru that I knew, anyway. Anger issues at all?"

"No! God, no! I... I don't fight. I mean, I didn't mean to hit him with the bottle. I only meant to slap his face. I really don't know how it happened. He grabbed me, I slapped him and there was blood and then he hit me and then I was on the floor. I don't.... I mean, this isn't really the kind of thing that…"

I trailed off as my breathing started to quicken and catch in my chest.

"Here, you're shaking. Let's get you a drink."

I looked down at my hands. They were shaking uncontrollably. It was almost fascinating the way they oscillated independently from anything I was doing. I turned them over and

231

looked at the palms of my hands. My right hand had a smooth line of crimson across the heel of my palm. I must have cut it on the bottle. I couldn't even feel the cut. I folded my arms and pushed my hands under my armpits to curb the trembling.

Eddie came back into the room surfing a solid wave of noise which became instantly muted with the closing of the door. I looked up to see a large shot of amber liquid floating in a tumbler before my face. I opened my mouth to tell him that I didn't drink spirits, but there were many things that I'd never done before tonight and I was in no position to object.

"Thanks." I took the precariously sloshing drink from him and smelled it. In his other hand he was holding a tea towel wrapped around something.

Answering my silently questioning eyes he said, "Ice. For that jaw. Here let me look at it. Jeez, that's nasty. Not broken though. You'll live. Right hold the ice onto here. Got it?"

I nodded and did as I was told. Aside from being mortified that he was seeing me in this state, I was pleased that I'd finally got him alone, although I wished the path I'd taken hadn't been quite so extreme. I took the opportunity to look closely at Eddie. He was wearing jeans and red converse trainers, which made him appear younger than I knew him to be. Across his broad chest he wore a Rolling Stones 40 licks T-shirt. There was no wedding ring on his left hand although that didn't necessarily mean he was single.

Meeting his gaze brazenly I took in his open face. Not many wrinkles but his blond hair was greying now. He had a couple of days' growth of stubble on his chin that was several shades darker than the hair on his head. I wouldn't say he looked cool exactly, but he had an ageing rocker style about him.

"How is she?" he asked quietly, looking away and interlocking his fingers behind his head, feigning nonchalance. "Pru, I mean."

"She's good thanks. You know... I was going to say that she doesn't change but maybe she has changed since... well, everything, you know. I'm normally a lot more erudite that this, trust me. I think that guy knocked the sense out of me."

"Does she know you're here?" Eddie asked, fixing me with his clear blue eyes.

"In Cyprus? Yes. With you? No."

"Right." He seemed to mull this over for a while as we both sat and wondered what to say next. "What did you want to talk about?" he asked with a troubled frown.

"Well, I don't know how much you know about me, about my birth and stuff. Wow! This is more awkward than I was expecting."

"That's okay. I know that you are *not* Pru's daughter."

This brought the hackles up on my neck. "I *am* her daughter. She might not have given birth to me but she has been a mother to me in every other way."

Eddie held up his hands in mock surrender.

"Okaaay," he said slowly.

"Look. I only found out a few weeks ago that she's not my *biological* mother. Until then, I thought you were my father. It's a long story, but basically, I'm trying to find out who my biological parents were and I was hoping you might know something and be able to help me. Mum either doesn't remember or doesn't want to tell me, so I was hoping you would tell me what it is that you know."

"No can do."

"What?"

"I told you before, in the bar, I can't help you. I don't want to get involved. Pru brought this on herself. If she doesn't want you snooping around then..." He paused and went silent as if remembering something. When he spoke again, his voice was barely more than a whisper. "She should never have taken you in the first place," he said with a surprising amount of sadness.

"Why are you so pissed? Wasn't it you who walked out on her?" I challenged.

"Is that what she told you? Is it?" he snorted and folded his arms. He laughed though it wasn't a warm sound.

"Well, yes. No. Oh, I don't know. Before I found out that you guys weren't my 'real' parents, she told me that you left the hospital just after I was born and never came back. Obviously, I now know there might be more to it than that, because I've now found out that I wasn't born in a hospital and certainly not to Mum. So why don't you tell me your side of it?"

"I've already told you, I don't want to get involved."

"Fine. Then I'll carry on thinking that you're the shit that walked out on my mum thirty-nine years ago when she needed you the most. Suits me."

"Y'know what? You need to work on your people skills." Eddie frowned at me like he was trying to work me out. He didn't look angry but it was very difficult to read his expression.

This evening wasn't turning out quite as I'd expected. I thought I'd track down Eddie, we'd catch up, talk about old times and he would swear to make amends for his absence by helping me find out more about my birth family. I certainly hadn't expected hostility or a bar brawl.

"I should have called the police, you know," he said at last.

"Huh?"

"You assaulted one of my customers with a beer bottle."

"You know it wasn't like that! I think you'll find that he sexually assaulted me first."

"I don't know anything. All I saw was you on the floor and some guy with blood running down his face."

"So call the police then," I dared him while trying to keep my face neutral from the panic growing in my chest.

He seemed to consider this possibility for a moment with his arms crossed over his chest.

"Nah. Don't think so."

"And why not?" I asked, keeping the obvious relief out of my voice.

"Because a) the bloke was a tosser and b) I am intrigued by why you'd come here. And c) and this is the tricky one… I'm not sure who to say you are. Are you Mrs Helen Jefferies from England or little Miss Kostas from Cyprus?"

I ignored the first two statements and latched onto the third.

"That's a good memory you've got there."

"Come again?" he puzzled.

"Remembering my name when I only told it to you once, in a noisy bar. Y'know, back when you pretended you didn't know who I was."

Eddie had the decency to be slightly abashed.

"Yeah, well, I'm a people person, I remember names. Either that or I've been checking up on Pru from time to time. But that sounds a little creepy so let's just stick with the 'people person' theory, shall we?"

"Yeah. Let's. Well *People Person,* thank you for your hospitality and for *not* calling in the police. And thank you for spending time talking to me. If you do change your mind and remember anything you think would interest me, I am staying at The Pleiades on Troodos Mountain."

I stood to make my dignified exit but the room span round and I found myself bent over at an awkward angle holding on to the back of the sofa for support.

Eddie chuckled. "Perhaps you should give it a minute."

"No, I'm okay. Thanks." I walked as steadily as I could to the door without looking behind me.

"I take it all back," came Eddie's voice behind me, saturated by amusement. "You *are* Pru's daughter – certainly as pig-headed as she is."

I tried to make a "humph" sound and then flounce out of the room but it sounded more like a snort as I stumbled towards the door with my hand outstretched to steady me.

"Why now?" he whispered so softly I could barely hear him.

"Sorry?" I turned at the unexpected change in tone, still with one hand on the door.

"I don't get why she's told you after all these years. She'd got away with it. I was the only one who knew and I wasn't going to tell anyone. So why now?"

I exhaled noisily. "You don't ask easy questions."

"Neither do you," he shot back.

I studied his face. He would have been handsome once, so I could see why Mum fell for him. He was still attractive now but in a softer way. His blue eyes were clear and startling but they held a touch of sadness to them. He was still well built and strong looking but the washboard stomach had been replaced by something a bit gentler.

Eddie smiled then, genuinely, and gestured to the sofa once more. I was still too wobbly to consider riding Rita up the hill so I returned to the sage green seat in defeat.

"Okay," I said, steeling myself. "I lost my baby." I didn't look at Eddie. I hated seeing sympathy or pain in other people's eyes. I could only keep my own emotions under control if they kept theirs. "My husband and I had fertility treatment, we'd been trying for a while. When I fell pregnant it was a dream come true. When I found that the pregnancy was ectopic the dream turned into a nightmare that I still haven't woken up from. They say I nearly died. Sometimes I wish I had."

I glanced up at him. He was listening intently.

"Mum was my rock. She was there when I came round from theatre and never left my side. She brought me home, tucked me up in bed and slept in the rocking-chair in the corner of the room. The next day I woke up to find her rocking backwards and forwards sobbing her eyes out but I couldn't get a word of sense out of her and she wouldn't talk to anyone. It got to a point where I started getting angry with her and I ended up yelling at her to pull herself together and that it was me that had lost a baby, not her. That was when she told me that she *had* lost a baby. She'd lost her *only* child. Eventually she told me the whole story and how she didn't have time to grieve for the baby she lost because she had to take care of me. What happened to me brought it all back to her. It was quite a blow, as you can imagine. I'd lost my baby and my mother in one week.

"I don't know who I am anymore. I'm no one's mother and I don't seem to be anyone's daughter either. I can't explain it, but I need to *know*. Just to know *something* about who I am. Pathetic, huh?"

"No. Not at all."

We sat and listened to the muted vibration of the music through the walls. This time it was Eddie's turn to fill the silence.

"I did walk out on Pru, but not how you think. I went to join the fighting. I wanted revenge on the Turks for shooting her, for killing my child. Now *that's* pathetic," he scoffed. "I thought she was still sedated in the hospital. When I came back, she was gone. I saw in the evacuation logs that she had been evacuated with a baby girl – you. I had no idea who you were at first, I thought she'd stolen a baby from the hospital or something.

Friends who saw her said she'd been in an agitated state so I thought anything was possible.

"When I eventually tracked her down she wouldn't talk about our son at all. I had to fill out his death certificate. I named him Edward and had him buried here in Cyprus. I thought she'd want to know but she wouldn't listen. I just wanted to share my grief but she cut me out completely. In order to keep her secret for her, I never told anyone that I'd lost my son. She took away my right to grieve openly for my own child."

Eddie's eyes glistened deeply with the ache of loss. It hurt my eyes to look into his pain. I had only just met this man but he was telling me about something that had ripped his heart in two and I knew exactly how that felt. I wondered whether I should reach out and touch him but our connection didn't need a physical touch. We were connected in that way that survivors often are. We both knew what it was like to lose a child. The difference between us was that I was allowed, and even expected, to grieve but he had had to keep his pain bottled up inside for years.

"I'm sorry," I said. "I didn't know. There's so much I didn't know." I blinked away the tears blurring my vision.

"Your mother's name was Helene Kostas. I expect you were named after her. Her husband was called Christos, but he never returned from the fighting and his body was never found. I presume he is dead but until his body is found no one will declare him deceased. As far as I know, there are no other living family members. I asked around a bit after Pru left mainly to satisfy myself that no one was looking for you. It seems that your birth was never registered here so there is no record of you being born to Helene Kostas. In the confusion of the evacuation nobody asked any questions and Pru claimed you as her own child. I can't tell you anything else, I'm afraid. I didn't really know Helene and I never met Christos."

I nodded, it was a lot to take in. I knew I should write these names down, but I was numb and unable to move.

"Thank you. That's... that's... Well, it's something. It's nice to have their names at least. Helene and Christos Kostas."

"You mentioned a husband?"

"Me? Yeah, Dom. He's back home in England. He's busy with work otherwise he would have..."

"Don't shut him out. He lost this baby too. And as trite as it sounds, you do have the opportunity to have more children; there are all kinds of things they can do nowadays. Unless you've married a complete shit, he's got to be hurting as much as you. He is the only other person who knows exactly what it felt like to lose *that* baby. You lose your husband and it'll be like losing that baby all over again. Trust me, I've been there."

"Have you always been this wise?" I smiled.

"Nah, ask Pru. This is from years of wisdom gained from hours polishing glasses behind the bar and hearing the woes of the world. If I'd known then half as much as I know now there might have been a chance for your mum and me, but I was drowning in a mixture of lager and self-pity. It wasn't a pretty sight."

"Thanks for talking about it Eddie. I appreciate it. I really do."

"S'okay. It's kinda nice to be able to talk about it. So she really is doing well then, Pru?"

"Yeah, good I think. Not spoken to her for a while. Things are a little bit awkward between us after the baby and her... news."

"She did what she thought was best, you know? But don't tell her I said that! If she hadn't found you, you'd have a very different life now and so would she. You'll never know for sure, but I think it's worked out better for both of you. She gave you the chance of a better future. What would you have done in her situation?"

"Okay, okay! I get it. She saved my life, I know. Can we leave it for now? I have a bastard headache."

"Let me drive you home. You need to rest. We can talk more tomorrow."

"Can we?"

"Yeah, you're not bad company. C'mon."

Eddie reached out his hand to me and, without hesitation, I took it.

Chapter fourteen

Cyprus, 1974

"Don't make any sudden movements or sounds. I'm going to let go now. Okay? Nod if you understand me."

Eddie nodded cautiously.

"Okay then. Easy now, soldier."

The strong hands released their iron grip tentatively at first and then completely disappeared as it became apparent that Eddie wasn't going to make a scene and give their position away.

"Into the hut," came the gruff voice.

Without turning, Eddie shuffled upright then walked steadily towards the rundown building, rubbing at his sore ribs. The pain was enough that he was aware of it with every hobbling step he took, but it was nothing compared to the agony that was the pointed end of humiliation at the hands of a man he knew to be almost twice his age.

The weathered planks of the shack door had never been painted or seen any colour but that of the tree they had been fashioned from. The overbite of sharp wooden teeth at the base of the door ground against the uneven stone floor as Eddie attempted to push at it. He turned sideways to inch into the damp and dark building, closely followed by the other man. The musty smell of years of abandonment by all except animal and insect was repellent in his nostrils.

"Ya idiot!"

Eddie turned towards the Geordie voice but couldn't see the man's face in impenetrable gloom.

"Bernie, what the f–"

"I could say the same to you, man!"

"Don't start. I'm not having a great day."

"So, coming oot here in a war zone is going to mek it better is it? What good is that gunna do yeh, eh?"

"I've got to do *something.*" Eddie ruffled his hands through his hair. He turned his back on the other man and looked out of a hole in the thick stone wall that served as a window but let in a scant amount of light.

"Tell me Einstein, what d'ya think yer gunna do now then? Take on the whole effing army?"

"Jeez, I don't bloody know." Eddie sighed and all the breath he had been holding poured out and deflated him. In a low voice he continued, "I want them to pay, Bernie. Pru is in some sort of state that she might never wake up from and... Shit!"

Eddie suddenly and violently thrust the heel of his hand into the wall. Stone crumbled to the floor and dusted his feet.

Both men stood in silence for a moment while Eddie put his hands in his pocket and kicked his toes at the dirt and brick dust covering the dingy floor.

"How d'ya find me?"

"Well, you're an idiot, and idiots are predictable. I had a hunch you were heading for those guns you told me about as soon as I saw you get on yer bike."

The two men faced each other in the cramped, dark space. "I won't let her down again," muttered Eddie. "I'm gonna make the Turks pay. They can't shoot my wife and walk away from it back to their families and their poxy fuckin' homes. If the army aren't going to get off their arses, I'll have to do it myself."

"Listen to yerself fer a minute. You're just going to wade into the middle of a war that's not yours? And what? Get yerself bloody killed? What good do you think that'll do Pru?" Bernie threw his arms up in exasperation.

"And if she dies, Bernie? What then?" Eddie was shouting now. "I wasn't there for her, Bern. Without Pru I really don't care if I die and this way at least I'll take a couple of Turks down with me when I go."

Eddie bumped his back down the uneven wall and slumped to the floor in a shower of sand and flaking paint.

"I don't know what to do Bern," he whispered, "I just don't know what the hell to do."

Bernie looked down onto the shell of the man before him and went to crouch beside him, laying a large clumsy hand on Eddie's shoulder.

"I know son. I know. But you *will* get through it. You say you weren't there when Pru needed you? Well, be there for her now. She needs you *now.* Together you'll find a way through this. Come on. You should be there when she wakes up."

"I don't know Bern..."

"Well *I* do, so get your arse in gear, and let's get you home."

"And just chalk this down to another catastrophic Eddie fuck up? Can't even shoot a Turk when he has a crate full of guns?"

"You would be failing yerself – and Pru – if you take revenge on some innocent man. You'll never find the man who shot her, so you'll be just taking a man away from his wife and children and then someone, his brother maybe, will want to take revenge on the British Army for the death of his brother and then the army will have to retaliate and we've got an out-and-out war on our hands. How many people need to die before you feel that it makes up for what you've lost? I know you, Eddie. Killing won't sit easy on yer conscience.

"I was here when EOKA was in full swing, remember? I saw, first hand, the attacks on the British and their families. I saw the bodies of women and children lying in the street. I was here when they shot a man was in the back when he was walking down the road with his two-year-old son. I had to take the boy back to his mother and tell her what had happened. No one wants to reopen those wounds, Eddie."

Both men fell silent, lost in their own thoughts.

Eddie was dragged back into the present by the sudden alertness of Bernie as he scampered into a crouched position by the door. Bernie held his hand up to halt Eddie, who sprung up in response.

Outside, a humming sound was getting louder. Peering through the crack in the door neither man could see anything but, judging by the increasing noise levels, whatever was making the sound was gaining in proximity. With growing unease, the men realised that the sound belonged to at least a dozen people murmuring to each other in low voices. There was something about the collective voice that was more unsettling than threatening. By the time the noise makers came into view it was too late for Eddie and Bernie to get out of the shack without being seen. The two men breathed slowly and waited as a column of men came into view about twenty yards away from them. All were in civilian clothes and unarmed. Their dejected eyes were downcast and they spoke to each other in voices that were soft but not suggesting any warmth or kindness. Then, coming into view, were at least a dozen soldiers, all of whom were heavily armed.

"Turkish soldiers," mouthed Eddie and Bernie nodded once in response. The soldiers didn't seem wary of any threat and, as such, were uninterested in scanning the horizon or investigating the rickety shepherd's hut.

"Civilians?" whispered Bernie.

Eddie shrugged in response and mouthed, "Greek." Eddie was keeping his eyes firmly on the narrow slit of the door which afforded him a glimpse of the unfolding scene. The caravan of people disappeared slowly from view with the last of the soldiers.

Eddie and Bernie looked quizzically at each other but stayed where they were, waiting for the threat to pass. Some sharp words were shouted in Turkish on the edge of earshot but neither man was familiar enough with the Turkish language to be able to understand what was being said. Silence followed for a couple of minutes, and just as Eddie was about to suggest they went out to investigate, a volley of machine gun fire was heard.

"Shit! What the–?" whispered Eddie.

"Sit tight," Bernie urgently whispered back.

"We're not armed! We're sitting ducks. I can get to the guns."

"Eddie, no!"

The two men hesitated as three more single shots were fired.

"Fuck this!" spat Eddie as he darted past Bernie and out through the fissure in the door.

Bernie was unable to stop the younger man from sprinting through the trees to where the crate was stashed in the shade. Cautiously, Bernie eased himself into the open and then slid from tree to tree until he was alongside Eddie who had retrieved his knife and was prising open the crate.

"You mad bastard. These guns probably won't even fire. They've not been oiled in... how long? Fifty years?"

"Well, they certainly won't fire themselves stuck in the box. Excellent!"

Eddie had opened the box and was looking onto at least ten Bren guns and several boxes of ammunition. Handing some of the small boxes to Bernie he stuffed the rest into his shirt pockets. He passed one gun to Bernie and picked up two for himself.

"Let's go." Eddie motioned his head in the direction of the gunshot.

Bernie inwardly groaned.

"I'm a bit long in the tooth for this."

"Bernie, there is meant to be a bloody ceasefire but these bastards don't care about that. I will not let them get away with killing innocent people. First Pru and now this? You can come with me or you can fuck off. This isn't just about Pru anymore. We can't sit by while they murder innocent people!"

"You don't know they were innocent! You don't know anything about them! Eddie, come back!"

Eddie stuck close to the narrow shadows of the olive trees. He didn't look to see whether the Bernie was following him but the occasional grunt and shuffling of feet let him know that his friend was behind him.

In the sun patches, Eddie could feel his skin prickle with the harsh, unrelenting furnace of the day and the shade didn't grant much respite either. It took about five minutes of stealthy progression until the soldiers were in their sights. Six men were standing on the top of a mound of earth looking down into a rock-strewn crater. They were talking happily and smoking cigarettes, completely unconcerned by the gunfire issued minutes before. Eddie had a feeling he knew what had happened but wanted to see the truth of it with his own eyes.

Slinging his gun over his shoulder so that the weight fell on his back he climbed up the tree, two branches at a time, until he could witness the scene for himself. Although he had been reasonably sure of what he would find when he got there, the confirmation of his worst fears still came as a shock to him and punched him in the gut.

Lying heaped in a pit where they had fallen were the men who had filed past him moments earlier. Limbs twisted at obscene angles, eyes open but unseeing. Several soldiers with guns at the ready were going round the bodies one by one, kicking them and pushing them over to ensure they were dead. Each one of these men was followed by another who, once he was assured of the victim's certain demise, would rifle through their pockets and take out any personal belongings. Anything of any value went in a beige jute bag while the rest was thrown down into the pit with the dead and dying. Already, birds were circling overhead keen to feast on the carrion below.

Eddie had seen dead bodies before but never this many all in one place. His mind was finding it difficult to make any sense of the scene in front of him. These men hadn't even been armed. They hadn't been a threat to these soldiers. This wasn't an honourable death in battle. This was genocide at its most basic level. Shock rooted Eddie to the spot until a noise from Bernie below brought him sliding down the narrow tree.

Eddie kept his voice low. "They're all dead. We need to check our weapons and take up our positions."

"And do what?" hissed Bernie. "Take on half the bloody Turkish Army?"

Eddie pulled himself up to his full height which was at least four inches higher than Bernie.

"You almost had me convinced back there that the Turks were normal men like you and me, simply doing their job. But from what I've just seen, they're barbarians. Maybe not all of them, but certainly the weak bastards up there who have murdered a group of men armed with nothing more than their faith. I might not get the same man who shot my wife but I can make these bastards pay for what they've done here, today.

"They are over there now, going through their pockets, taking money out of their wallets and casting aside pictures of their children and their sweethearts. They are standing around laughing and smoking like they're out for a walk in the countryside. I am going to show them that there are consequences to their actions. I will hold them responsible. Now, are you with me?"

Bernie took a deep breath while he composed himself.

"It's war, Eddie. Shit like this happens. The Greeks are no angels either but I'm with ya lad. Not for the reasons you think, but aye."

Eddie and Bernie stood facing each other for a long time until Eddie finally broke the icy silence. "If that's as good as I'm gonna get, I'll take it. Now let's go. If we head round to the right we'll be covered by the dense shrubs until we're pretty much on top of them. From there we'll have the sun at our backs and they'll be dazzled and effectively blinded as they look to our position. They're in no hurry to leave so take it steady and wait until we are safely in a strong position before opening fire."

Bernie nodded curtly and followed in Eddie's dusty footprints. Both men were aware that the likelihood of Bernie opening fire was thinner than Eddie's receding patience. Progress was slow as they tried to move silently through the brittle bushes. The more Bernie tried to move silently through the scrub, the more his trousers got caught on the bushes and his black shoes kicked the loose stones from under his feet.

The dark birds that were circling overhead made no cries to each other and the absence of the usual incessant hum of crickets amplified the stillness. The pall of silence surrounding the bodies was dense. It appeared to have a solid mass of its own making, as if the horror experienced here had to exist in a vacuum so as not to pollute the rest of humankind.

As they neared the voices, Eddie's pace quickened and his heart hammered adrenaline through his body. Taking up position on their stomachs on the cracked and scorched ground, Eddie inched forward. Both men set their weapons in front of them, with Bernie putting the spare one at his side. There were fourteen men either walking around the pit or sitting chatting on the side of the embankment. Behind Eddie and Bernie the slope fell away towards the expanse of open fields sheltered on one side by steep mountains.

A distant sound and a dusty haze attracted Bernie's attention and he reluctantly took his sights off the milling soldiers. He could see about one hundred people moving swiftly across the field below him, some carrying bags and others carrying children. There were four carts being pulled by donkeys.

From somewhere in the distance plumes were starting their ascent to the sky from darkly burning trees. He didn't have the luxury of wondering where they were heading or why they were doing so, right now he just had to try and stop Eddie getting killed. A trickle of fear edged down his spine as he realised the smoke and the sounds below them would soon be attracting the attention of the soldiers and reveal his and Eddie's position. If they were going to do anything it was going to have to be soon.

Bernie's eyes closed momentarily and his lips moved in silent prayer. Then, with a brief shared look of agreement, both men eased the safety catch off their guns. Eddie paused for a moment and looked over at Bernie with eyes brimming with loss and pain. It tormented Bernie to see the young man he regarded with such fondness with a mask of immovable anger. He barely recognised the granite eyes looking out from the prematurely lined face. He held his breath as Eddie nodded and turned back to the scene in front of him. The soldiers made no reference to the carnage at their feet and acted as though they were catching up with friends after a hard day's work. Bernie kept his finger away from the trigger and the muzzle of his gun pointed towards the ground. He wanted to use this gun to defend them, nothing else.

The world moved in slow motion as Eddie eased his finger onto the trigger and began to squeeze. Eddie's body tensed and, after what felt like an age, there was a loud razor-edged 'click'. Both men held their breath and one of the Turks jerked his head up in their direction. He scanned the horizon but then looked away again before heading to the assembled men in the shade.

Eddie lay his body flat. "We've been made," he hissed

"What happened?"

"S'jammed. Hand me yours. Quick."

"You sure they've spotted us?" asked Bernie in a barely audible whisper.

Eddie shrugged then slowly nodded. "Pass me the other gun"

"They're fifty years old. If this thing misfires... We need to get out of here now."

"Gun." Eddie held out his hand, jaws set firmly and teeth gritted. Bernie could see that the group of men were now all squinting in their direction and lifting up their rifles.

"Shit!"

"Bernie." Eddie's voice held a note of warning in it.

"No. We need to get clear."

Eddie snatched the gun and started positioning himself.

"Wait!"

Bernie put his hand on Eddie's arm and looked back to the Turkish men who were now on their feet. They weren't looking directly at them anymore but off to one side. Bernie looked over his shoulder in the direction the men were looking and saw at once what had caught their attention. Eddie had heard the sound and snapped his head around for the briefest of moments and then back to his targets.

"What's happening?"

In the sky a Turkish plane was flying on a direct course to where they lay in the dust.

"Turkish I think. They can't have spotted us."

Bernie pushed himself out from the low lying shrub and part way down the dirty slope catching his trouser pockets on sticks and boulders. It quickly became apparent what the pilot's mission was.

The screams preceded the bullets as the plane opened fire and strafed the fields in front of the scattering crowds of people. The convoy of villagers on the plain below started running in all directions, flinging themselves and their belongings wide as the bullets hit the earth behind them. Some families cowered low to the ground huddled and crying but they were easy targets for the unrelenting bullets. The donkeys bucked their carts and ran back the way they came, creating more confusion and entropy. There was chaos as bodies sank to the dirt. Insentient corpses lay where living breathing people had been walking only moments earlier. Eddie and Bernie gasped in horror as, even from this distance, they could see crimson daubing the cinnamon soil where the men and women lay sprawled.

"No, no, no," Eddie murmured and skidded down to where Bernie sat transfixed.

Some of the men had reached the shelter of the ravine now and had un-shouldered their guns firing futile bullets at the metal predator.

Everyone watched on in trepidation as a man retraced his steps in haste to pick up two children, one wrapped its arms around his neck but he flung the smaller one under his arm. Alongside him a small boy ran to keep up. Eddie and Bernie both watched with impotence as the bullets cut up this man's footsteps. The plane shot past before circling and coming back but all eyes were on this man and his children. There were thirty feet now to the asylum of the ravine. More people were jumping into the sheltered crevice to claim sanctuary. Twenty feet. The young boy was lagging behind. Fifteen feet. Mentally urging them speed, Eddie sat forward, poised as if to run to them.

"C'mon. C'mon!" he murmured.

The bullets seemed to be coming faster now and raked up the dried earth creating an orange cloud around those fleeing to safety. The man and his children were all but obscured by the dust and Eddie strained to see whether any of them were still on their feet. From the mountains a response was heard to answer the plane's searching bullets as anti-aircraft guns opened fire. This brought renewed screams from those in the ravine and some cheers as some realised the 'ack-ack' was a Greek response to the Turkish projectiles.

The jet took evasive action, dipped its wing and turned away. Eddie squinted through the dust as it lost momentum, hovered, then floated to the ground, overlaying the hurried footsteps of those fleeing to safety. There were no bodies where the man and his children had been. Please God that they made it to safety. Eddie had just opened his mouth to speak to Bernie when a scorching flash of light heralded an almighty explosion. Eddie flinched involuntarily and cowered with the noise. He looked up in time to see the Turkish jet spinning into the distant mountain and disintegrating in the explosion.

A cheer went up from some of those who had made it to safety while others rushed across the field to where friends and family lay injured and dying. Remembering what had initially brought them to this parched hillside, Eddie scrambled back up the incline back to the Turkish soldiers but they were gone.

"Where'd they go?" he whispered to Bernie

"Left when the fighting started. Do you want to go after them?"

"Nah." Eddie collapsed onto his back and looked up into the cloudless blue. How could the sun still be shining over what had happened here? "I think I've lost my stomach for death."

"Jesus Eddie, yer a lucky man. I really thought they'd spotted us then. If that gun had backfired… Well, I wouldn't like to have been the one holding it. Lucky man, I tell ya."

"Not feeling like luck is on my side right now" muttered Eddie with some petulance. "We should go and see if we can help down there." He was looking down onto the few figures who were crawling out into the open now.

"No." Bernie's response surprised Eddie. "They're shit scared. We blunder in there now and we'll get shot. They're on the defensive. There's nothing we can do anyway."

"But we can't just leave them, pretend like we didn't see what happened."

"We'd only be getting in the way. Let's get home."

"Not yet."

Gripping his weapon firmly now, Eddie stood and pushed himself over the edge of the crater to where the dead bodies lay in a heap. The birds and the flies had not yet come to take their meal from the flesh that lay open to their hunger. The sweet cloying scent of blood hung stratus-like in the air. Eddie tried to breathe through his mouth to stop the smell from registering but instead he tasted death upon his tongue.

A moan brought Bernie rushing into the fray.

"This one's alive! Shit Ed, he's alive. Help me!"

Eddie ran over, stumbling against flaccid limbs and dropped to his knees. There was a lot of blood but it was difficult to see where it stemmed from.

"Here!" Bernie applied pressure on the immobile man's upper arm. "I need your shirt."

Eddie ripped it in two sharp movements and tied it in a tourniquet above the seeping wound. With what remained of his shirt he dabbed away the blood from the Greek man's face to reveal a bullet graze on his left temple. It didn't look deep and the blood had already started clotting.

"We need to get him out of here." Eddie said to Bernie. "Help me get him onto my shoulders. There's a village not far from here."

"Can you manage?" asked Bernie as they positioned the limp body of the man across Eddie's back.

"Yeah, just about." Luckily the Greek man was small and slight and weighed less that Eddie did.

Bernie pushed Eddie up out of the crater and they staggered back to where Eddie had left his motorbike. They tugged at the prone man until they had him sitting astride the vehicle.

"How the hell are we gonna do this?" asked Bernie.

"Strap him to my back as well as you can and I'll ride him down to the village. What about you?"

"Don't worry, you're not the only one with wheels. Mine are stashed further down the track. I'll follow you."

Bernie used his own shirt to create strips of material to tie Eddie's passenger to him.

"It's not brilliant, but it's the best we can do. You go on and I'll follow you. Take it easy, his weight can have you off the back of that bike if yer not careful."

They came across the Greek village to the south just as the sun started to set. Their arrival was greeted with quiet, strong efficiency as bandages were cut and the man carried away to be treated. No one seemed surprised or upset. There was a job to be done and no one questioned that the women would do it. Eddie and Bernie were taken off to the taverna with thanks and pats on the back. In some regards, it felt that there wasn't a war going on at all. The village tavernas still had tables outside with bowls full of pitta bread and olives. The only difference was the fact that the radio was on constantly with groups of silver-streaked heads huddled around it waiting for news.

The two weary men were brought food and drink even though they explained that they had no money but the Greek owner merely shrugged and muttered under his white moustache, "What good will your money do us now?"

Groups of young men from the National Guard arrived by truck down the mountain and were met with cheers and kisses on each cheek by the assembled villagers. They obviously saw the downing of the Turkish jet as a sign of a small victory and were treated like heroes, even though the fighters barely looked old enough to shave. The scene could have been from any warm evening that summer if it had not been for the glow of the fires still burning in the forests above him. Perhaps Eddie could go home to Pru with his head held high after all.

As he slipped away into the dusk, Eddie took one last look at the assembled men and wondered how many, if any, of them would still be alive tomorrow.

Chapter fifteen

Eddie was sitting in the shade of a fig tree when I got to the beach.

"Hi!"

"Whoa, nice bruise!"

"Thanks."

"You're welcome."

We smiled at each other awkwardly.

"So..." I prompted.

"So, this is where Pru and I used to spend our weekends."

"Is it?"

"Yep. This is the 'fabled' Fig Tree of the bay that is supposed to be renowned for its fertility giving properties. We had a lot of fun here. We'd swim, snorkel, drink beer. It was quite a nice life when we first got out here. Everything was so new. None of these hotels were here then." He waved at the buildings behind us. "And none of these bars and cafés. There was one place to get a drink from round here and that was it. You never knew what day they'd be open either. There weren't all these people back then. Sometimes it'd literally just be me and yer mum so I guess it wasn't worth staying open every day, but if they were around, taking deliveries or whatever, they'd always get us a bottle of beer or something. At weekends we'd have lunch here and at the end of the day the bloke would ask us what we'd had cos he wouldn't have been keeping track. He relied on our honesty back then. 'Course, it's all changed now."

I slumped down into the sand beside him. "Sounds like a lot of fun."

"It was, yeah. It was so different from back home. When we first got here we went straight in the sea in February. The locals thought we were crazy. I was so hot that first summer I

272

used to lie in a bath of cold water to cool down." He laughed at himself and shook his head. "She was always searching for something, your mum, some new adventure. I hope she found it."

"I'm not sure that she has. I think that everything got a bit dull when she moved back to England. Certainly not so much snorkelling."

"Did she go back to Bedford? See her mum?" Eddie asked genuinely interested.

"No. Well, not that I know of. After her mum died she had to head back a couple of times to arrange the sale of the house and stuff but I don't think there was any love lost between the two of them from what I can gather. But you'd know more about that than I do."

"Her mum was a piece of work. She never approved of me. But then, if I'd had a daughter I wouldn't have approved of me either." He chuckled. His face suddenly dropped as he looked to me. "So she's remarried then?"

"What?"

"The divorce. The solicitor said she was getting remarried."

"Oh. No. It didn't happen. They split up not long after that. No she's happily single. Her and her cats. She's worried she's going to end up as an old woman living on her own, talking to cats all day long. She'd love someone in her life but she likes things done exactly her way and she's not very good at compromise."

"She's not changed that much then," he commented dryly.

"And what about you, Eddie? Did you find what you were looking for?"

"Up to a point. I've come to terms with a lot over the last few years and I've not got a bad life here."

"Why have you never left Cyprus?"

"I did leave it. Several times in fact, it's, well, I could never stay away for very long."

"Why? Do you love it that much?"

Eddie looked to the sea and moistened his lips, thinking carefully.

"Which answer do you want?" he asked. "The one I give the tourists or the truth?"

"Hit me with the truth, I think I can take it."

"Well...." Eddie took a deep breath and looked into his hands. "I don't want to leave Edward. I know it might sound stupid to you, but I'm the only one who even acknowledges that he ever existed. I still visit his grave and put flowers on it. If I wasn't here then who'd do that? I know he's not really here anymore but it's the only link I've got to my son and I don't know how I'd go about remembering him if I left. I've got no photos. No one to talk to about him. Stupid really."

"That doesn't sound stupid at all," I answered quietly.

"I held him, after they'd delivered him. They wrapped him in a blanket and handed him to me. He was warm. He was the most perfect thing I'd ever seen. I kept willing him to open his eyes. I'd never prayed so hard in my life."

"I'm sorry."

"No. Don't be. It was a long time ago. I can at least hold onto the fact that I got to see him and to hold him. Your mum never did. She never got to say goodbye. Not really."

I looked down at our hands clasped together. Did I take hold of his hand or did he take hold of mine? I didn't even remember it happening. It was an odd experience, being with a stranger who you had known all your life. He wasn't really what I had expected, but then my expectations had been pretty low.

He suddenly shook himself like he had come to his senses. "You hungry?"

"Ravenous."

"Come on then, let's eat. I hear on the grapevine that you write about food," he stated. "You are about to have the world's greatest mezze."

"I hear that a lot."

"Yeah, but not from me. When I say it, I mean it."

I laughed as he helped me to my feet and we walked up the beach to where his car was parked.

"Get in," he motioned to the car.

"We're not eating here?"

"No chance. This is watered down for the British appetite. No, tonight you dine with the Cypriots. I just wanted to show you the tree that your mum spent her time sitting under. I thought you'd like to see it."

"Thank you." I slid into the passenger seat of the battered blue Ford.

"What? You're not impressed by the wheels?"

"I didn't say that."

"No, but the way your nose wrinkles up like you've just stood in dog dirt betrays you."

I laughed at that. He wasn't the first person to tell me that my face was easy to read.

"Don't get me wrong, you're a lovely woman but, Jeez, you say it all with one look. There's the 'I'm disgusted look', there's the 'you're an idiot' look and there! There's another one, that's the 'you're pushing your luck, Eddie' look!"

I feigned mock indignation but Eddie laughed at me. "The upside is, you do light up the room when you smile. Just like Pru."

"Thank you. And now you've succeeded in embarrassing me, do you want to tell me where you are taking me?"

"A little village up Troodos mountain. It's all plastic tables and chairs, cheap cutlery and 'rustic' decor. It's not really one of your upmarket gaffs but the food is pretty much top-notch. I think you'll like it."

When Eddie said it wasn't upmarket he wasn't joking, but it was full of old-world charm. There was no flashy sign or welcoming party. If I hadn't been with Eddie, I wouldn't have even noticed that it was there. We double-parked behind another car which gave me a slight attack of anxiety but I followed Eddie into the restaurant nonetheless.

He greeted the proprietor in Greek like they were old friends and led me to a table out back. There were eight square tables with matching white tablecloths. At the centre of each table was the lit stub of a candle, even though there was still a fair amount of light left in the day. Next to it was a jug of water. There was no roof out here on the terrace but there were beams entwined with vines above our heads dripping with green opals of fruit. We sat on neighbouring sides of the table so that we could both take in the view down the mountainside. The lush green valley stretched out before us like a languorous cat in front of the fire.

Beneath us the insects that come alive at dusk were beginning to move and call to each other. I was so lost in the view that I almost forgot that I was sitting there with Eddie and so when he spoke to me I jumped.

"I ordered us a selection of dishes. I hope that's ok."

"Great, thanks."

"So what's the plan now?" he asked.

"How do you mean?"

"Well, you're not just here for the food and the sun. You've got the names of your biological parents but I get the feeling that you still aren't satisfied. So, what next?"

"Tomorrow I'm going into Famagusta to see what's left of Varosha. I want to see your old flat and where Helene died."

"Well, it's been nice knowing you," he smirked. "You do know that's likely to get you shot, don't you?"

"So I've been told. But I'm not that easily deterred."

I was spared the task of having to elaborate by the arrival of tsatsiki, hummus and taramasalata with finger-scalding pitta breads. Before these bowls were finished, souvlaki, stiffado, kleftico and afelia were placed before us. I didn't know where to start so I grabbed the dish closest to me.

"Ummm. Stiffado." I inhaled deeply. There were the usual scents of beef, tomatoes, red wine and wine vinegar but something else was tripping over the hunks of meat. I took a mouthful and savoured the taste: cinnamon and fresh parsley. Nice additions. The meat was so tender it threatened to dissolve on my tongue before I could even chew it. It was exactly what I needed with my still-sore and swollen jaw.

I followed that with the afelia it seemed an obvious choice given the inclusion of red wine in this dish also. The coriander seeds crunched and popped in my mouth almost sensually and so I moved onto the kleftico with something approximating the food equivalent of lust.

"This is delicious," I said with a mouth half full of lamb.

"Isn't it?"

"Do you come up here a lot?"

"Yeah. It's where I bring all my hot dates."

I raised my eyebrows at him and he laughed.

"Don't flatter yerself! Apart from the fact that I'm old enough to be your father, I nearly *was* your father. No, actually I don't get that many dates. I can't compete with the Greek men on charm or looks. It's a good job I enjoy my own company."

"Well, it's great here. I love it. Can we get some wine?"

"Knock yourself out. Not for me though."

"Of course, you're driving."

"Yes, but it's not only that. I don't drink. I'm teetotal."

"But you run a bar," I said, stating the obvious.

"I am well aware of the irony."

The waiter came over when I motioned for him.

"Could I get a glass of red wine, please?"

He just looked at me and Eddie laughed.

They spoke to each other in Greek and then Eddie said to me, "He doesn't speak English. Or at least, he pretends not to."

"Sorry. I thought everyone on the island did."

"Most do, but I don't think that Statos wants to attract Brits to the restaurant so he stubbornly refuses to speak the language of the tourist."

The proprietor brought the wine to me and I made a point of thanking him in Greek.

Dishes of calamari came and went, dolmades were dispatched without effort and I even requested another serving of the divine stiffado. As we came haltingly to the end of our meal the sun slipped away, transferring our attention back to each other.

"Why are you so intent on getting to the old flat? It's just bricks. There is nothing there of any consequence. People and memories are all that matters."

"That's it though." I leant forward onto the table. "I don't have any memories of Cyprus, do I?"

"So you'll get memories of a rundown building covered in dust. What good's that, really? We all have to let go of the past, Leni."

"Says the man who won't leave his son's grave."

Eddie looked sharply at me, his eyes showing their hurt like beacons in the dark.

"Shit! Sorry Eddie, sorry! Oh God, I shouldn't have said that. Sorry. Truly I am. I'm not good at taking advice. It makes me prickly. Sorry. I can't believe I just said that. I can be such a cow."

"Yes you can. But at least you know it," he smiled at me. I couldn't believe how nice this man was being to me. I had insulted him, churned up painful memories for him and turned his life upside-down and yet here he was sharing his favourite taverna with me.

"For what it's worth Eddie. I wish Mum had stayed with you. I don't think she ever got over you."

"You never get over your first love," he said wistfully.

We didn't talk about anything particularly deep for the rest of the evening, we just drank and chatted. It was nice. Comfortable.

When Eddie dropped me back home later that night he handed me a folded note.

"What's this?"

"You might need it at some point. It's as much as I can do to help you, I'm afraid."

I went to unfold it but his hand was upon mine. "Wait until later."

"Sure."

"Come and see me again before you leave Cyprus?"

"Of course! Of course I will. Thanks for this evening. It has been lovely. I've really enjoyed myself." I leant in and gave him a peck on his cheek.

"Goodnight."

"'Night"

The main house was in darkness except for a small, low light coming from the kitchen. I stole slowly past the kitchen door as soundlessly as possible.

Clouds had covered the stars for the first time since my arrival in Cyprus and it gave the night a claustrophobic feel as if a heavy blanket was being draped over my head. There was no breeze and barely any light as I stumbled my way down the uneven and precarious path, desperate to lay my head on the soft feather pillows of my borrowed bed.

As I neared the cottage on heavy feet I was aware of a golden glow of light. I thought it was unlikely that I would have left the light on. My overfilled head couldn't make any sense of it and I was too tired to be either intrigued or concerned. There before me on the table were lit tea-lights encircling a simple white vase with white and purple flowers in it. They were beautiful, bold blooms. Propped up against the vase was a modest card. In simple writing it said: *I am sorry*. It wasn't Dom's writing but I wondered if perhaps he had somehow got hold of Antheia to do it for him. I allowed myself to be carried along by this impossibility and I turned quickly, with barely concealed excitement, towards the footsteps that I could now hear crunching my way.

"You like the flowers?" The voice was heavily accented with Greek and my heart deflated. I peered into the darkness as Stefanos came into view.

"Thank you. They're very pretty."

"Pretty flowers for a pretty woman."

Despite myself, I blushed and turned away looking at the flowers. "What are they called?"

"Anemones. In Greek the name means 'Daughter of the winds'. They made me think of you. Bold, fearless flowers. They are important for my family and we buy them for special occasions. My mother's niece was called Anemone, of course."

"Yes, of course. Daughter of the winds? That's nice." I stroked the blooms with ill-disguised fatigue. "I don't mean to be rude but it's been a long night, Stefanos. What do you want?"

He stepped closer and frowned. It appeared that even in the velvet of the night my bruises could be seen clearly enough.

"What happened to your face?" he asked reaching out a hand.

I instinctively ducked backwards out of his reach. "Oh, I got into a fight last night in a bar. It looks worse than it is."

"Really?" He seemed to consider this for a moment with his hand hovering above my cheek. "Police?"

"No. And I don't want to involve them. It's nothing really."

"Why did she hit you?"

"He. It was a *man* that hit me."

"No! Who was it?"

"I don't know his name. And to be fair to him, I *did* hit him first... With a bottle."

Stefanos let out a soft whistle from between his teeth as his eyebrows disappeared into his hairline in surprise and, from the twitch in his cheek, he appeared to be choking on a smile.

"This seems an odd thing for you to do?" he questioned, seeking reassurance and with it, more details.

"He grabbed my... He grabbed me and I hit him instinctively. I happened to have a bottle in my hand at the time. Look, I'm embarrassed, to be honest. I goaded him into behaving badly, so I am as responsible as he is."

"No, no, no." Stefanos shook his head and held up his hands to stop me in my tracks. "There is never an excuse for a man to hit a woman."

"Stefanos, please, I'll discuss the morals with you another day but right now I would like to go to bed. Do you mind?"

"Of course." He stepped in closer to me so our bodies were almost touching, "But I don't have to leave," he said, suddenly very serious and looking at me with his head slightly bowed so that he had to look at me through his long, dark eyelashes.

"Yes. Yes, you do have to leave." I was self-conscious as I said it, but even more ashamed by the fact that I was a little sorry that was the case.

He stroked my swollen cheek with a gentleness that didn't look possible with his big hands but this time I didn't flinch away.

"If you need anything, Antheia can get hold of me. Okay? And I'll come back."

"Okay. That's very kind of you. Now go." I placed my hands on his chest and gently pushed him away. He was warm and steady under my palms and I let my hands linger for longer than was necessary. The temptation to give into him, to be held and comforted, was like a glowing coal only needing a little more oxygen to flame brightly.

Stefanos put his hand under my chin and for a moment I thought he was going to kiss me so I took a step backwards, scared that I might do something I was certain to regret.

"Goodnight, Stefanos." I tried to keep my voice steady.

"*Kalinichta.*" He took my hand and kissed the back of it, inhaling my scent.

I pulled my hand out of his, turned and walked into my room closing and locking the door behind me. I pushed my back to the door and listened to my heart booming in the darkness. I thought about placing the chair under the door handle for added security but knew that I wasn't so desirable that someone would break down a door to get to me.

I made my way over to the bed in complete darkness and slumped on it after I found it with my shins. What on earth just happened there? Had a guy fifteen years younger than me really looked at me with brown eyes brimming with desire? I must have concussion. After I was sure that Stefanos had left, I turned on the little lamp by the side of the bed and retrieved the note Eddie had given me from my bag. What I saw made me smile and I clasped it to chest smiling.

"Eddie," I muttered to myself, "you are a star!"

Chapter sixteen

Cyprus, 1974

There was no one to see Pru as she slumped with her forehead against the warm rough wall of her apartment building. No one was there to puzzle about her oversized housecoat or the visible blue hospital gown that hung limply below the hem of Betty's coat. Not one person could see that she was barefoot and dishevelled.

"Not long now," she thought, and pushed herself upright.

The pain in her stomach was making her sweat now, but at least it was helping to focus her mind. The painkillers were beginning to wear off, and Pru hoped that some clarity would return to her mind now that she was no longer under the influence of their prescription drugs, designed to keep her quiet and compliant. Even though she was dripping with perspiration, she shivered against the cold. Goosebumps sprung from her skin, catapulting her fair hair to attention along her arms. The backs of her hands ached where needles and tubes had been forced into her veins. She could still smell the disinfected air of the hospital clinging to her hair and it made her want to vomit.

She put her hands in the coat pockets to warm her bruised hands and found a set of house keys and some used tissues. Pru felt a pang of guilt. She was many things, but she'd never been a thief before. Would Betty have a spare set of keys somewhere? Would she be sitting outside her own home now unable to get in? Pru sighed and swallowed back her tears. Now was not the time to start worrying about other people. She had a job to do. She pulled herself upright and tried to smooth down her matted hair. She used her middle finger to wipe underneath her eyes, in the hopes that any melting makeup would be smoothed away. She steadied herself against the wall and looked around her.

Everything looked different today; the yellow light made her surroundings look like a sepia tinted photograph. There was no breeze and little noise. She felt like she was in a bubble, a giant blister surrounding her anguished soul.

Pru was battling the fog of confusion. They had given her so many drugs that she was barely able to string two words together. They said that the medication was for the pain but she didn't believe them. They told her that she had been shot in the stomach and her baby had died. They told her she would never have children. They told her she was lucky to be alive. They lied.

Eddie was gone by the time Pru woke up. Nobody knew where he was. It was obvious that the doctor had some bad news but he seemed to want Eddie there before he told her. In the end Betty had been the one holding her hand when they told her that her baby had gone. Pru had stayed in bed staring at the ceiling for hours trying to make sense of what had happened. She'd managed to piece together enough of it to know that there had been a baby and that she had held it in her arms. She also knew with absolute certainty that the last time she saw the baby, Mrs Kostas had it.

She sent Betty to get her some cheese on toast before slipping unnoticed from behind the closed curtains of the ward and out into the blindingly bright street. They couldn't keep her here. She knew what they were trying to do and it wasn't going to work.

Outside the hospital Marjorie had picked her up and driven her home.

"Are you sure you're okay?" she kept asking, as if she didn't quite believe Pru's answers.

"Oh yes, a false alarm that's all. They've told me to go home and rest."

"Can't be long now. You're riding, lower aren't you? Always a sign that baby's on its way."

"Yes, I suppose so."

"I can't believe that Eddie was going to let you catch the bus home. What a dick! Call me if you need anything, yeah?"

Pru couldn't remember how she got to the hospital, or why for that matter. But she remembered the baby in her arms in the home of Kyria Kostas. She could remember the labour that had lasted most of the day and she remembered Helene being there. She didn't know why they had stolen her baby but she was going to get him back. When she had woken up in hospital they told her that they had performed a hysterectomy. They said they were sorry, but that it couldn't be helped. But Pru knew things like that didn't happen to her.

She pushed herself away from the cool wall with a grunt, and headed to the Kostas' door. A quiet busyness emanated from within the dark, terracotta tiled home that stopped Pru mid-stride. She could hear the slow, rhythmic 'swish, swish' of someone working away, sweeping the floor. Pru tip-toed closer to the entrance, not wanting to be spotted just yet. Looking into the vaguely lit kitchen, Pru couldn't make out much except blurry forms and deepening shadows. The only light came from a single lamp that did nothing to dispel the growing darkness in the angles of the room.

Taking a silent step backwards, Pru looked all around her and then up at the beautiful building that had been her home for the last five months. Its cream walls and blue painted doors and windows used to please her, but now she was all but consumed with sadness when she imagined living there. She knew that whatever happened tonight there was no way that she was ever going to step foot in that apartment again. She was going to get her baby back and then head back to England where nobody could hurt her or her baby ever again.

If she had had her wits about her she would have realised that the roads were abnormally quiet and that she had barely seen a soul since she'd left the hospital. She didn't know how long she'd been in the hospital so couldn't be sure what day it was. It could possibly be a Sunday but somehow it felt different. On a Sunday, while cafés and shops were shut, you still had the impression of a trembling life force behind the walls as people relaxed, chatted, ate or slept. But tonight she could feel nothing at all. Maybe, she pondered, that was because she wasn't capable of feeling anything anymore. She felt like all her empathy had been swiped away. If anything, instead of feeling any curiosity, Pru merely nodded with relief at the realisation that there was no one around to witness what she was about to do. They couldn't steal her baby and get away with it. She was tired and weak but she wouldn't rest until she had her son back in her arms.

Looking back through the poorly lit doorway, Pru could see Mrs Kostas gently sweeping the floor while there, on the sturdy kitchen table, a wicker cradle stood. There was no noise from the basket but she was certain that her son was asleep in that nest.

The pictures in her head were out of sequence but she clearly remembered being in this house. There was blood, there were screams and then, after an interminable afternoon, there was *him*. She remembered clearly the dark-haired little baby, tongue darting in and out of his mouth, tasting the air around him, like a snake. She remembered him opening his eyes to reveal chestnut lagoons with ebony atolls.

Pru could still feel the ghost of his weight in her arms and the warmth of the body beneath the yellow sheet and she ached to be able to hold him once more. Pru remembered holding him in her arms when he was first born and still covered in the fluid that had been his sustenance over the previous nine months. She could remember the smell of him, all milky and sweet. She could picture, with perfect clarity, his tiny domed finger-nails crowning long wrinkled fingers.

After that, it was all muddled in her mind. She could remember Helene and Mrs Kostas being there. Perhaps they had helped deliver the baby. She grabbed handfuls of her own hair in frustration. Her fingers stuck in the tangled mess that evidently hadn't seen a brush in some time. She wondered again, with increasing frustration, how long she'd been away. Her stomach ached, and where her stitches brushed against her hospital gown her skin burned and itched. She couldn't get it clear in her head. Why had the doctor lied to her? And where was Eddie? Did he know what they'd done?

Pru's head began to spin and suddenly she was looking down upon herself from somewhere upon high. From her elevated position floating above her other self she could see everything in startling clarity but in deathly slow motion. She watched her other self rubbing her temples in distress. Images started to strobe through her mind, one after another, not making any sense to her. Water, glass, blood, Betty, Helene, baby, pain, Eddie. Water. Glass. Blood. As she rushed back into her own failing body she felt the ground careen beneath her and the last thing she saw as she fell through the curtains was the stunned

expression on Mrs Kostas' face.

Chapter seventeen

Famagusta. The name tastes exotic on my tongue. It is a place my mother has mentioned in passing over the years, but never in detail. Her vagueness added to the mysterious and hazy aura ever present when she alluded to Cyprus. The word conjures up fairy-tales of dusky damsels imprisoned in crumbling sandstone towers. Just the mere mention of the Ghost Town in Famagusta evokes feelings of poignant sadness, lost souls endlessly searching dusty abandoned streets for the disappeared and the dead.

In reality Famagusta was a scorching, harried and odorous city like any other in the Mediterranean. Brash shops and overconfident shopkeepers clanged in my ears as I scurried forward trying to look purposeful. The Ghost Town, that the locals knew as Varosha, sat silently and inert off to the side like the forgotten relative at a boisterous family wedding.

I slipped away from the heaving mass of bodies and into the dusty streets of Famagusta's old city. The walls should have been impressive, and in their hey-day would undoubtedly have been so, but now they protected nothing and no one from the rest of the world. They leered over me unaware of their impotence. The yells of roadside vendors raised such a cacophony that their cries became an indistinct babble. Domes of mosques held the sky aloft and open-fronted shops boasted the best Turkish Delight in Cyprus. I slowed, without stopping, tempted by the powdered confectionary.

Ostensibly the Turkish inhabitants of Famagusta were the same as their dark-skinned, thick-haired Greek counterparts in the south, but the Muslim presence was palpable and I felt like I really had crossed into another country which, according to the Turkish, I had. I hadn't gone far when a wiry man with a pitted face was grabbing my elbow to escort me into his shop selling leather jackets and shoes.

"No, thank you. Too hot," I mimed, flapping my t-shirt and blowing my fringe off my face.

He persevered and this time held out a hot, sweet, apple-scented brew in a glass which I declined.

"Thank you. But no," I answered firmly but politely and quickened my pace until he turned his attention to another pasty-legged passer-by.

I had been walking for about thirty minutes when I found what I was looking for. The streets were largely deserted here. Buildings that had been damaged in years gone by, probably with the shells of the war in 1974, had been left to falter and decay. There were no flashy shops here and no residents creating homes for their growing families. This seemed to be the domain of cats and stray dogs alone.

"Don't do it."

I wheeled round, guilt flowing from my pores.

"Shit, Stefanos! You gave me a heart attack! What are you doing here?"

"I thought you might be up to something. I was right, wasn't I?" He smirked at me triumphantly like a head boy who'd caught me smoking behind the bike sheds.

"Have you been following me?" I blustered, trying to deflect the attention back on to him.

He inclined his head and shrugged in response.

"Stefanos, please don't do this."

"What?"

"You know what. Don't get in my way, Stefanos, not today."

"You shouldn't be doing this." He stepped closer to me, peering into my eyes with such deep intensity. "You are going to get yourself in trouble and I can't let that happen to you." He picked up a strand of my hair and rolled it between his fingers.

"I know what I'm doing. Trust me." I don't whether I was trying to convince myself or him but either way, neither of us bought the act. "This might be the only chance I get," I continued.

"You don't even know where you're going."

"I do. I've got this." I reached into my bag triumphantly, pleased to be able to prove him wrong for once.

"What is it?"

"A map. See? Eddie drew me a map last night. I know exactly where I'm going."

Stefanos went to take the paper from my hand but I snatched it out of his reach. This was all I had; I couldn't risk Stefanos destroying my only clue to what lay behind the sandbags and rusting barbed-wire fences.

He scratched at his lightly stubbled cheek and sighed dramatically. "At least wait until dark. And take me with you."

My impatience was getting the better of me. And I stepped from one foot to another, mulling it over. I was desperate to get my own way but knew that Stefanos could make it difficult for me if I didn't acquiesce.

"Okay," I dropped my shoulders in defeat. "I'll wait until dusk but you are *not* coming with me."

"As you wish. Come with me now." Then, as an afterthought, he added, "Please."

He held out his hand, which I ignored, but I walked alongside him anyway both hands gripped on the shoulder strap of my bag. I didn't trust Stefanos enough to assume that he wouldn't try and take my map from me.

After five minutes of taciturn silence, Stefanos took me to Ledra Street which was now packed full of shoppers, both locals and tourists alike.

"Do you know this place?" he asked. His polite tourist-guide voice had returned.

I shook my head in reply, still sulking slightly and not feeling particularly loquacious.

"Do you know how long I have been able to walk down this road?"

I shook my head once more.

"Since 2008."

I raised my eyebrows in surprise and looked down the busy street. It could have been any pedestrianised city centre in England. There was a Starbucks and a McDonald's for a start.

"Come."

I followed Stefanos into the Starbucks and sat at a table in the window while he ordered two coffees. I tried to imagine how different this scene would have been just a few years ago. It was unfathomable. But that wasn't the only thing that was troubling me.

"What?" he asked when he looked at my furrowed forehead and questioning eyes.

"It's just..." I began, wondering which conundrum to begin with, "I wouldn't expect you to want to drink coffee somewhere like this. It isn't the kind of place that I would choose to drink coffee while on holiday in Cyprus. Are you trying to make a point?"

"What point exactly?" Ignoring the handle, Stefanos picked up the mug with both hands and looked at me over the steaming rim.

"I don't know. *You* tell *me*."

"What is it that you people want?" he challenged.

"So I'm *'you people'* now, am I?" I asked, not attempting to hide how offended I felt.

"Do you only feel that you have your money's worth if you see an old woman dressed in black leading a donkey by a rope?" He slammed his mug back on the table and the deep brown liquid sloshed over the side onto the wooden table.

I bit back a retort. How dare he? But part of me wondered if he might have a point so I sat patiently while he continued in the same fashion.

"You think that you're better than the tourists that come here and want their nightclubs and their British beer, but people like *you* are just as bad."

"People like me?" I tried to ask evenly.

He nodded.

"Explain," I said, trying to keep my voice calm against yet another unwarranted attack by Stefanos.

"People like you think they are above the average tourist. You come for the 'real' country and to soak up the 'culture'. But you do not want to see that we too eat burgers and pizza and listen to popular music. You do not want to know us as westernised civilised people, you want us to be quaint caricatures of ourselves."

"Whoa! Slow down. I hardly think that's fair!" I raised my voice, unable to contain myself any longer. People at nearby tables turned to look in our direction. "When have I asked you to be anything other than what you are?"

"You–"

"No! That was a rhetorical question, Stefanos. It's your turn to listen for a change. Every conversation we have ends in you criticising me for the way I behave or my lack of understanding. I may have been born here but I did *not* grow up here, I do *not* know about the history of the island. I do *not* know about the reality of living here on a day-to-day basis. That's why I'm here, that's why I ask all of these questions: I am trying to learn. I *want* to learn. Cypriot blood runs through my veins too, like it or not, and my biological parents are dead. They can't answer my questions so I'm trying my sodding best here to piece together what I can about my heritage."

I stopped for breath and waited for what I expected would be his counter-attack.

"Well?" I asked, goading him into a response.

Stefanos kept his eyes firmly on mine. My hands were shaking and my heart was quivering in my throat.

"The coffee here is shit. Let's go."

I had to run to catch up with him as he took long strides out of the café. I almost didn't bother but I knew he was far too valuable as a guide, and besides, I was shocked at how easily he had backed down from our fight.

Stefanos was difficult to work out. On one hand he was arrogant, narrow-minded and argumentative but on the other he was fascinating, passionate and exciting. He wasn't the type of person I should spend time with. His personality and mine were inflammatory when mixed together. It was definitely a safety goggles and gloves relationship.

We walked side by side as Stefanos marched me around the city explaining as much about the history as he could. Our earlier fight might not have been forgotten, or at least not by me, but Stefanos had moved on from it with remarkable ease and was back in his persona as charming and affable tour guide. Ledra Street, he explained, had run through the UN buffer zone and had been barricaded until a few years back when it became another crossing point between the North and South of the island.

During the EOKA struggle it had been known as the 'Murder Mile' due to the fact that so many of the British military and their families had been targeted in this area. I didn't want to dwell on that too much. My imagination has always been overactive and the last thing I wanted to do was to imagine dead bodies in the street where people now ate their Big Macs.

What surprised me most about this information was that this barricade was in place long before the Turkish invasion of 1974. The barricade had stood since 1963 following clashes between the Greek and Turkish Cypriots.

"1963? Why hadn't I heard that before? It must have been a serious dispute."

Stefanos shrugged. "If you ask a Turkish Cypriot, they will say 'Yes' but the Greeks don't remember it with such... ah... *importance.* It led to the Turkish Cypriots setting up areas where they could live safely. They called these places 'enclaves'. North Nicosia was one of these."

"Why were there clashes? Come on, you are not normally so reticent to share information, so spill it."

"I'm not sure I know all of the details," he lied.

"Nah, I'm not buying it. Come on, get chatty." I nudged him playfully in the ribs with my elbow.

"I am not trying to be evasive." He lowered his voice and I realised that his views could possibly get him into trouble with those around him. He placed his hand on my arm and ushered me to a table outside a nearby café. The coffee shop looked almost British with its green and white striped canopy and white plastic chairs set around round plastic tables with English menus propped up between tomato sauce and vinegar bottles.

Stefanos ordered us two coffees and a jug of water without even consulting me on what I would like to drink. I bristled at the assumption. I calmed myself down by reasoning with myself that if he had asked me what I wanted I would have said exactly the same, but it was the arrogance of his actions that irritated me. If he noticed my discomfort he didn't acknowledge it. He waited for the drinks to be placed in front of us before he continued talking.

"There were some suggestions about amendments to the constitution which were not well received by the Turkish Cypriots. They rejected these suggestions and it led to some heavy fighting. Mainly between extremists though, not really fights between Greek and Turkish neighbours. Many Turkish people chose to live in enclaves where they thought they were safer. But remember, it was their choice." His words were self-assured but they were spoken quietly.

"How much of a choice do any of us really have though, Stefanos?" I asked gently. "They wouldn't have left their homes to live in enclaves unless they felt that they didn't have any other option or that their families were in danger."

Stefanos shrugged. I was beginning to hate that shrug. It really meant he didn't agree with me but was trying to bite his lip. I appreciated the effort but I didn't back down.

"So if all this was happening back in... when? '63? The problems were rife long before the Turkish invasion in 1974, right? So the invasion can't be taken as an isolated incident, can it? It was just the culmination of many attacks against the Turkish Cypriots."

I knew I was playing devil's advocate and was likely to be shot down but it was the fastest way to get an answer from him.

Stefanos chose his words carefully. "Certainly you *could* see it that way. However, you could also conclude that the Turkish have a history of overreacting and that the strength of their overreactions showed they were waiting for an excuse to start a war."

"No one wants to start a war!" I said louder than intended.

"I used to think no one wanted to start an argument either and yet, here you are, Leni."

That silenced me for a minute and I sipped at my scalding coffee wondering whether he was right. A reluctant smile edged its way up my face. Generally I shied away from any kind of quarrel but I was enjoying bantering with Stefanos.

"Please remember Leni, that sometimes people *want* to play the victim. Some see problems where there are none, fights where there is apathy, hate where there is dispassion."

"Eloquent. Why's your English so good?"

"I study at University in England. I come back in the busy season to help my father and work on my tan. The rest of the time I study English and History and dream of a unified country."

"Can it though? Can the island be unified? I mean, can Turkish Cypriots and Greek Cypriots forgive each other and live side by side again? Is that even possible?"

"I don't know. You talk to individuals such as my parents and the answer is 'yes'. They do not hold a grudge against any individual Turkish man or woman. And yet..."

"What?" With my eyes I urged him to continue.

"My mother still weeps for the niece that she lost. Our churches have been knocked down in the North to be turned into mosques or to make way for Turkish hotels. Our graveyards that once held our families have been built upon. How do we move on from that? Forgiveness is something that does not just happen once. You have to forgive every day. My mother wakes up every day and forgives the men that killed her sister and her niece. I don't find it quite as easy."

"So you don't think you can live side by side then?"

"Actually I do. There are places where Greek Cypriots and Turkish Cypriots live side by side today."

"Really? Where?"

"Pyla. It is not far from here," he said, pointing off to his left. "It is now the only place where we live harmoniously side by side. There are about eight hundred Greek Cypriots and five hundred Turkish Cypriots."

"I would love to see that. Could you take me there?"

Stefanos nodded. "Let's go today."

I ignored his blatant attempt to sidetrack me from my foray into Varosha.

"So, if a resolution can be reached about the Ghost Town, you think unification would be possible then?"

"Anything is possible, Leni."

Stefanos took my hand and looked at me softly, his simple words loaded with meaning.

I snatched my hand back from him as if stung. "Stefanos, I'm married!"

He smirked. "Yes. But he is not here with you. I am."

He leaned in closer to me as I pushed myself as far back in my chair as I could. Even at this enhanced distance though I could feel his warm breath on my face.

"Sorry Stefanos. No," I frowned. I wasn't entirely sure if his overtures were genuine but nonetheless it was disconcerting.

"You are an interesting woman, Leni." He laughed and sat back in his chair in bafflement. "Never have I been attracted to a woman who annoys me quite so much."

"If this is your way of seducing me, it really isn't working."

He laughed even more at that, his ego not showing the slightest dent. "You argue with me all the time, you think that you are always right about *everything*, and half the time you look at me like you think I am an idiot. And yet, I still want you. Why is that?"

It was my turn to shrug.

"You know, I meet a lot of English girls here in the summer. They are younger than you and they agree with everything I say, they hang on every word and they cry when they have to leave me to go home. I could have any one of them, you know."

"Don't let me stop you."

He smiled broadly and turned his attention to the women passing a few feet away from us. Within seconds he was attracting admiring glances and second looks from a variety of ladies. At least he didn't seem heartbroken at my rebuff. Even though his attention was unwarranted, I felt aggrieved that he had so swiftly extinguished his ardour. I got the impression that he was trying to make me jealous and, angrily, I acknowledged he had succeeded.

I took the correct change out of my purse to pay for our coffees and placed them on the saucer by my side.

"Stefanos!"

He snapped his head round to look at me. "Huh?"

"Whilst I might not be about to leap into bed with you, could you at least wait until I've finished my coffee before you snare my replacement?"

"Sure. Drink up."

"Are you that desperate?"

He scoffed. "No. I want you to meet someone, that's all. C'mon."

He stood up and started walking away with his hands in his pockets. I picked up my bag and nodded my thanks at our waitress and followed him into the sunshine.

"Where are we going?" I asked as I trotted after him.

"I've told you, there is someone I want you to meet. I was in Famagusta to meet a friend. See? Not to spy on you. We have a little business to take care of but after that I am sure he will be happy to talk to you about the problems between the Greek Cypriots and the Turkish Cypriots."

"Is he as biased as you are?"

"No. He sees things more clearly than I do."

"Greek or Turkish?"

"Neither. He is British but he has been in Cyprus for a long time. He does a little work with the UN and the rest of the time he works at the museum. Do a little shopping or something, huh? Meet me in front of the museum in one hour. It is down this road to your right hand side. Okay?"

"Okay. That'd be great."

317

Stefanos smiled and started to walk away from me, looking at his watch.

"Stefanos?" I called after him.

"Yes?"

"How do I know you'll come back for me? What if you meet up with one of these women who are more interested in your company than I am?"

"Ha! Then she can wait. They are always happy to wait for me." He grinned "They are well rewarded for their patience."

He walked backwards a few paces to see what effect his remark had on me then turned and continued on his way with a smile.

Picking a direction at random I began to move cautiously through the unfamiliar streets. People jostled me out of the way on their way to meet friends or to go to work. Twice people spoke to me in Greek or Turkish and I had to reply that I didn't understand them. They looked surprised that I was British. In just a few days the sun had coloured my skin mocha. The only thing that gave me away as a foreigner was that I was wandering aimlessly through streets that I should have known well.

Once or twice people looked at me and smiled, their eyes holding onto mine for a fraction longer than was usual. Each time I wondered if they were going to say something. I thought there might be a flicker of recognition, a spark of kinship, but then they were carried away on the tide of people.

I don't know quite what I'd been expecting but perhaps, deep down, there was a part of me that hoped for a sudden embrace from a stocky stranger with cries of, "You are the spitting image of my good friend Helene. God rest her. You must be her daughter." I wondered, as I looked into the sea of brown eyes whether I might see my own peeping back at me in mirror image. Where was the fanfare? Where was the welcoming party proclaiming that Helene Kostas' lost baby had returned?

Laughing inwardly at my own deflated sense of self-worth and my pointless drive to belong somewhere, I suddenly realised that there were no longer any people in the streets or any shops or boutiques. I had obviously come to the end of the shopping district and I found myself back at the Green Line looking at the fence that divided North from South. For a moment I panicked, scared that I wouldn't be able to find my way back to Stefanos. I sucked the air into my lungs and forced it out again to make way for the next.

I looked back to the fence and pushed my fingers through it. Was Stefanos right? Was there any point to me going into the Ghost Town? What was I trying to prove? There was unlikely to be a large book on the kitchen side entitled *The Kostas family – our life story*. There wouldn't be a box full of old family photos with a gift tag saying *For Leni, with love*. I stood by the fence, my fingers entwined in the diamond of wires separating me from the place where I was born. What is this drive in us to visit the place of our birth? Is the same thing that drives salmon upstream? Was I nothing more than a fish? I had to be capable of more than reacting to a vague idea that I should be somewhere else.

The sound of falling stones caught my attention and I snapped my hands back as if an electric current was now pulsing through the wire. Was I even allowed to touch the fence? Was I about to get confronted by a Turkish soldier? No one came out of the shadows and all was silent again. It was difficult to see much of interest from where I was standing. The buildings themselves weren't that impressive or noteworthy but their direct contrast with the inhabited buildings behind me was stark and foreboding.

A strong breeze suddenly sprung up and caressed me with its soft fingers, teasing my scalp until the hairs on my head and neck stood on end. I shuddered at the sudden chill. I surveyed the buildings for any sign of life at all. I was sure that someone was watching me. I don't know how a gaze can connect with someone as clearly as a hand but sometimes there is as much touch and solidity in both. I knew that the 'sensible' me would leave here now and go back to Stefanos before I was late, but I couldn't shake the nagging feeling that I was missing something important.

My heart was thrumming too loudly as my eyes darted from building to building. Mum or Helene might have stepped foot in any one of them. Their feet would have travelled these roads when both of their futures were filled with promise. Life had once suggested endless opportunities ahead of them and their unborn children.

I shook the fence in frustration and the ripples came to an abrupt halt at the metal poles either side of me with a 'clank'. I'd never known such confusion. I needed someone to talk to but the only two people who knew what I intended to do were both set against the idea of me exploring the Ghost Town. Right now I wanted my husband. I needed him so much that it felt like a physical blow to my gut. He was my best friend, my lover and my soul mate. Since I'd lost the baby, I'd done nothing but push him away. I couldn't bear to look into that strong face and see the reflection of my aching heart. I'd closed down the vulnerable part of me that used to love unreservedly.

Perhaps it was time to not only get back to Stefanos but to get back on an airplane and go home. All of a sudden I was desperately tired and I slumped over, deflated and de-energised. If I'd had the energy I would probably have cried, but even that seemed beyond my capabilities right now.

I was no longer so sure that I could find any answers here in Cyprus. The only people I could trust to help me with the turmoil I was in were at home waiting patiently for me to pull myself together. As I lowered my gaze and started to turn away a rush of wind caught my hair and blew dust in my eyes.

"Leni!"

I blinked away the dust but my vision wasn't clearing as quickly as I needed it too.

"Hello? Who's there?"

"Leni!" The voice shouted again. An impatient wind carried the noise from afar. It was a little girl's voice. At last my vision cleared enough for me to peer around into the deserted street. Nothing moved. I turned back to the wasteland behind the fence and there, standing in the doorway of a building that had been left half completed, was a beautiful little girl with plaits hanging over her narrow shoulders. Anna was waving to me.

Chapter eighteen

Cyprus, 1974

Whispering through the fog in her head, Pru heard urgent voices. Hushed. Greek. She tried to ask what had happened to her but it felt like a long walk back to consciousness. When eventually she pushed open her eyes, Helene and Mrs Kostas were crouched over her. Helene put her hand behind Pru's neck and lifted her head off the hard cold floor.

"Here. Drink." A glass was pushed into Pru's sore lips where the icy liquid stung her cracked mouth. As she sipped, she could feel the progress of the water down her throat and spreading across her chest. The water tasted stale. Stagnant. Dust danced in the pellucid liquid and grit stung her throat. She tried to look more closely at the women but their images swam in front of her eyes and her pulse hammered out an uneven beat inside her head.

"Seet up!" commanded the old woman.

Pru was too tired to move but equally too tired to fight with the imposing Greek woman. She tried to push herself up using her elbows but she lurched to one side. The glass tumbled from her hand onto the hard stone floor and smashed, sending shards of glass across the tiles as it crumbled. Suddenly, as if the scales had fallen from her eyes, Pru saw it all. Time froze as she retreated within her own mind unable and unwilling to stop the memories flashing before her face.

She saw herself having just returned from helping deliver Helene's baby. She was tired and thirsty standing at the kitchen sink. Then she was lying on the floor of her apartment amid jagged splinters of glass. There was deep black blood oozing across her abdomen. She was shouting and screaming for help. "Somebody save my baby!" No came. She remembered the feeling of desperation as she had tried to cling onto her fragile consciousness as it was being drawn away from her.

Pru's hands flew to her stomach as the images bombarded her. The wrenching in her chest threatened to split her in two as the sob she had been holding back all day unexpectedly burst from her in a voice that she didn't recognise. The acidic realisation of grief burned through her veins and made her scream. "Noooooo!"

She balled her fists up and pressed them against her eyes to blot out the burning images. Pru grunted and hummed with no rhythm or tune in the hope that the voices would quieten in her head. But still she could hear them whisper. "You lost your baby. He's dead. Gone. Forever. What will you do now you useless piece of shit?"

"Nooooooooo! No! No! No!"

Pru rubbed her hand across her sagging, deflated stomach and the cotton material of her hospital gown snagged against her barbed wire stitches marking out the perimeter of Pru's own personal war zone.

"Is he dead? My baby?" Pru whispered looking at the two worried looking women in front of her. "Please, can you tell me the truth? I don't trust them at the hospital. Is he really gone?"

Helene stood and held onto the worn kitchen table, swallowing with difficulty. Her face told Pru everything that she needed to know. Mrs Kostas placed her fat hands on Pru's shoulders and nodded twice. The last of the fight left in Pru fled her body at that very moment. The only thing that Pru possessed now was body-numbing apathy. Pru could have sat, unfeeling and unflinching until the sun rose and the seasons changed, had it not been for the gurgle and bleating from the cradle on the table-top. All three women looked towards the wicker cocoon and then Helene looked back to Pru with pain and guilt etched all over her face.

"It's okay. Go to him. None of this is your fault and it isn't his either." Pru wiped her face on the sleeve of the borrowed coat she was wearing and was surprised at the lack of tears adorning her face.

"Ees a girl. You remember?" asked Helene as if talking to a simple child.

"A girl, yes, of course. I do remember now." Her voice was uncertain and shaky but she was sure now that this couldn't be her baby. Her baby had been a boy. She'd known it all along, throughout her pregnancy. Pru closed her eyes as she opened her arms to the tsunami of realisation and understanding that her baby was dead. Her son had died. She was all alone in the world.

Carefully placing her hand behind the baby's tender head, Helene lifted the baby out of the cradle and after a moment's hesitation, offered the baby to Pru.

"God, no." Pru wrapped her arms around herself to keep her arms for reaching for the child. There was no doubt, thought Pru, that everything she touched withered under her hand. Her existence was noxious, poisoning everyone who came into contact with her.

Helene smiled sympathetically but failed to hide her relief in her face entirely. Mrs Kostas started clearing up the broken glass carefully and silently as if this was the kind of thing that happened daily.

"I'm sorry. About the glass, I mean. And everything else. Sorry. So," said Pru trying to lighten the mood "does she have a name yet?"

Mrs Kostas helped her to her feet and into the chair by the table.

"No," smiled Helene sadly. "I am waiting for my husband. He not know he has daughter. I have sent letter to the villages."

Even though the words were sad, Helene still wore happiness on her face as she looked down at the squirming pink bundle in her arms. Settling down in the arm-chair she deftly unbuttoned her dress with one hand and settled the baby at her breast. Pru's own breasts started to ache and throb at the sight of this natural maternal act and another pang of grief coursed through her body when she realised there was another momentous event she would be missing out on.

"You have more baby," Mrs Kostas asserted.

"Actually, I won't."

"Tsk. You will."

Swallowing down the unwelcome lump of agonising despair in her throat she concentrated on the now empty bassinet rather than the old woman's milky brown eyes.

"No. I won't." And stopping the other woman before she could interject she continued "They did an operation at the hospital. I will *never* be able to have children." Her voice cracked as the words came out of her mouth for the first time.

To Pru's annoyance Mrs Kostas swatted away this information with her hand.

"I see you weeth baby like this. A girl. I never wrong."

Pru's anger was beginning to burn with a searing heat which was gathering intensity. She needed to get some fresh air or she was going to be sick.

"I'm feeling a bit hot. I think I shall sit outside for a minute, if that's okay?"

Mrs Kostas nodded. "I breeng you brandy."

Helene nodded briefly in her direction and then went back to looking at the baby. Pru couldn't bear to look directly at the little girl, for fear she would collapse again and never get up. She hadn't even realised how much she wanted her unborn child until he was gone. The pain of witnessing a scene that she would never experience was too much for her to bear. She pushed her way through the kitchen to the door and held on to the doorframe. Unseasonably, there was a crispness in the clear night and Pru pulled her borrowed coat tightly around her and tied the belt an extra notch tighter at her middle. What would Betty think when she realised that Pru had stolen her coat and left the hospital? How would she explain this to everyone. To Marjorie? To Eddie? What would they think of her if they knew that she had intended to take another woman's baby?

Pru nursed the shame in her heart. She allowed herself to feel every ounce of pain and humiliation that she deserved. What kind of person was she who, not only lost her baby, but intended to take someone else's too? She was disgusted at herself. No wonder Eddie was nowhere to be found. He couldn't stand the sight of her either. She had spent most of her life blaming other people. She blamed Mam's bitterness at her own miserable life for her kicking Pru out of home. She blamed Dad's weakness for him not getting in touch with her before he died. And Eddie. She blamed him for pretty much everything else. But as she stood in the night air in the coat she'd stolen from a well-meaning friend, outside the house where she'd been planning on taking her neighbour's baby, she realised that *she* was the common denominator in all of these relationships. They'd all failed because of her. That, she realised with a snort, was why the 'powers that be' had decided she shouldn't be able to bear any children. It was all starting to make sense now.

Pru furtively looked about her. She had to get away from it all. Get some distance between herself and that baby. Before Mrs Kostas could come out and stop her, Pru launched herself down the dusky road in the direction of the sea. This was a walk she had completed many times before but today the distance seemed insurmountable. Her legs thrummed with fatigue and her knees threatened to give way with every step but she pushed on until there was enough distance between her and the house.

She had to sit a couple of times on walls and benches before she reached the beach. Mrs Kostas would have discovered by now that she wasn't sitting outside. She hoped that they wouldn't come out to try to find her. She desperately needed to be alone. On the empty shoreline, there was meagre light being thrown out by the taverna and the noise was bearably low. Pru slumped just above the tide-line on to the welcoming sand and rolled onto her side. She pulled her knees up to her chest as much as she could, ignoring the angry pains in her stomach as her stitches rubbed and pulled. At first she tried to clear her mind of all thoughts but as she felt calmness lapping at her toes with every tender caress of the sea, she allowed herself to think more clearly.

She sank deeper into the pool of her own pity as she concluded that there was no point in her existence. If she wasn't able to have children, what could she possibly achieve with her life? When she died no one would mourn her passing, even if she lived to be one hundred years old. She was alone and would never be anything else. She couldn't see the point of going on any more.

Her mind landed lightly upon Mrs Kostas' comment about her having a baby in the future and she permitted herself to be momentarily led down the path that the doctors could perhaps perform a miracle that would allow her to have a baby. "Please Lord, I will do anything you ask of me if I could just..." but she couldn't stand to hear her own whining voice, calling out to a God that she hadn't served in many years.

From somewhere in the distance, a sharp rapport of laughter pierced the silence but then died down just as quickly. Pru was confused at how people could still be laughing and joking and getting on with their lives when Pru's own was in tatters. She felt entirely removed from the world around her, but in a peaceful way. There were no tears left to fall. Her well of emotions had run dry. She didn't want to be part of this world anymore. She had no place in it.

It took some time for her to manoeuvre herself into a standing position. She didn't seem to have functioning stomach muscles anymore. She brushed the sand off her clammy bare legs and fixed her sights on the sea in front of her. Pru felt her pain become part of her, rather than a sensation to be fought, as she walked towards the sea. She could barely see it now that the darkness had fallen in earnest. The sky held aloft a sliver of moon which cast little illumination on the sea below but she could hear the water rushing impatiently to and fro and whispering to her. She headed down the slight incline into the sea and felt the tide soothe its gentle fingers around her aching legs as if encouraging her to come in deeper. She was surprised by how cold the water felt on her legs but did not find the sensation unpleasant. She loosened her coat and tossed it up further onto the beach, hoping it wouldn't get wet. She didn't want to ruin Betty's coat after all she had done for her.

Pru took a step forward and then another as the tide ebbed and flowed around her, pulling and pushing her in turn. The sea, however, was so shallow that she would have to walk some way out to be completely submerged. Her mind made up, Pru now felt entirely at peace. She had made the one decision that would free her entirely from all of her pain. It would also free Eddie up to be able to marry someone who was worthy of him and have children of his own some day. Everyone would be better off.

She inhaled deeply as she waded out towards the thin moon's reflection. The smell of salty sea air was comforting and she was pleased that it would be the last thing that she would ever smell. A few more steps now and she could join nature and perpetually swim in the arms of the shadowy depths.

Chapter nineteen

"What are you doing?" I whispered urgently. "You can't be in there! Anna, come here now!" I beckoned her towards me. "Come!"

She fluttered her hand at me in a childish wave and then disappeared around the side of the building.

"Bollocks!" They wouldn't shoot a young girl would they? She was almost certainly safe. *Almost* certainly. I should probably alert someone so that she could be found and escorted to safety. I looked frantically around me not knowing what I should do next.

"Where's a UN patrol when you need one?" I whispered to no one in particular.

I made my way along the fence, shaking it as I went. At last I found where the fence had been loosened at the ground. It didn't look like anyone had been through this way recently, so there had to be somewhere else that Anna had managed to get in but I didn't know whether I had enough time to find it. I dropped my bag to the floor and fell to my stomach muttering "Bugger, bugger, bugger" under my breath.

As I pulled myself under the fence it caught on the back of my top and I wriggled to free it, hearing the material rip. Of course, if I was caught by the Turkish Army now, the holes in my top would be the least of my worries. I'd be worrying about holes of another nature – bullet holes. I dug my toes into the soil and pushed myself further through the opening. I looked back at my overstuffed bag. There was no way it was going to fit through that slim gap so it would have to stay there. I pushed myself into a crouching position. What the hell was I doing? I half ran, half crawled to the building where I'd seen the little girl.

"Anna!" I hissed. "Where are you?"

337

I worked my way around the back of the building and peered about me. I could see Anna skipping down the street before me with her plaits swinging in her wake and her arms windmilling at her sides. I started to jog as quietly as I could, keeping my stride wide and feet soft. I didn't want to shout out from this distance, in case it alerted any Turkish patrols.

She rounded a corner just as I inhaled about to call her name. I quickened my pace, so as not to lose her, but slowed as I reached the corner and ducked down. Anna was nowhere to be seen in the dark, narrow street. I paused, listening out for any movement at all but there was nothing. Even the breeze had died down now and silence was the only pedestrian meandering down the vacant streets.

"Anna!" I growled. "Where are you?"

I looked behind me. Should I go back to the fence and call someone for help? I was likely to get us both shot at this rate. She was almost certainly safer on her own anyway. Almost. I gazed longingly the way I came but couldn't leave this innocent little girl here alone. I felt responsible for her, and who knew

338

what dangers were lurking here? Snakes? Collapsing buildings? Worse?

I pulled myself up and started walking softly up the street trailing the cool, brittle walls, under my sweating hands. I warily looked up at the hollow-eyed buildings. There were unlikely to be soldiers in these buildings, otherwise they would have spotted Anna. I also believed, naively perhaps, they wouldn't be expecting anyone to enter the Ghost Town during daylight hours and either wouldn't be particularly vigilant or, at the least, wouldn't bother concealing their positions. I hoped to God that I was right as I quickened my step to a silent jog.

There were several streets leading off this one. None of them were wide enough for two cars to pass but they were too wide to be called alleyways. There were no sounds from these streets either. They held their breath in anticipation of what I might do next. I stood motionless, hoping to hear some footsteps from Anna but still there was nothing but a solid rampart of silence.

I walked tentatively to the end of the street and came out onto a wide road that would have, at one time, been a busy thoroughfare. There were shops and restaurants lining up tattily down each side of the street. Metal signs advertised Coca-Cola and souvlaki in styles reminiscent of the 1970s. It seemed too exposing to try to cross the road so I headed cautiously along the boulevard, hugging the walls. Torn between searching for Anna, keeping an eye out for Turkish patrols, and the sheer amazement of being so close to buildings that had been left abandoned for so many years, I stumbled warily along the road.

"Anna?"

A sound from a building ahead of me made my heart lurch and I melted back into the shadows. I had to will myself to move on in case it was the brown-haired girl but my feet were rooted to the spot. I clenched and unclenched my fists, digging my nails into the palms of my hands to keep me focussed. I slid along the wall, holding on to it for misplaced security. When I reached the bones of what had once been a store of some description, I could see that part of the metal shutter had been torn back, formally saluting the street. I had very little inclination to go in there so got to my knees in front of the gap.

"Anna, are you in there? Anna?"

The sound of breathing and light footsteps inside started coming closer to the sunlight. I peered in but could see nothing in the gloom.

"Anna? Please come here now. I'm not cross with you, I just want to take you home."

The footsteps quickened and rushed out of the small gap, knocking me on my back with surprise. As I fell I saw the brown blur of a small dog running across the street with newspaper hanging from its mouth. I lay there for a moment with my hand cupped over my eyes staring into the grey-blue sky as my heart calmed down and the sour taste of bile subsided.

I was going to have to head back to the gap in the fence. I had absolutely no idea where Anna was now. I could be wandering around the city for hours to no avail. I had no choice but to go and get Stefanos and then he would alert someone to find her. He must have some contacts within the UN. I had no idea if Anna had skipped down this way or if she was still in Varosha. I felt guilty at the thought of abandoning her but I was sure that I was absolutely no use to anyone if I got shot or arrested now. There was a part of me that wanted to stay here a little longer; after all, I had inadvertently succeeded in my plan to get into Varosha, but I really should alert someone to Anna's presence here.

I was panting heavily as I sat up and wrapped my arms around my knees. Rocking backwards and forwards I took in the truly incredible sight before me. I felt like I was in an old Western. All I needed now was tumbleweed rolling down the dusty deserted street before the bad guys rode in to town. It was difficult to accept that there was no one living here anymore. How often would I come across a conurbation of this size absolutely devoid of any residents except wild dogs? My mind refused to shake the feeling that there must be some home-makers behind those shutters, or hiding out in the back of the shops. It was simply unfathomable that all of this could be left to decay. One day it had been full of bustle and thriving businesses and the next day jilted like an unwanted bride and left to age, alone and unloved, like Miss Haversham.

Directly opposite me was a clothes shop with yellow plastic sheeting covering the inside of the window, supposedly to stop the sun from fading the clothes. The clothes stood like wallflowers in neat rows. Dresses that would never find a dancing partner and shoes that would never know what it was like to walk down a road, skipping over puddles from an unseasonable shower.

There was something so abjectly miserable about the sight I felt the urge to go over and try some of the clothes on, just to give them an outing. I smiled to myself at the thought, but shoplifting, even thirty-odd years since the shop had closed, wasn't something I would ever feel comfortable with.

I pushed myself to my feet and brushed the dirt off my denim shorts. On my way here I had been so intent on searching for Anna that I hadn't taken stock of my surroundings.

I was becoming a schizophrenic. I wasn't just in two minds, I was two almost separate people. The me of old – British me – was hyperventilating at the thought of trespassing and breaking the rules. She was consumed by the fear of being caught and shot. She was convinced that she would never find her way out of here and if the Turkish soldiers didn't shoot her, then she would find herself at the mercy of rabid dogs and feral cats. The new me – Greek me – demanded to know her birth right and dared anyone to stop her from retracing the steps of her mother. *That* me wanted to make the most of the serendipitous opportunity that had presented itself and explore a little.

I stopped my spinning head from thinking about what to do next and stood at the side of the dusty street, sticky with perspiration. In a concept that was alien to me, I allowed myself to simply 'feel'. I switched off my mind and let my heart propel my feet down the street towards the magnetic lure of the sea. There were more houses now, interspersed with the shops. The terraces showcased bountiful fig trees which were clearly flourishing with neglect. I began to reach out for one of the lusciously green and purple fruits but stopped myself before I could stroke the velvety skin. There was still that ingrained thought that someone would come rushing out from their home shaking their fists at me for purloining their pride and joy. The curtains were drawn in some of the windows as if some of the inhabitants were merely asleep. Perhaps they were. The curtains now hung in rags behind the begrimed, mottled windows.

I turned to my right and walked up a cracked and uneven path between the houses. Here I could see washing strung out between sun-washed homes sagging on bright plastic lines. Strips of rags unrecognisable as garments hung side by side while a solitary pair of trousers still hung there intact, impervious to the elements and the bombs. They stood still and straight, a lone sentry in defiance of the Turkish presence in these streets. I no longer felt any fear at being discovered. I felt like I belonged here. My feet knew where I was going even though I had never set foot on any of these roads. I was being guided now by something other than my curiosity.

The road in front of me wasn't in as bad a condition as I had feared, even though low growing, lush green foliage with yellow flowers seeped over the hot grey thoroughfare. A building to my left housed a strip of shops with apartments on top. Each shop was open to the elements and completely empty inside. Panes of glass littered the pavement and dusty puddles of bottles and twigs pooled in the corners. Signs indicating that these had once been hairdressing salons and beauty parlours hung limply from above.

To my right I could see a church down the end of an alleyway. Never had a house of God looked so uninviting.

Rusting barrels and oil drums piled high behind thick iron railings and barbed wire conveyed a clear message that I was not welcome there. I carried on walking in the silence past a beautiful house which, in its day, would have housed one of Varosha's elite and wealthy inhabitants. Terraces and archways were dotted pink with the rice-paper flowers of Bougainvillea. A half-hearted attempt to board up the windows and doors with a wire mesh had been dismissed by either hand or wind. I allowed myself a brief moment to picture the home in its full glory and how I would develop it, imagining myself sipping gin and tonic on the terrace with a slice of lemon from my own tree.

Ahead of me down the broadening road was what was left of a hotel. Even from here I could see the devastation the war had wrought on its once imposing walls. The missing walls exposed pink wallpaper that was never meant to be unmasked to the outside world. In the courtyard of the hotel, chairs and bits of wood congregated in the empty swimming pool. I'd read that somewhere in Varosha there was a car showroom with cars sitting idle, never to be driven. It was unlikely that I'd be able to locate it, even though it intrigued me.

I picked my way over the detritus and stepped into what would have once been the foyer of the hotel. Chairs squatted in armless huddles. Something bulky and long lay on the floor by the front desk. Nervously I approached it to try and take a closer look. It was what was left of a grand piano. The inner workings of the piano were still there but the keys were all missing and most of the wood had been taken away. I backtracked out of there, stumbling over a mislaid shoe. I chose a road at random and started jogging down it, keen to leave the hotel behind.

In front of me I could see the golden blossoming of the open, unshadowed street up ahead but my path was now blocked. Thick, prickly, thistle-like weeds had punched their way through the walkway, demanding their day in the sun. A small white fridge lay rusting and pock-marked on its side. The door was open, lying flat against the floor. Leaves and cardboard had taken up residence in its shelter. I picked my way over the obstacles, ignoring the barbed spikes of the monstrous plants. Dirt and twigs had drifted to the walls in neglected brown peaks.

Placing both hands on the white peeling wall beside me I saw what I knew would be there all along. The buckled metal sign on the wall opposite me read 'Lakira Street'.

I was buzzing with equal quantities of excitement and trepidation. I took a deep breath to steady myself and to arrest my urge to sprint across the road. It would be all too easy to make a mistake now. I remained immobile holding onto the wall a moment or two longer while I steadied myself and looked about me.

These were the streets where Mum and Eddie had walked as a newly married couple in love. This was where my other mother, Helene, had lived and died. I'm not sure what emotion I expected to feel but it certainly wasn't this. I felt elated. I'd made it, I'd found the place. But now what did I do? I'd not really thought any further than the need to get into Varosha unnoticed. My concerns for Anna had vanished now and there was no way I was going back to Famagusta to find Stefanos. This was where I was meant to be. I drummed my fingers on the wall, considering my next move. Instinct had brought me this far and it seemed churlish to stop listening to it now.

I pushed myself away from the wall, noting the white flakes of paint clinging to my sweating palms, and stepped boldly into the weakening sunshine. The hairs on my arms rippled even though there was no breeze. There were clouds in the sky but they were skirting around the sun for now and the rays were still warm. I didn't know exactly where the old flat was so I picked my way carefully to my left down the street, touching everything I could: the leaves on the overgrown bushes, the low lying walls, the miniature dunes of sand which had gusted up against the sides of the houses. Lizards stuck to the sides of sun-warmed homes which would still be throwing out warmth even as the sun set. Untrusting of this anachronistic outsider they darted away as I drew near.

I was trying to conjure up the image in my head of the map that Eddie had drawn for me. I had stared and stared at it last night and this morning, but even so, it was difficult to equate these perishing edifices with the neat blue biro lines drawn in Eddie's hand.

There was a pretty building on my left that showed the ravage of almost four lonely decades of sun and rain but still held an aged, ragged beauty. Round balconies of black wrought iron railings stood before tall doors and windows. On the ground floor window boxes held dried brown offerings, which would have obscured the view if anyone had been looking. I gazed at it for a long time. I was as sure as I could be that this wasn't Mum's old flat although, I confess, I'm not entirely sure I'd recognise Mum's apartment if it fell on me. Now I was here I wanted to look around a bit more. The hotel had been an impersonal space and I itched to see someone's home from all those years ago.

"Just five minutes," I told myself.

It was difficult to find the path that led to it but I picked my way through the weeds and up the cracked, bowing steps. As I stood on the top step it crumbled beneath me with all the solidity of a meringue. It was enough to make me stumble and grab at the rutted railings but otherwise I was unharmed. I found my right hand covering my heart, as if that would help stop the hammering in my chest.

There is an eeriness about knowing that you are the first person to set foot in a place for many years. I could feel it like an imprint of a previous life. I fancied that the inhabitants were just round the corner, out of reach of my outstretched hands, and their voices a little too quiet to hear.

The first door that I tried was unlocked. Was I surprised by that? It seemed amiss by the previous inhabitants to go out and leave their home unprotected, but then, the kind of things that they needed protection against were unlikely to be stopped by a standard house lock.

Even though I knew that no one was in there, it felt like I was intruding and I almost knocked before easing the door open as quietly as I could and tip-toeing into the stale and time-frozen room. I expected to see a mound of unread mail and flyers in a heap on the floor as often happens in a house that has lain uninhabited. But I shook my head, there was nobody to deliver the mail and takeaway menus here. No postman would be traipsing up to the door with letters bundled by a red elastic band.

I absent-mindedly wondered if there was an office somewhere holding onto the mail for when the people of Varosha returned. Had their mail been redirected? Of course, having a mail service wouldn't have been a priority in Famagusta during the invasion. I mused that it would be a priority in England. There is something so innately British about the Royal Mail and letters. I would still be "Tsk-ing" if my mail wasn't delivered by mid-morning even in the middle of a war. Some things are just the British way.

My feet padded into what looked like the living room. I looked down, expecting to see carpet, but the cushioning under foot was forty years of dust. The imprint of my footsteps could be seen clearly behind me, complete with the wavy lines of the tread from the underside of my shoe. There was an oval table, with one side folded down, pushed against a wall with four chairs arcing round it. Three of the chairs were pushed out from the table around the open sides but one was pushed firmly into place.

Two coffee cups and an old coffee pot sat on one side of the table next to a sepia coloured newspaper. Two small glasses with pink and orange flowers and two forks sat flanking two empty white plates on the other side of the table. The set-up suggested this was the home of a family of four people with two young children.

The fact that the breakfast things were still laid out suggested these people had been in a hurry. Perhaps they stayed as long as they could, telling each other that it would never happen, they would never leave their home. It wouldn't come to that. They all sat down to breakfast together and enjoyed a cup of coffee, pretending all was normal until... Until what? They heard tanks? Voices? Gunfire? Perhaps they left at the urgings of their neighbours. Perhaps they were dragged from their home.

The other side of the room held two hard-looking sofas facing a low oblong coffee table. There was more wood than padding in the seats and the rough orange-brown fabric had bobbled with age. There were no cushions to soften the effect of the austere furniture. On the wall there was a painting of a lioness and cubs lying supine on a dark green background. The painting was at a slight angle and I couldn't resist straightening it a little. My fingers came away black with dust and I wiped them on my shorts.

I walked through a doorless archway into the kitchen. There was no glass in the windows and the shutters were wide open. Where a back door once was, there was nothing but air. This room had taken a lot of the battering from the elements. One wall had been once covered with framed photographs, but now some lay on the floor, faces smiling up through the shattered glass pinned down by splintered wooden frames.

I picked up one of the pictures and its frame came apart in my hand. I let the dark wood fall to the floor but held firmly onto the photo. I turned it over to see illegible angular Greek writing on the back. The snapshot showed an angelic little girl of about five years old on the shoulders of a muscly dark man with an age-masking beard. Her hair was loose in rat-tails around her shoulders. And she was displaying two cavernous holes where her front teeth should have been. The camera had caught her in the middle of a shriek of glee.

The man, her father I assumed, was holding her knees and she was gripping the sides of his head. The joy on their faces radiated from the picture and filled the little kitchen with sunshine.

"And where are you now?" I asked the picture out loud. The child would be older than me, perhaps with children, perhaps even grandchildren. Maybe she now carries children on her own shoulders. Does she remember this picture? Does she long for her childhood home? Did they get out of Famagusta safely?

I turned then to take in the kitchen and frowned. It wasn't only the wind and the rain that had been through this room. I could now see that that all of the drawers and cupboards were open and everything had been taken. Green squares on white walls showed where cupboards had been removed from above the sink. I puzzled over why the inhabitants would have taken their cupboards with them and then I saw the green glass beer bottles on the side. There was no doubt that someone had been in here since the Greek family had fled.

I placed the photograph in the back pocket of my shorts – I don't know why – and headed towards the stairs. Nervously sticking to the outside of the steps, where I hoped they would be more stable, I slowly picked my way up to the landing using the ornate bannister as support. The style seemed more French than Greek.

At the bedrooms I noticed the doors were missing here too but I didn't step over the threshold. The first room came alive as cockroaches scuttled into the corners and I shrank backwards instinctively. There were two stripped beds in the centre of the room. A filthy blanket and pillow were on one of the beds. On the floor were more beer bottles, some teaspoons and aluminium foil. Drug users.

Pink curtains danced around the floor-to-ceiling windows with the deftness of ballerinas as the breeze picked up outside. Their movements caused me to feel uneasy and I went back towards the stairs, unable to stay here any longer now I knew what had been going on in the child's bedroom. I had expected everything to be frozen in time, a snapshot of perfect 1970s' family life. Instead, I had seen that nothing is sacred. These houses had been looted, used and destroyed. Nature wasn't the biggest enemy of this town. Man was. I snorted at my own naivety, thinking that anyone respected the lives of the previous inhabitants here.

The day had lost none of its warmth but it was mercifully overcast now as I rushed back into the open air. The clouds had sneaked up on the sun and smothered it. It felt like the spotlight had been turned off at last and I was free to explore the Ghost Town in anonymity.

I closed the door carefully behind me, even though there was no one there to complain if I left it ajar. I could almost hear my mum's voice shouting, "Were you born in a barn?" Some habits die hard. From my vantage point at the top of the steps I looked across the street and imagined the neighbours of this family. Did they know Mum and Eddie? Did they exchange pleasantries on a morning or did they pass by on the street, too caught up in their own lives to be interested in the English woman and her army husband?

The light wind stirred up sand, litter and memories, spinning them in the air indiscriminately. I sucked in the air which was both fresh and oppressive. No food smells pervaded the air from houses or cafés. There was no lingering odour from

357

cars and motorbikes thickening the air. There were no well-heeled ladies sweeping by leaving a wake of perfume and hairspray. And yet, although the air was untainted, there was something unbearably heavy in the ether. Hints of war and hatred still lingered on street corners and loitered in the abandoned buildings. Menace and slyness beckoned you round corners and into deserted alleyways.

The end of the pitted road opened up into a larger square which contained a few shops and two identical apartment blocks, two storeys high, each housing four families by the looks of it. I carefully descended the steps, taking care to walk on the edges to avoid the cratered concrete blocks. I was about to turn and head back up the street to explore the top end when it loomed at me. The rest of the world dropped away for a minute as I saw with unwavering clarity the apartment block where I had been born. It looked at me expectantly like it was thinking, "It's about time."

Chapter twenty

Cyprus, 1974

Pru swayed in the inky water. She opened her arms wide and threw her face up to the purple sky. This was her last goodbye to the world. She looked at the stars blinking at her. Her father had taught her the names of the stars and the constellations. She turned her head slightly and spotted the Plough, the Great Bear and acknowledged the orange glow of Mars. She wondered if Dad was up there somewhere, watching her. Wasn't that what some people thought happened to you when you died? If it was true, she'd be seeing him again soon enough. And what of her baby? What happened to those who died before even taking their first breath? Where does God stand on what constitutes a life, she wondered. At conception? When its heart starts beating? Or when it takes its first gulp of air in its mother's arms? It was too late to be considering theology now. She'd either see her baby boy in the afterlife or she wouldn't. There was certainly no chance of seeing him again in this world. As far as she could see, there was only one option open to her now.

She nodded to the Seven Sisters, spotted the Milky Way and then pinned her sights on the scimitar moon. She would walk to her death while fixing her gaze upon that glimmer of light. A silver chink in the darkness that would deliver her from perpetual grief. She walked forwards, her feet finding cold rippled sand under her toes. There were no stones to impede her progress on the welcome mat spread before her.

A flash of intense golden light illuminated the beach and coloured the air orange. Pru felt the explosion rather than heard it and was thrown forward into the water. Shock and fatigue rendered her arms unable to hold her up and her face plunged into the salty liquid. Coughing she remerged from the shallow water wiping the strands of wet hair from her face. She turned with terror as a percussion of explosions boomed through the clear night and stung her ears. Pru was frozen to the spot and unable to do anything but kneel in the water and sway with the tide.

Her pulse was pounding in her ears like the aftershocks of an earthquake. She couldn't hear anything except a ringing like the distant peels of cathedral bells. She watched as people came running out of the taverna and looked towards the throbbing glow in the distance. They didn't see Pru sitting on her heels up to her chin in the water, nor would they have cared if they did. Two of the younger men set off at a sprint up the beach and Pru dragged herself out of the water to do the same. The sea didn't want to give up its prize so easily and it pulled on her hospital gown, wrapping it round its watery fingers and yanking her into the deep. She struggled to her feet but fell sideways with a splash and felt the stitches on her stomach give way.

Pru fumbled with the tie on the gown at her neck and ripped the blue material off her battered body. Naked, she pushed herself to her feet and looked up the beach towards the orange glow in the sky and the fast moving would-be heroes. She was searching her mind, trying to get her bearings, so that she could work out exactly which building had been hit. She kept coming back to the same answer but didn't want it to be true.

"The baby," she whispered.

Rivulets of liquid ran cold from her hair over her bare body. Pru started wading back to the dry sand but her progress was slow and cumbersome. She reached the tide-line and collapsed with a muffled thud on to her front. The cool sand clung to her wet body and scratched at her raw skin. It took a Herculean effort to get herself into a standing position and she staggered to the discarded housecoat. At first she carried it by her side unencumbered by embarrassment at her naked body. She only realised that she was cold when her teeth started to chatter. It was then that Pru struggled into its limp arms and closed it around her, thankful for its protection once more.

"Not the baby. Not the baby," she kept murmuring to herself over and over again.

She stumbled and almost fell to the sand again. Her legs were too weak to carry her any further but she could see where the bomb had hit. Pru sank to her knees in dismay. Through heavy lidded eyes she expected to see fire crews and ambulances

362

but eerily, few people were around. The apartment where she had been sitting earlier that night was now a singed, hollow husk. A shell had passed straight through the building leaving a hole right through its heart. The men she had seen jog up the beach were standing by a group of older men and, some feet in front of them on the ground, there was a huddle of bodies covered in dirty cloths. The smell of burning thickened the air even though nothing appeared to be alight anymore. Pru closed her eyes as tears formed around her eyelashes, stinging her raw face.

The men had gone by the time Pru opened her eyes again. Some time had passed but she couldn't tell how much. The bodies were still there lying in the street where they had been dragged. Propelled by the need to look at them, to see whether it really was who she feared, she pushed herself upright. Pru willed her feet up the slight incline to where the bodies lay under the trees.

Helene's profile was easily recognisable under the cover. Her black wavy hair spilled out from its cotton tomb and Pru suddenly retched without warning. The pain of her empty stomach did little to slow down the reflex action of her muscles convulsing and causing her to heave. Warm water splattered her toes and she hunched over the puddle of vomit percolating the dusty ground.

When she was spent, Pru staggered to one side and rolled onto her back. She gingerly straightened out her legs, concentrating on slowing down her breathing to stop her stomach from trying to eject everything it had ever had in it. Every inch of her limbs ached and screamed at her. The nausea was slackening its hold on her now and the tears started to trickle down her face. She wasn't sure what she was crying for; there was no particular thought associated with the weeping. They needed no urging to spring forth from her eyes and she was soaked in her unnamed grief within minutes.

Pru wanted to experience the numb feeling that she'd harboured earlier. Anything would be better than this desperate feeling lying heavy on her chest. She was struck by the futility of life. Her baby had died but *she*, Pru, had lived. Helene's baby had been born safely but then Helene had died. In the depths of her self-pity, Pru felt that Helene was the lucky one as she did not have to wake up in the morning knowing that her baby was dead. She had been spared that gut-wrenching knowledge that she had been unable to protect her only child. Pru wished that she had stayed with Helene and her mother, then all of this pain would be over for her. She too would have been lying beneath a white sheet, stripped of grief and pain.

Again, Pru wondered at the eerie silence of the streets surrounding her and sat upright. This was normally a busy area and if people weren't rushing to some place, they were sitting out under the stars, telling stories and drinking ouzo. She snorted to herself. "They knew," she thought. "They knew another attack was coming and they've already left the area, leaving the Kostas to fend for themselves. How *could* they?"

Once more the sea invited her to sleep in its clutches for eternity and she steeled herself to make the walk back down to the seafront. The sea promised peace, a release from the pain. Its soothing whispers told her it understood what she was experiencing and didn't blame her for ending her life. It knew she had done all she could and no longer had anything to live for.

The Turkish soldiers had taken away her future and that of the Kostas and there was nothing more she could do here.

The line between the sky and the sea was becoming visible again as somewhere over the horizon the sun was starting to make an appearance. Black was starting to give way to purple as the night began to lose her dominance.

"Now or never," Pru thought.

In a trance-like state, Pru stood up, trying her best not to notice the pain flowing through body as readily as blood through her veins. "It won't be hurting for much longer," she told herself. Standing by the shell of her former house, Pru afforded a last glance backwards and fancied she heard a soft cry from the debris. Sighing she turned and started to walk towards the sand.

Her steps faltered, she wasn't getting any strength to her muscles and she was finding it increasingly difficult to propel herself forward. At this rate it would be dawn before she reached the sea.

"What *was* that noise?" For a moment Pru contemplated whether it was the weaker part of her mind playing tricks on her or something more compelling. She no longer felt in control of her body or her mind. It was as if the part of her that was essentially Pru was shrinking and, if she didn't do something decisive now, she would be lost forever.

She stared at the rubble but no further sound came, and yet, she had the feeling that she should retrace her steps and investigate.

"God, tell me what I should do. I am so tired" she whispered.

She strained her ears but couldn't hear anything over the inviting shushing of the waves like a mother soothing a fretful child. In spite of her resolve to receive the embrace of the sea, another noise had Pru starting back towards the building.

"Hello? Is anyone there?"

She couldn't make out anything from the gloom and chaos that greeted her at the hole in the wall. An acrid smell seized her nostrils and she wrinkled her face against the unpleasant smell.

"Hello?" she asked again softly, feeling slightly scared by her own voice echoing back to her to amplify her intrusion.

A shrill bleat from the middle of the room alerted Pru to something still living amongst the stones and dust. And again, that same noise.

"Oh my God! The baby!" Abandoning any pain and doubts she had, Pru stumbled in the darkness towards the sound and listened again. This time the cries were more insistent. She pulled aside the table and found a basinet lying on its side. Inside its cushioned shell was a pink pearl. A baby girl.

Pru had trouble getting her hands underneath the squirming mass and it took a couple of attempts to ease the baby out of the confines of her wicker bomb-shelter. She clutched the baby to her chest, terrified of dropping the priceless package, and made her way out of the building, more carefully this time, fearful of tripping or the building collapsing in its entirety around her. By now the baby's crying was more insistent even though it wasn't very loud.

"Shhhhhh. Shhhhhhh. Are you hurt? Where does it hurt, baby?"

She rushed round to the front of the building ignoring the shrouded bodies and hurried to where the street was lit so she could see the baby better. Falling to her knees she placed the swaddled baby on the floor and unwrapped the blanket. She ran her hands over the baby girl's smooth arms and bucking legs but could find no marks or injuries.

"Shhhhhh. You're okay now, you're okay."

Pru clasped the baby tightly and rocked her but the crying didn't stop. Her little rosebud mouth opened and closed at Pru's breast.

"Are you hungry, baby girl? But I haven't got anything for you."

Looking around her, Pru could see no alternative. She needed to get Helene's baby to a hospital, but until then, Pru would have to feed her herself. She tentatively loosened her coat and let it slip down to expose her left breast still full of the milk that should have been sustaining her own son. Instinctively the baby searched for her nipple, latched on and began to suck. In a sensation that was both painful and euphoric, Pru allowed the baby to feed from her as she looked on in wonder.

Pru didn't know how long she sat there cradling the baby at her bosom before she heard the rumbling of the truck and saw the headlights coming up Lakira Street. She glanced over her shoulder at the oncoming vehicle and assumed it had come to take away the bodies of Helene and her mother. She wrapped the coat around her and the baby, tucking in the blanket to preserve her dignity. The truck stopped beside her, and she was about to point to where the bodies lay when an abrupt yelp took her by surprise.

"Oh sweet Jesus! Pru!" Marjorie was on the floor beside her with her arm around her shoulders. "Are you okay? I can't believe you did this all on your own. Someone help me here!"

Strong arms hoisted her to her feet but she kept both of hers around the suckling baby.

"I'm fine Marjorie, really."

Pru could hear murmurs coming from inside the truck and realised she must look quite a sight.

"I knew I should have stayed with you. Were you in the building when it was hit? Sweet Jesus. You two are lucky to be alive!"

"Yes," whispered Pru stroking the baby's cheek with the side of her thumb. "It's a miracle. We saved each other's lives."

Pru felt a blanket being draped around her shoulders and someone helping her up into the truck.

"We're being evacuated" explained Marjorie. "They're taking us to Episcopi where there are Hercules planes waiting to take us back to England. Are you okay to travel? Is the baby okay?"

The questions kept raining down on Pru's ears but she could only hear the gurgle and murmur of a contented baby in her arms. Pru looked up long enough to notice that she was back on the same bus as a few days ago, with largely the same people, and yet, the world was markedly different now. She had been through something so life-changing, and so nearly life-ending, that she felt entirely removed from the circus around her.

"Where's Eddie? Does he even know?" asked Marjorie.

"I honestly don't know," sighed Pru, finding her voice at last but never taking her eyes from the baby who had now fallen into a peaceful satiated sleep. "I think he's working."

Both women sat in silence looking at the sleeping baby until Marjorie spoke.

"She's gorgeous Pru. What's her name?"

"She doesn't have one yet."

"Well, I guess it's all been a bit of a rush, hasn't it? Mine were without names for three or four days before we decided what suited them."

Pru bent over and kissed the baby's forehead. This poor baby no longer had a mother or grandmother and didn't even have a name and yet she looked so content. She was blissfully unaware of the war that was unfolding around her that had already claimed the lives of at least two members of her family. Pru supposed the army might be able to track down the baby's father, if he was still alive, but she was reluctant to leave the baby to the whims of the administrative system. She was going to see if she could stay in Cyprus and help track down the baby's father. She couldn't bear the thought of leaving her all alone.

Pru sat back in her seat and waited for the bumpy journey to conclude. Each bump and pot hole in the unevenly tarmacked road reminded her of her physical ordeal over the last twenty-four hours. She pulled the blanket around the baby and then covered herself up, suddenly aware that she was woefully underdressed and completely naked under the ill-fitting coat. As if sensing her discomfort, Marjorie was tapping Pru on the shoulder.

"Here."

Pru looked down at the bundle of clothes in Marjorie's hands.

"It's obvious that you weren't able to pack any clothes in the circumstances. So, everyone has donated an item of clothing out of their bags for you."

Pru looked around at the women and children in the crowded truck.

"Thank you. That's so..." Pru's eyes instantly flooded and overflowed down her cheeks. "I don't know what to say. Thank you. I don't know why I'm crying."

"Hormones. Don't fret about it. The knickers are mine. They're clean, don't worry! Claire has given you a top and a cardigan." Marjorie leaned in and whispered conspiratorially "Silk! Here let me hold the baby while you get dressed."

"Hello, little dumpling. Are you coming for a cuddle with your Auntie Marjorie? Are you? Are you? Who's a beautiful girl, then? Eh, eh? Yes you are."

Pru slipped into the borrowed clothes with some difficulty due to the bumpy terrain and her aching body. The bell-bottomed jeans wouldn't do up over her still-swollen tummy, but a hastily-applied elastic hairband managed to bridge the gap between button and hole. The cardigan was soft against her battered skin and the well- worn flip-flops she eased her toes into were a perfect fit. She pulled a brush through her knotted hair and was starting to feel a little bit more like herself again when the bus pulled into the air base. There must have been over one hundred people sitting in the hangar next to a hotchpotch of bags and boxes. Men in uniform were pounding about with clip-boards and urgency.

"Here you go, dumpling, back to Mummy," Marjorie said as she handed the baby back to Pru.

"Oh Marjorie, no. You don't understand. You see, she's not my–"

"No, don't make me hold her any more, I'm already getting broody again! Look honey, I can see Jason over there so I'm going to grab him while I can. Come on kids, stay with Mummy please. Okay Pru, I'll see you later love. And make sure

you get the two of you checked over by the doctor, okay?"
Marjorie flowed into the crowds.

Pru saw Eddie's Commanding Officer moving through
the crowds and hastened to him.

"Excuse me?"

"Mrs Clarke. Well, that explains why Eddie didn't turn
up for his shift tonight then! Boy or girl?"

"Erm... girl. So, you haven't seen Eddie tonight then?"

"No. Well, congratulations to you both. Unfortunately I
can't stay and talk. Do excuse me."

"Of course." Where was Eddie? He wasn't at home and
he wasn't at work either. She had needed Eddie more than ever
today, and not only had he left her at the hospital, but he hadn't
even gone to work. He was probably drunk somewhere and
talking about how his wife had let him down. And in a way, Pru
supposed he was right. She would never be able to give him
children and they had little or no future together now anyway.

If she was sure of anything, it was that her marriage was
effectively over and she was leaving Cyprus without Eddie.
Mind made up, Pru walked over to the registration desk to add

her name to the list of those being shipped out to Oxfordshire that day.

"Name?"

"Prudence Clarke. And this," she said without hesitation, "is my daughter Helene."

Chapter twenty-one

Leering at me from across the road, I could clearly see the half-shelled building where I was born. When I say that I saw it clearly, I don't mean just that my vision was unimpaired, I mean that my gaze pinpointed the building and faded out everything around it. I knew without any trace of doubt that this was the building that I was looking for. Where it had all began. Where it had all ended.

I bit down the urge to run to it and looked around myself cautiously. Now was not the time to get caught. It was unlikely that there were guards in these buildings; they seemed to patrol the points by the fence, and this building was away from the sagging wire fence but even so, I had to be careful. To get this close to the building and then not be able to go inside would be unbearable.

It took me longer to cover those final yards than it had to walk the previous mile. I tried my best to savour these final steps leading to the realisation of my quest. Even though this was the reason that I'd come to Cyprus, the circuitous route that had led me to this point meant that it was all taking an unnaturally long interval to sink in.

My feet carried me soundlessly under the trees and to the front of the building. The upper floor of the building looked remarkably intact, unaware of what had happened beneath its floor. In the bottom right of the building, there was a gaping hole as if the house had opened its mouth wide in shock. The shell that had hit it appeared to have gone straight through the middle of the apartment leaving an almost perfect cylinder like a cored apple.

I couldn't make out anything inside the building, just darkness and debris. If the building over the road was anything to go by, there was very little chance that this had been left as a shrine to my dead mother and grandmother. The sun was still obscured by a stubborn mantle of cloud and there was hardly any light permeating the gloom. Above, and to the left, I saw Mum's old apartment exactly as Eddie had described it to me. It stood perfectly still, untouched by the tragedy that had befallen its neighbour. The curtains hung still and straight at the missing window. The front door was a light blue. It hadn't been painted that shade, of that I was sure, but decades of sun had bleached everything to a shadow of its former self.

I waited for fifteen minutes silently before I broke free from my trance. The heat that had built up through the day was oppressive and barred everything but slow and stately progress through its mire. Now that I was close enough to touch the bricks I didn't know what I was going to do next. I thought I would start with the building closest. There was no door to walk through, only a gaping cavernous hole. I stepped over the threshold and looked around me. I expected to feel some of the memory of Helene's death lingering in the air, but there was nothing. This was the place that I was born and the place that my biological mother and grandmother had died. And yet, there was nothing that separated this building from any other building in Varosha except the wormhole shot through its centre.

Any one of these buildings could be hiding a painful history. With nobody around to tell their stories, the secrets would stay unearthed, untold and, to those too young to remember the conflict, unfathomable. I stepped carefully over the brick-strewn floor. I didn't want to risk disturbing anything and have the entire building come crashing down around my ears.

The walls of the large room that had once been a kitchen-come-living room were remarkably untouched by the devastation of the bomb. They still held the pattern of the wallpaper in muted greens. The physical carnage was straight through the middle of the room, like a cyclone had passed through. There was an overturned dining chair and table to one side but all other furniture seemed to have been removed, or used for firewood. I placed the chair on all four spindly legs and sat down delicately upon it. It groaned but showed no sign of surrendering under my weight so I relaxed my back into it. I willed something to happen then – something to link me to this room – but I was coming up empty. The elation at finding the building had been replaced by a heavy feeling of numbing anti-climax. Now what?

I sat and looked closely at the dirty rubble under my feet. It was nothing but bricks and mortar. I tried to conjure up distasteful images in my head. I wanted to feel something. I expected to sit here and cry over my lamented mother. I tried to imagine her lying prone among these bricks but nothing moved me to any form of emotion.

My eyes travelled across the floor and, I'm ashamed to say, I was searching for a physical sign of Helene Kostas' death: a blood stain, a blast-torn locket, a waylaid shoe. Nothing I saw gave any indication of what had happened to the inhabitants here. Did it matter that no one heard her dying words? Did she realise that her child was alive and safe and would be loved and adored by a strong, courageous mother?

If she could see me now, would she be pleased at how I'd turned out or would she be disappointed that I knew nothing of my heritage and knew only a smattering of Greek words? Did I look like her? Did I have any of her characteristics? Did we like any of the same things? I bowed my head and shoulders as I realised how little I would ever know and how pointless it was sitting here in this husk of a home.

There was no bond between this woman and me. She may have given birth to me, but it was Mum who had plucked me from the carnage and given me my life in more ways than one. Pru hadn't given birth to me, but without her intervention I would have almost certainly perished. It took two mothers to bring me into this world. One to bear me, and one to rescue me from the rubble and give me sustenance. I was indebted to both of my mothers. I was a product of them both.

I suddenly felt so very guilty for coming here to find out more about Helene Kostas. It was a terrible slap in the face for Mum. I had no memories of Helene, no photographs and I felt sad that she was nothing to me. I had so wanted to feel a connection with her. Now I realised that the reason I felt nothing was that she had never been my mother. It was Pru who had held me, fed me from her own breast, nursed me when I was sick, attended every sports day and school play. She sat with me every night to help with my homework and stroked my hair when my heart was broken for the first time. And the second. And the third.

It was her that had instilled in me my strong sense of fairness and morals and it was her that gave me the encouragement to go out and follow my dreams. Should she have told me sooner that I wasn't her biological daughter? I had thought so, but now I wasn't so sure. What good would that have done me except land issues on me that I would have been even more ill-equipped to deal with than I was now? She did the best thing for me that any mother could do; she brought me up in a secure environment feeling loved and wanted. She provided everything I needed, not everything I wanted. She taught me how to love other people unconditionally. It was my solid and loving relationship with her that was the driving force behind me wanting children of my own. I wanted the same relationship with my children as my mum had with me.

Suddenly I was hit with the realisation that I didn't need to carry the child myself for me to love it. I think that's what Mum had been trying to tell me all along. Dom and I could look into adopting. I had absolutely no doubt in my mind that Mum loved me above anything and everything else in the world, so it stood to reason that I would love a child in my arms as much as if I'd given birth to it myself. I smiled to myself. I'd travelled a long way to discover that everything I needed was back home waiting for me. It was only then that the tears welled up inside of me and gushed down my face. I felt bulbous droplets thud onto my bare legs but I did nothing to wipe them away. There was no one to hide them from and no shame in these tears even if there was.

I stood up feeling lighter than I had done in weeks and stepped out into the heat which spread over me like warm butter. It was darker now than I had ever seen it during the day in Cyprus. Drops of rain as big as walnuts were intermittently plop-plopping onto the cracked dirt as if the clouds were finally letting go of the build-up of pressure. I moved swiftly up the concrete steps two at a time as the rain started to fall a little heavier, and a little heavier still. I reached Mum and Eddie's splintered front door and threw it open just as a flash of lightening split the sky in two overhead. The door clattered backwards, smacked off the wall behind it and swung back into my shoulder as I entered. I closed the door quickly behind me as thunder rattled the deserted streets like coins in a collection tin. I knew the door wouldn't be locked. It had never been in doubt. It felt like the home had been waiting for me and knew that I would visit one day.

I walked tentatively down the short white-tiled corridor passing a bathroom on my left and the kitchen on my right and then a door that led to the single bedroom. I continued past it until I reached the open but small living room. I could imagine Mum in here as easily as if she were sitting here in front of me now. The window before me was opaque with years of looking out over the deserted streets, but at least it wasn't broken. With no one to take in the view, it had been lost to high reaching trees which grew too close to the window and were now tapping out the mournful rhythm of a funeral dirge. Where cobwebs had once lightly dusted the corners, grey streamers now hung from the ceiling and down the walls. I reached out to swat away an offending spider's web but it clung stickily to my fingers. I shook my hand vigorously and then wiped it on my top, repulsed by its adherence to my form like I was a troublesome fly.

On the right side of the room was a plain table with a white Formica top and metal legs. Three matching chairs were sat at each open side. Where was the fourth? There was a low, chunky sideboard taking up most of the opposite wall. A comfortable chair was angled towards the balcony, ignoring the rest of the room. I could imagine Mum sitting there.

On top of the sideboard was a record player and a bulky black machine. I wondered if it was a video player but on closer inspection I could see that it was an 8-track machine. They hadn't really been used since the late 1970s and I remember Mum telling me about having to leave this beloved possession behind. I'd never heard one play and idly turned the knobs on the machine. It was a shame that there was no electricity here anymore. I would have loved to listen to some of Mum and Eddie's music.

I looked to the side and saw just five 8-track cartridges beside it. I turned my head sideways so that I could read the names more easily. I smiled as I went through them. Rolling stones *Exile on Main Street*; Curved Air *Airconditioning*; Bob Dylan *Planet Waves*; Mike Oldfield *Tubular Bells* and Jethro

Tull *Aqualung*. Interesting mix of pop and progressive rock. Mum still liked those old bands. I wasn't sure about Eddie.

I looked around me. Why hadn't this place been looted like pretty much everywhere else in Varosha? It wasn't difficult to get in to but perhaps the half missing building acted as a deterrent.

I opened the sliding doors of the cupboard beneath and saw a stack of records. They would probably be worth a fortune now at collectors' fairs but there was no time to think about that now. I didn't really know what I was looking for as I sat on the floor and opened the other sliding cupboard door. On the top shelf were two photo albums.

One was entirely in black and white. It was Mum and Eddie's wedding photos. They had an abundance of youth, so fresh and so naïve. Mum was beautiful, hair pinned back from her slender face with long white-gold curls cascading down her back. She wore a high-necked, empire-line lace dress. The flowers were roses but it was difficult to tell which colour in the black and white pictures. My best guess would have been pink. She looked delicate and blonde and even through the black and white pictures you could see the blush of her cheeks and the turquoise of her eyes.

Eddie looked dapper in his army uniform with his hat under his arm. His severe haircut and rigid stance was a credit to his position. That was a man exploding with pride. They had so much to look forward to then. I felt sorry for the young couple in the photograph as I knew what hardship would befall them. But would they thank me for warning them? I doubted it. And if they were forewarned, what would they have done differently? I would probably have died in the rubble downstairs.

The other photos had the same signature smiles beaming from them. Cutting the cake, signing the register and standing under confetti held permanently aloft by the snap of the camera's lens. There was one picture of a stern looking older woman with black-rimmed horned glasses and a hat perched on her head. She was unsmiling but she was holding horseshoes on ribbons, no doubt a gift of luck for the happy couple.

I placed the thin photo album in my lap and reached for the other one. It was a fatter album this time with a seascape on the front of it inked in midnight blue. Most of these photos were in pale water-colours and a lot less formal. The album held four small square photos per page. The first page showed Mum in a short white dress in front of a float covered in oranges, Mum standing by a fence stroking the nose of a chestnut brown horse, and there were two of her sitting in a red bikini on the beach with an enviable figure.

"Wow Mum, look at you!" I muttered.

Over the next few pages there were pictures of Mum and Eddie at formal dances, Mum in a floor-length mauve dress with a matching short floral cape around her shoulders. There were photos of Eddie on his motorbike, Eddie in uniform, Eddie kissing a budgie, Eddie smoking a cigarette.

Back to the pictures and I could see that these were snapshots of a simple life, when they still thought that they were living in paradise with a bright future in front of them. I wondered if either of them had expected any fighting on this posting. Eddie was trained for battle, but had he really expected to see a war unfold around his family and ultimately involve his family so tragically? I doubted that Mum had realised there was a serious threat otherwise she wouldn't have considered having her baby here.

It was becoming difficult to see the photographs and I squinted at them, realising that most of the light had gone out of the day. I didn't have a watch on, but I was pretty sure it wasn't as late in the day as it felt. I could hear the rain hammering down outside, but it was almost comforting, like a blanket had been wrapped around me, blocking out the outside world. I could have been the only person on the planet for all I knew at that moment.

I pulled myself up using the sideboard as leverage. I carried the photo albums with me as I went to look at the rest of the house. If the light was fading fast then I needed to see all I could of this place before the light was gone completely. I seriously doubted that there would be any electricity still live in Varosha for me to turn a light on, and even if I knew where to locate candles, I would be afraid to light them in case the glow alerted anyone to my presence here.

With no streetlights, and a heavy covering of cloud to obliterate the stars and moon, it could be pitch black in less than an hour. I wandered into the kitchen. The first thing that I noticed was the rain coming in through the broken window and slapping the window ledge. I took another step and my foot crunched on something. I stepped back immediately, recognising the sound of broken glass. However, it wasn't glass from the window, it was curved like a tumbler. It rolled gently from side to side before coming completely to a halt. It lay next to a dark patch on the ground. Even in the gathering gloom I could see the deep rust colour. My first thought was that something had spilled out of the glass, red wine perhaps, but it covered too much of the floor for that to be the case. A bolt of realisation shot through me as it occurred to me that I was looking down at Mum's blood on the floor from when she was shot in the stomach.

I crouched down and went to feel it. I stopped just short of the stain and took my hand back, rubbing my fingers on my shorts as if I'd touched something unpalatable.

"Oh Mum," I whispered. "I am so sorry."

I wasn't entirely sure what I was sorry for. Sorry for the loss of her baby, because she was shot or that this signified the beginning of the end of her dreams and her marriage? Or sorry for the fact that I had reacted so badly when she told me? Either way, I was sorry.

A gust of wind blew suddenly through the window and an inner door slammed shut. I jumped and let out an involuntary squeak.

"It's just the wind. Just the wind," I told myself.

Green tiles had fallen from the walls in groups of four or five but still more clung onto the plaster, refusing to let go. I opened the nearest cupboard to find piles of plates and cups. The shelves were lined with patterned wallpaper that had curled and greyed at the edges.

I was suddenly very cold. Goosebumps stood to attention up and down my arms. I had an idea and went back down the corridor towards the bedroom. A slight hesitation on the threshold allowed me to take in the gaudy colours of oranges, purples and browns. There was no colour co-ordination in here. Twenty-first century Pru would never have allowed these strong colours in a bedroom. I smiled at the idea of my Mum as a young girl, inexperienced and inelegant. I wish I'd known her better.

Paperback books were stacked up on the floor like the leaning tower of Pisa, pages fattened and yellowed with age.

I stepped through the door and went straight to the wardrobe. The door was hanging limply on its hinges so I opened it with care. The wardrobe seemed full, no empty hangers where clothes had been hastily packed and no gaping holes where once favoured clothes had hung. When Mum left this flat for the last time she couldn't have known she would never be coming back.

The clothes smelled fusty as I ran my finger over their shoulders. It was a stale, smoky smell tinged with something vaguely citrus. Already the dust was aggravating my nose to try to provoke a sneeze. I squeezed my nose and wriggled it. There were some beautiful tops in here, mostly in blues and greens, always a good colour on my mother. There were kaftans and sun-dresses and two pairs of ridiculously bell-bottomed trousers. I placed the photo albums on the bed as I rummaged through the clothes. Didn't Mum own anything warm at all? A cardigan or something? Then on the top shelf of the wardrobe, I spotted a pile of folded woollens.

"Aha."

I reached for a soft purple towelling one but three fell out at once with a thud. I frowned at the sound, they didn't look heavy enough to make that impact, I lifted them up gingerly, half expecting to see a decomposing bird, but as I shook out the purple top a bundle of letters tied with a red elastic band tumbled to the floor. I swallowed down my thudding heart that leapt into my throat at the unexpected movement and let out a soothing sigh of relief.

I stooped for both the top and the letters. I didn't recognise the handwriting on the envelopes. They were written on fine, almost transparent, shiny blue paper with red and blue airmail markings on the front. Some were addressed to my mother in Bedford and some were addressed, in a hand I was familiar with, to Cprl Edward Clarke in Cyprus. These had to be love letters. I so wanted to tear them open and devour their contents but I stopped short of doing so. I had intruded enough on my mother's life for now. Besides, there might be things in there that I did not want to see.

I squeezed the wad of paper into my pocket and pulled the jumper over my head. It was a loose, round-necked jumper, hanging below the hips with two square front pockets low down on the front with splits up either side. I inhaled deeply, hoping to still be able to smell my Mum's scent but all that was left was the pathetic smell of years of neglect.

Picking up the photos I went back into the living room. On the table were blank postcards, three pens and a small, brown, unopened parcel. Curious, I turned the parcel over in my hands, hesitating. There was only so much that I could carry back with me so I would have to open it to be sure it was worth smuggling out of here. Conscience calmed I eased the string off the parcel and ripped open the brittle brown paper. A plain brown square box was inside. I fumbled with it in my haste to open it and when I did I saw a folded piece of paper. I opened it and read: *Dear Prudence. Going through your Dad's things I found this and thought you might like to have it back. Thinking of you. Mam*

I reached into the box and plucked out a delicate watch with thin white straps. I turned it over and saw that it was inscribed on the back. It was difficult to read in the bleak light and I turned it to one side and then the other trying to decipher the message.

Happy 18th Little Bean. Dad and Mam.

I couldn't help but let out an involuntary 'Ahhhhh!' into the empty room which sounded too loud to my ears. The face read 12.15 but had stopped working many years ago. As useless as it was as a tool for telling me the time, I strapped it to my own slender wrist and stared at it some more.

With the sound of muffled rain outside, I picked up the photo albums and began to think about getting home. Would I be able to find my way back in the dark? If not, I'd have to stay here until dawn and then get out as quickly as possible. I stopped to have a last look around the flat. It was unlikely I would ever step foot here again and even though I felt a little bit sad about that, I was gratified and humbled that I'd had the opportunity to have a look around the place that Mum and Eddie had lived in as a young couple.

Just as I was about to leave, I spotted a clothes horse the other side of the table on the far wall with what looked like baby clothes on it. I felt a wave of sadness for Mum. She had so many plans for her baby. She had started getting in baby clothes ahead of the birth with no reason to think that her baby wouldn't be born safely. I found myself in front of the clothes running my fingers over the cloth even though I hadn't been aware of moving towards them at all. I lifted up the white wool and saw that it was a hand knitted blanket. It was a little bumpy but knitted with love. It was a perfect square with yellow flowers around the edges.

The sadness I felt in my heart right then was like a physical pain. I knew what it was like to plan for a baby and to think of the future you would have with that child for it only to be taken away from you. It tore me apart to think about what I had lost, and I hadn't even seen it on a scan or felt it move under my hand. I don't know how Mum managed to stay so strong for so long.

Boom! Lightening flashed and thunder roared simultaneously. I involuntarily ducked as the room lit up like a lighthouse had suddenly shone into it before turning away. I didn't know whether I should go out into the storm that was raging outside. There was a sudden gust of wind and I heard the sound of metal scraping on concrete and the tumbling of a heavy object on the road below. I went to look out of the window to get a better view of the scene outside when I suddenly felt unsteady. For a horrible moment I thought that I was going to faint; the room seemed to be shaking around me. I realised a second too late what was happening and the floor beneath me vanished into the chasm below. I screamed as the building swallowed me up, knocked me unconscious and turned my world black.

Chapter twenty-two

I opened my eyes but couldn't move my head. It was completely dark and I couldn't see a thing. Panic gripped me and I tried to scream. Was I blind? I knew I was trapped but apart from that, I had no idea what had happened. I tried to move my legs but they were weighed down. Worryingly I could feel no pain. I tried to call out but there was no breath in my body capable of making a sound. I just started thinking in my head over and over again, "Please God, help me. Help me Lord."

I had to get back to Dom. I needed to tell him I loved him. I needed to touch his face and hear his voice. And I certainly was not going to die here without telling Mum how sorry I was for everything. The last conversations I'd had with both of them weren't exactly arguments but they had been devoid of any warmth from my side.

There was a cool breeze on my face like someone lying next to me exhaling. Before I could puzzle over what that meant, a sudden flash of intense light burned in my eyes just like it always did following a nightmare. In relief that I wasn't sightless, I instinctively snapped my eyes firmly shut. The memory of the luminescence danced in reds and greens on the back of my eyelids.

"She's here! She's here! Help me," a man's voice shouted.

I swayed like I was on a boat and then cool air rushed at me like a tidal wave.

"Can you hear me?"

I tried my best to nod.

"We need to move you, okay?"

This time I didn't even bother to nod or try to make a sound. Someone was here to take care of me and that was all that mattered.

"Take it slowly, c'mon, try sitting up for me."

"She okay?" a second voice came from somewhere, shouting over the rain.

"I think so. I can't see any blood but..."

"You get her other arm. On three. One. Two. THREE."

I felt myself being dragged to my feet but just as I was about to put my weight on my feet, I was hoisted in the air and carried into the rain.

"You'll have to put her in the back."

I could hear a car engine running somewhere.

"I'll sit with her."

"Good. Let's get out of here."

I dozed off at that point. I didn't care if I was safe or not, there was no way I could stay awake any longer. I was so tired. As I drifted off I could hear someone's voice saying, "Do not sleep. Do *NOT* sleep."

The first thing I noticed when I woke up was that I wasn't dead. There had been a point where I wasn't sure that I would ever see daylight again, so just waking up held a certain pleasure for me. I blinked open my eyes to see what else was new. I was in a hospital bed, no surprises there, with a drip in my arm connected to a half-full bag of clear liquid hanging from a metal stand. I wasn't in any pain, so I was assuming that I was shot through with some pretty good painkillers.

At the foot of my bed was quite a crowd but without craning my neck I couldn't tell who any of them were. They were definitely not speaking English though.

Shit! I thought as my situation started to dawn on me. Was I still on the Turkish side of the island? Was this a Turkish hospital? Was I about to get arrested? *Crap. What now?* I toyed with the idea of pretending to be asleep until I could be sure of my situation. I couldn't quite piece together the last few hours. There were images in my head like pieces of a jigsaw but, try as I might, I couldn't seem to slot them together. *Stop panicking. Breath. Think clearly. In through the nose, out through the mouth.*

"Leni?"

Shit! They know my name. Time to face the music.

I looked at the face of the woman who had just spoken my name. My vision blurred a little and then focused again. In front of me was that woman. What was her name? She was my landlady I think. Relief spread through my body.

"It's Antheia. How are you feeling?"

Ah yes, Antheia. That was it. I smiled at her but it hurt my head. It felt like I had imbibed several bottles of cheap red wine.

"Shoo! Shoo! She needs rest."

I watched as all but one of the others left the room. The young man who was left was familiar but I couldn't place him. He was very good looking and had worry marks between his eyebrows.

"Are you in any pain?" he asked.

I started to shake my head but winced at the motion.

"Yes and no." My voice didn't sound like my own, it was rasping and quiet. "Who found me?"

"Stefanos, his father George, and Nick," the kindly woman answered.

Stefanos. That's his name. I was starting to remember.

"You found me. Thank you Stefanos."

"Yes. Thank God."

"How did you?"

"Find you?"

"Uh-huh." I was learning that all communication was going to have to be verbal. It hurt too much to move my head.

"We found your bag by the fence. It had that map in it that you had shown me. Nick pulled some strings with his friends at the UN and when it got dark my father brought his truck and we went in to find you, using that map."

"Nick? Do I know him?"

"You were meant to be meeting us outside the museum, remember? When you stood us up, we went to find you."

Right. It still didn't make much sense.

"How did you know that I was stuck in the building?"

"We didn't. A girl flagged us down, pointed at the building and then ran away again."

"Anna," I whispered. "She must have been so scared."

"Then we saw your light and we pulled you free."

"Light?"

"Yes. A torch or something?"

"I don't know. I don't think it was me. I remember seeing it too but it wasn't me."

Stefanos sighed and exchanged a glance with the plump, older woman. What was her name again?

"Leni," started the older woman, "You need rest. I will bring food. We will fatten you up, and get you strong. Yes? Antheia will make it all right." She leant in and smothered me with her bosom as she kissed my forehead.

"Wait! Where is Anna?" I croaked.

"Eh?"

"The girl, Stefanos." I sighed at him. "Did you get her too?"

"No. She disappeared."

"Is she home?"

"I don't know," he shrugged.

"Antheia? *Is* she?" I demanded as firmly as I could manage.

"I do not know."

"But she's your daughter!" I gritted my teeth. I was getting impatient with their slow-wittedness.

They both looked at me in puzzlement. I had to make them understand.

"It was Anna that I saw in Varosha. She was the reason I went in, I followed her in there. I was worried about her, I was going to bring her back home. You've got to go back Stefanos, she's all alone. She might be in danger, the buildings aren't safe."

"Tell me again. Who is she?" he asked softly, like he was talking to a distressed child.

"Stefanos!" I was getting exasperated. "It's Antheia's daughter, Anna." I looked at Antheia. Surely she could understand what I was saying. She picked up my hand and leaned in close.

"My daughter's name is Erato."

"I'm talking about your *other* daughter."

"I do not..." her eyes narrowed but she looked concerned.

"Yes! I've met her – at your house!"

"No."

"Yes! Her name is Anna!"

Antheia looked at Stefanos and he frowned, shaking his head. Unperturbed, Antheia lowered her voice.

"Tell me what she look like."

"I don't know. She just looks like a girl. She's about ten years old, maybe twelve? Brown eyes, hair in plaits, red ribbons. She's usually wearing a blue and white dress, she doesn't speak much English. I don't know, she looks like a normal Greek girl."

Antheia whispered something to Stefanos in Greek. Her eyes were wide with what? Fear? Amazement?

Stefanos looked at me but addressed Antheia.

"No. Absolutely not. She has banged her head, that is all."

"Excuse me? I might have a headache but I DO know what I'm saying." I was becoming more and more infuriated with them. There was a little girl out there on her own. I should have saved her instead of continuing on my selfish dead-end journey. "She *is* your daughter, isn't she?" I asked Antheia, starting to doubt myself now.

"No."

"Then who is she?" I asked in confusion. Perhaps I had banged my head after all.

"Anna is my niece. She died many years ago."

Antheia and I looked at each other across the bed in silence. I looked deep into her warm brown eyes to see if she was joking. I wouldn't put it past them to be making fun of me but there was something earnest in her eyes that suggested honesty. But, even so, I could not believe that I had seen a ghost. Concussion I could accept, but apparitions I could not.

"I... But I thought your niece was called..." I struggled to remember the name.

"Anemone. We called her Anna."

No. This couldn't be happening. Maybe Stefanos was right. I had taken a bang on the head. There had to be a plausible explanation for this. There always is.

"Please. I need to speak to Dom. Could you get me a telephone?" I asked, my voice shaking as much as my hands, which were knotted in the hard cotton sheets.

"What did she say?" asked Antheia, with eagerness in her eyes.

"I need to talk to Dom. Please. I can't deal with this right now."

"Here. Use my mobile," said Stefanos. He reached out his hand to Antheia, who took it reluctantly.

The phone took an age to connect, I kept checking the mobile's display in case it had disconnected. Eventually I heard the phone ringing. I could see the phone clearly in my mind. It would be next to the television, Dom would be padding over to it bare-footed, he hated slippers.

"Come on baby. Please. Please."

A click and my heart lifted for a moment, but instead of Dom's smooth deep tone I heard my own tinny voice saying, "I'm sorry, we're not available to take your call at the moment..."

I pressed the red button on the phone and disconnected the call.

"Shit!" I couldn't remember his mobile number off the top of my head. Tears stung my eyes and I could feel the restrictive vice of panic sitting on my chest. He was listed on my mobile telephone under 'Hubbie', I never actually dialled the digits.

I cradled the mobile to my chest and thought for a moment. *Mum.* I could remember Mum's mobile number. It hadn't changed in over ten years.

No ringing at all this time, it went straight to voicemail. Mum's voice came into my ears. "You've reached Pru. Please leave a message after the tone."

I cried out in anguish.

"Mum?" My voice sounded too high in a bid to sound normal. "It's me. I really need to talk to you. I'm okay but had a bit of an accident. I'll call you again later. I think I'll be out of hospital later today. I'm okay. Don't worry, I just wanted to talk to you that's all. I love you. Bye-bye." I sighed as I hung up the phone.

I felt suddenly so alone and vulnerable. I imagined Dom and my mum getting on with their busy lives, probably not missing me at all. I wanted to be home with Dom's arms around me. He would know what to do right now, he would help me make sense of it all.

I couldn't comprehend anything that had happened today. I knew that Anna wasn't a figment of my imagination. We'd had conversations. I'd held her hand. She was *not* a ghost. I could remember the touch of her small warm hand in mine and the lavender scent of her hair when I kissed the top of her head. There must be an explanation for it. But I strained to remember seeing her talk to anyone else. That first day I saw her in the kitchen, she stood away from everybody else. Whenever she came to my room, she was alone.

If what Stefanos said was true, she had led him to find me in the ruins of the old apartment. Could a ghost do that? It was hurting my head to think about it. I tried to sit up but every muscle in my body ached. I let out an involuntary cry as I felt the pain burn through my muscles.

Two men appeared at the bottom of my bed. They smiled pleasantly at me as I pulled the sheet up around me. The two men were polar opposites. One man, who was obviously a doctor, was unusually fair and stood at about six feet four inches and was uncomfortably scrawny. The other man, in normal clothes, was about a foot shorter, dark with a comfortably round belly.

"How are you feeling?" asked the doctor.

"Good, thanks."

"Sore?"

"A little."

"You are lucky that you were not seriously injured. Those mopeds are lethal. They should ban tourists from riding them. But that is just my opinion. I am only a doctor." There was no humour in his eyes even though the soft smile remained.

I looked at the other man who was almost imperceptibly shaking his head. I couldn't tell what was in those twinkling brown eyes, but I had a strong sense that I wasn't meant to enlighten the doctor as to the exact nature of my injuries.

"I will send a nurse in to change your dressings and then you will be free to go home. Stay off the bike. Fill in this form before you leave and give it to the nurse at the desk." He dropped a clip-board onto the table at the end of the bed and nodded to the other man, said something in Greek and then left.

The short man smiled prodigiously at me. "We think it is better to not say where you were. So if anyone asks, you came off your moped. Okay?" Now he was smiling I recognised him as being Stefanos's father, George.

I nodded. "Whatever you say. Where's everyone gone?"

412

"Stefanos has taken his aunt home. She is... a little emotional."

"Right. Yeah, she would be. Do you believe in ghosts, George?"

He sat on the side of my bed without answering and folded his arms. He stared off into the distance and at first I thought he hadn't heard me. I studied his face. At this proximity I could see that he had hair sprouting from his ears and his nose. His stubble on his chin was a thick, short carpet of bristles. If there was anything this man was lacking it certainly wasn't hair.

"Yes," came the staccato response. I waited for him to continue. "I have not seen one. But you have seen Anemone. She has been dead for many years. I cannot say that you are wrong in what you say. I believe you."

"I'm not sure I believe my own eyes, George."

He smiled and rubbed my arm.

"We cannot know everything about the world, Writer Lady. Accept that there is much we cannot understand. Do not think so much! Waaa-ha-haaaa!"

"Okay. No more thinking. It's a deal." I smiled at George's laughter. It was a nice sound. So wholesome. So alive.

A nurse bustled in then with a trolley on wheels.

"I will be outside if you need me. Okay?" George slid from the room.

The nurse worked in silence. I guess she didn't speak English and I didn't attempt to use any of my scant Greek vocabulary. I bit my lip as she recleaned my wounds and covered them with gauze and cotton wool wadding. It wasn't an unbearable pain but I could have done without it.

When she was finished, I hobbled out of the hospital, doing my best to walk normally, and failing. I was relieved to see George leaning against the railings blowing cigarette smoke skyward in front of the hospital.

"You good?"

"Yep. Free to go."

"I drive you home."

I climbed into the passenger seat of George's truck and closed my eyes to ward off any further conversations or admonishments. It turned out that we were quite some way from

The Pleiades and, in spite of the uncomfortable seats and the non-existent suspension, I dozed most of the way back.

I opened my eyes as the engine cut off. Yaiyai was back in her usual spot but with the addition of a coffee in her brown bony hands today.

"Thanks for the lift, George," I said through a yawn.

"S'okay."

"And, more importantly, thanks for saving my life"

"It was nothing. I save lives every day. I am Superman. Waa-haaaa!"

I smiled at him but felt suddenly sad. I felt that I owed him an explanation. He had risked his life for me.

"You know it's actually the second time in my life I've been buried in rubble in that building? That was where my mother found me, after the building was shelled in '74. She saved me and took me home with her to England."

"Your father?"

"Dead. Well, missing. So I think it's safe to assume that he's dead."

"If the body has not been found, he cannot be dead. Not in the law. There are women whose husbands went missing during the fighting who are still married to them. I know a man who keeps his son's bike clean and shiny in the corner of his café for the day that he comes home. People offer him money but he says it is not for sale. It belongs to his son. It is difficult to move on if you have not buried your dead. After many years there are still people who hope that the people they love will come home."

"That's understandable, I guess." We sat for a moment before I said. "You coming in?"

"No. The boss needs me in work today. She is very angry that I ran off with a writer lady yesterday! She had no one to hit with saucepan. Waa-haaa-haaa-ha!"

"Thanks for everything George. Really, I mean it."

I half-stumbled out of the car and slammed the car door harder than I needed to. The force of the action shot spears of burning pain through my shoulder. I waved as much as I could while keeping my elbow tight to my side as George drove away. I caught Yaiyai's deep black eyes on my face and just as I expected to see her spit at the soil, she nodded at me. From her that was tantamount to a warm embrace. Perhaps she was starting to forgive my fellow countrymen or, at the very least, starting to tolerate my presence here.

I rolled my shoulders slightly to ease the tension but instead was rewarded for my thoughtfulness with a crunching sound in my neck. I was about to walk around the side of the house when the front door flung open. Antheia was on top of me instantly, smothering me in her arms. She took my face in both her large, soft hands and kissed the top of my head. Saying something in Greek she beamed at me and led me into the house by the hand.

"I will bring you food, yes? Tonight is celebration, I cook special meal. You do not need to come back up to the house tonight though." She winked at me.

I didn't have the energy to argue with her so I simply nodded. I followed her into the kitchen where heavenly smells were pervading the air. When the flood of saliva into my mouth threatened to drown me I realised just how hungry I was. Even so, I wasn't sure that I would be able to keep my eyes open long enough to eat a thing.

"Is she here now?" Antheia asked me.

"Who?" I asked, dreading the answer.

"Anna."

I glanced around the room for effect more than anything. I already knew she wasn't here.

"Sorry. No."

Antheia waved her pudgy hand through the air.

"Pfft! No matter. She will be back. Now go." She handed me a single red rose.

"For me?" I asked stupidly. She laughed a loud braying laugh.

"Yes. Yes. You go."

My heart sank. Was this Stefanos again?

I noticed a card gift label attached to the spiky stem and read it with a certain amount of trepidation.

My heart missed a beat. It read simply, "I love you." I knew that stocky confident script anywhere.

Walking in a daze, I stepped through the back door into the courtyard. On the side of the well was another red rose. "Because of the way you smile at me in the mornings." I wasn't really sure that I'd been doing much of that recently. At the top of the stone steps there was another rose. As I bent to pick it up I saw a rose on each of the three stone steps going down beneath it. "Because of your dirty laugh!" "Because of the way you support me in my career." "Because of the way you dance in the kitchen when you think that no one is looking." "Because of the way you cry at romantic films." "Because you are an amazing lover." This one made me blush, even though I was on my own in the mid-afternoon sun.

I stepped down the stone steps, my weakened legs threatening to give out beneath me. Another rose, and another, signposted their way towards the shack. "Because you thought the Elgin Marbles were actually small round stones." All right, was he ever going to let me forget that one?

As I neared the cottage, I thought I could smell him. That heady scent on his skin, half musky, half citrus. I was sure that I could feel the thrum of his heartbeat rising in time with my own. I imagined him sitting outside with the sun glinting off the copper strands in his hair, but when I cornered the building there was no one there. My heart sank a little. What if he wasn't here?

He did say that he was too busy to come and we hadn't parted on the best of terms.

Even if this was only a delivery from Interflora, at least it showed that he was thinking of me. I tried to console myself with this thought as I spotted a final red rose on what passed for a doorstep. The final note was "Because of the way you feel in my arms." I pushed open the door with my shaking hand and stood for a moment peering into the comparatively dark room, trying to make some sense of it. As my eyes adjusted I saw, sitting in the bed with a rose between his teeth, Dom.

It is no exaggeration to say that he took my breath away. My heart boomed inside my chest and my nerves came to life all at once. He was sitting back against the pillows completely naked from the waist up. It was difficult to tell from the way the sheet was across his lap, but I had a sneaky feeling that he was naked from the waist down too. He was broad shouldered with a small splattering of hair around each nipple and that fine line of hair that trailed down the centre of his torso towards his groin. He was naturally tanned and his skin glowed like it had been kissed repeatedly by an adoring sun.

I knew from experience that he tasted as good as he looked; his skin was a warm caramel, smooth and soft. I stood on the threshold of the shack drinking him in. The air was electrically charged around him. This room had never felt like it had any energy in it before. Without Dom it had felt drab and sparse but seeing him there in my bed, the room was suddenly brighter and more alive. The atmosphere was thicker and ebbed and flowed between the two of us in caressing waves.

His eyes of the deepest blue were reflecting a light that wasn't there. They twinkled like they were moving, as if I could see the thoughts behind his eyes taking formation and trying to communicate with mine. He moved to take the rose out of his mouth and the spell that had rooted me to the spot was broken. It took all my strength not to run and jump on him. I kicked off my shoes and within three strides I was by his side and on the bed.

His dark eyebrows sloped together as he noticed my bruises and he opened his mouth to speak. Before any sound could come out I knelt and placed my mouth against his. He tried gently to push me back to speak to me but I clung on and he gave up without a fight. From my kneeling position I was slightly higher than him and he had to turn his handsome face up to me as I kissed him. My hair fell across his face and I held the palms of my hands against his strong jaw.

Our tongues explored each other's mouths tentatively, like it was our first kiss. He closed his eyes and leant into the kiss but I kept my eyes open, scarcely believing that he was here in front of me. I pulled away from the kiss and looked at his face. He kept his eyes closed for a moment longer and his lips still parted like he was still living the kiss. When he finally opened his eyes he was smiling.

"Hello," he said.

I laughed gently. "Well, hello there."

He sat upright then and took my head in his hands and pulled me towards him. He balled his fists in my hair and kissed me harder this time, sucking on my lower lip. I held on to his wrists as he kissed me, not wanting to quite let go of myself completely.

"Wait," I said.

"What's wrong, darling?" He let go of my head then and took my hands in his. I smoothed my thumbs over his knuckles. Such strong hands.

"I've not been fair to you, I..."

"Hold on. Is this going to be an apology?" he mocked.

I half smiled, half glared at him then.

"Maybe."

"Then can it wait until later? I need to give it my full attention and, if I'm completely honest, my mind is elsewhere right now." He pulled my hands then so that I fell on top of him. "Now, where were we?"

Epilogue

Dom and I stayed on the island for three more weeks. Mum flew out to join us and I gave her all of the things I'd rescued from her flat. She sobbed when she saw the watch. It was the last thing her parents had ever given her and showed that her mother had been thinking about her after all. She wished she'd forgiven her before she'd died.

I reintroduced her to Eddie. That was an awkward day, but they soon got to talking and she asked him to take her to see their son's grave. I think it's too much to hope that they will get back together again but who knows what the future will hold? They also went out for dinner with Betty and Bernie, some old friends from back in the day. Bernie had retired back to England after the war but they still came for a holiday in Cyprus once a year to stay with Eddie. Mum cried when she saw Betty and they promised they would never lose touch again.

I only saw Anna once more. I followed her against the strong breeze which I now realised was always present when she was there. She took me to a steep hill on the outskirts of a deserted village. She bobbed ahead of me with her plaits swinging behind her, smiling as she led me to a dried-up well. The same blinding light that had saved my life in Varosha exploded through the remote hillside and I shielded my face. When I glanced back in her direction Anna was gone. I never saw her sweet smile again.

It took three days before we could get someone to come and investigate the well. When they did, they found six bodies. All the bodies had bullet wounds to the head. They laid the yellowed bones out on white sheets under a tent. One body was a lot smaller than the rest. A young girl.

Antheia has given samples of her DNA and we're waiting now for confirmation of the identity of the bodies. We know that Anna and her mother are among those bones. Antheia has asked us to stay for the funeral but it might be months and possibly years before the bones are formally identified and then released to the family.

Dom and I are heading back to England to face whatever the future might hold for us. He is treating me like I am made of glass. He won't let me lift a thing. You see, I've been feeling sick for the last week; it seems that we are smuggling a passenger home with us. I feel sure that it is a girl, and if it is, she will be named after the girl who saved my life: Anemone, 'Daughter of the winds'.

THE END

Acknowledgements

Thank you to everyone who gave me their time and their memories in order to add colour to this novel. It would have been much paler without you.

Special thanks should go to my mum for dodging that bullet in Varosha in 1974 otherwise there would be no-one to write this story.

Steff@edit-my-book did a great job of editing and proofreading and I shall be forever grateful. Andy Cameron of Karate Graphics, local Rock God and all round great guy, thank you for the book cover design.

Credit should be given to my boys Alex and Danny for keeping out of the way (and not squabbling) for just long enough for me to put the finishing touches to this, my debut novel.

Finally, James, my wonderful husband who has been amazingly supportive throughout this project and been far more patient than I deserved. Without him I wouldn't have had the confidence to follow my dreams to Varosha.

About the author.

Jo Bunt was born in Cyprus the year following the Turkish invasion of Cyprus. After a career in Recruitment Consultancy in the City of London she turned her hand to motherhood and writing. She is still working hard to perfect both.

She now lives in Derbyshire with her husband and twin boys.

Daughter of the Winds is Jo's first novel. 'Eye of the Beholder', her second novel will be published on Kindle in September 2014.

Printed in Great Britain
by Amazon.co.uk, Ltd.,
Marston Gate.